FRANCINE P

SWEET V
High

ELIZABETH'S
SECRET DIARY

A hidden letter,
a forbidden kiss,
a passionate
secret
romance . . .

I saw Ken tonight—we drove down the coast to the Moon Beach Cafe for a burger. I felt even more guilty than usual when I got home, because Todd called while I was out. I wish I had someone to talk to about this, Diary, but I don't dare tell anyone—not even Enid. Ken is as torn up about it as I am, and over dinner tonight we both agreed that we had to end it. We had this really calm and reasonable discussion—we even shook hands to seal the deal. From now on, no more secret rendezvous, no more late-night phone calls. But the next thing we knew, we were strolling along this deserted strip of beach near the restaurant, and Ken took my hand, and suddenly all our resolutions flew out the window. We just crumpled to the sand in a passionate embrace—he kissed me like no one's ever kissed me before. . . .

ELIZABETH'S SECRET DIARY

Written by
Kate William

Created by
FRANCINE PASCAL

BANTAM BOOKS
NEW YORK · TORONTO · LONDON · SYDNEY · AUCKLAND

RL 6, age 12 and up

ELIZABETH'S SECRET DIARY
A Bantam Book / September 1994

Sweet Valley High® is a registered trademark of Francine Pascal
Conceived by Francine Pascal
Produced by Daniel Weiss Associates, Inc.
33 West 17th Street
New York, NY 10011
Cover art by Bruce Emmett

ISBN: 0-553-56658-X

Published simultaneously in the United States and Canada

Bantam Books are published by Bantam Books, a division of Bantam
Doubleday Dell Publishing Group, Inc. Its trademark, consisting of the
words "Bantam Books" and the portrayal of a rooster, is Registered in
U.S. Patent and Trademark Office and in other countries. Marca
Registrada. Bantam Books, 1540 Broadway, New York, New York 10036.

PRINTED IN THE UNITED STATES OF AMERICA

OPM   0 9 8 7 6 5 4 3 2 1

To Jordan David Adler

Prologue

"Todd!" I cried as my boyfriend picked me up and sat me down on his desk, right on top of the science lab report we were supposed to be working on. "What are you doing? Your parents are downstairs!"

Todd smiled—one of those sexy, crooked grins that always melts my bones like butter. I should say right here that Todd Wilkins is probably the best-looking sixteen-year-old guy on the face of the planet. He's tall and athletic without an ounce of fat on him *anywhere;* being captain and star forward of the Sweet Valley High basketball team keeps him fit. He has adorable brown eyes that I could gaze into for hours at a time—sometimes I do, actually—and curly dark hair that I love to run my fingers through. Not that looks are everything, of course. What makes Todd special is his personality: he's sweet, funny, warm, generous. . . . Well, I'm a writer, I could list about a thousand adjectives that describe him. Let's just say

1

he's a dream come true. And the way he makes me feel . . . that's another long list of adjectives!

Todd wrapped his muscular arms around me and pressed a kiss on the side of my neck right under my left ear. "They think we're doing homework," he said huskily. "This *could* be a scientific experiment, you know. I'm trying to find out what happens to Elizabeth Wakefield's body temperature when I kiss her like this . . . and like this . . ."

I laughed, shivering, as Todd's lips traveled across the line of my jaw to the corner of my mouth. "It shoots up," I whispered as our lips met. "*Way* up."

We usually don't let ourselves do this—be alone together in one of our bedrooms—and as Todd sat on the desk next to me, I remembered why. It's too dangerous! We didn't even notice when we knocked a couple of books onto the floor. We were holding each other so close, all I could hear was my own heart pounding, and all I could feel was the heat flowing from his body into mine as the kiss grew longer, deeper, more passionate. . . .

The phone rang and we jumped apart, laughing. "Must be the make-out patrol," Todd joked, hopping off the desk and crossing the room. "They'll catch you in the act every time!"

The phone was on his night table. He picked up the receiver. "Yo. Hey, Matthews! What's happening?"

Todd sat down on the edge of the bed, his back to me, and started gabbing with Ken Matthews, a classmate of ours and Todd's best friend. Now that I wasn't levitating with delight from Todd's kisses, I re-

2

alized I was sitting on a bunch of papers, a ruler, and couple of ballpoint pens. I shifted onto one hip to sweep the stuff out from under me. I'd totally crumpled our lab report and another piece of paper as well—a sheet of pale-pink stationery.

A letter. I smoothed out the paper, and a light floral fragrance drifted up to me. A letter . . . from a girl.

I glanced quickly at Todd, but he still had his back to me. Ken must have launched into a long story; Todd was saying things like, "Uh-huh. I hear ya. Ha ha! Yeah, uh-huh."

I'll just see who it's from, I thought, glancing at the return address on the matching envelope. Michelle Thomas, Burlington, Vermont. Then I started reading the letter. It was a nosy thing to do, an invasion of Todd's privacy. But I couldn't help myself. Todd and his family had lived in Burlington for a while, but who was Michelle? I couldn't recall his ever mentioning her.

"Hey, cute-buns!" the letter began. My eyebrows shot up. Cute-buns? Who did this chick think she was, calling *my* boyfriend cute-buns?

I wasn't about to put the letter down now, and fortunately, Todd was still yukking it up with Ken. I read on. The chatty letter was full of references to Todd's Vermont friends, and Michelle concluded every anecdote with "Wish you'd been there!! It just isn't the same without you!!" *She uses too many exclamation points,* I thought critically, turning the page over.

Too many exclamation points . . . and too many

3

endearments. The tone was affectionate, playful, familiar. I wanted to believe that Michelle was just one of Todd's old pals, but suddenly I felt queasy. Clearly, she'd known Todd well . . . *very* well. "Come back and visit me sometime soon," she pleaded. "Lots of love and a hundred kisses, Michelle."

This is the kind of letter you write to your boyfriend, I realized, fear and insecurity tying my stomach in knots. In fact, it was a lot like the letters *I'd* written when Todd first moved to Burlington from Sweet Valley. Quickly, I checked the date on the front side of the sheet, hoping it would turn out to be an old letter—hoping Michelle was an old flame, long since snuffed out. We'd both dated other people while we were apart, before Todd moved back to Sweet Valley and I broke up with Jeffrey French so we could pick up our relationship where we'd left off.

The letter was dated a week ago. I grew cold down to my toes. Michelle Thomas had sent lots of love and a hundred kisses to "cute-buns" just one week ago. Apparently, the flame was still burning bright and hot.

A clattering sound brought me back to the present moment. Todd had hung up with Ken and was striding toward me, his eyes alight with love. *But it's not* all *his love,* I thought, fighting back tears. *He's holding some of it back . . . for Michelle.*

Maybe I should have stuck the letter back underneath the lab report. I shouldn't have read it in the first place, and besides, Michelle lived three thousand miles away. Could she really be a threat? But in my mind at that moment, that wasn't the point.

Todd noticed my expression and stopped in his tracks. "Liz, is something wrong?"

"Yes." I held up the letter, my hand shaking. "Who's Michelle? Why didn't you ever tell me about her?"

"Michelle? What the—" He stared at the piece of pink stationery, a frown wrinkling his forehead. "Did you *read* that?"

"So what if I did?" I countered hotly. "Don't you think I deserve to know that there's another girl in your life? I guess you don't, or you would have told me yourself. I can't believe you had someone special in Vermont and you never told me! You're still in love with her, aren't you?"

Todd gaped at me. "*Still* in love with her?" he spluttered. "I was never—it wasn't like that. You're getting the wrong—"

"Don't tell me it wasn't like that, *cute-buns,*" I declared, my eyes flashing.

"She was just kidding around," said Todd defensively. "How can you accuse me like this, Liz? I can't believe you read my mail. I'd never pry into your private life that way!"

"Well, you wouldn't find anything like this if you did," I said, choking on a sob. "I trusted you, Todd. When you moved back and we started over, I thought we'd both wiped the slate clean. In a million years I never thought you'd two-time on me."

"I'm not two-timing!" he shouted. "Geez, Liz, you could at least give me the benefit of the doubt and let me explain what really—"

5

I couldn't bear to listen to lies about Michelle. The letter had told me everything I needed to know, and it had turned my world upside down. "You don't have to pretend you care about me and only me anymore," I cried, jumping down from the desk. "It's all out in the open now, Todd. Why don't you just go back to Vermont?" I threw the crumpled letter at him and stormed from the room. "Go back to the girl you really love."

"This is really pathetic, Liz," declared my twin sister Jessica as she barged into my room that evening and flicked on the light. "Lying here in the dark—get a grip!"

I pulled a pillow over my tearstained face. "Go away," I mumbled. "I want to be alone, OK?"

I heard Jessica bound across the room. The pillow was snatched away and she stared down at me. "No, it's not OK," she said. "You've been moping for hours, and I won't be able to have any fun at the Beach Disco tonight if I think you're alone in the dark bawling like a newborn."

"You're so sympathetic, Jess," I said dryly.

She shrugged, grinning. "Being sympathetic to someone else doesn't mean you have to *completely* stop thinking about yourself, does it?"

I had to smile. "No, I guess it doesn't."

"I'm thinking about both of us," she promised, tugging on my arm. "So get up and get dressed. You're going to the Beach Disco."

"I'm not in the mood to dance," I protested.

6

"It's the only thing to do." Jessica dragged me over to the closet. "Having a good time is the best revenge, take my word for it. As soon as you're dancing under the stars with some cute guy, you'll forget all about Todd and what's-her-name."

When Jessica makes up her mind about something, she's like a freight train barreling full speed ahead. Don't bother pulling the emergency brake—there's no stopping her. Half an hour later she had me at the Beach Disco, wearing my new swirly rayon dress and a pair of her platform sandals. It was Friday night, so everybody was there: Ken and Terri, Amy and Barry, Aaron, Lila, Olivia, Robin, DeeDee and Bill, Bruce and Pamela, Maria and Winston. Well, *almost* everybody. Everybody but Todd.

The Beach Disco has an open-air dance floor surrounded by palm trees, and they play the best new music. We're really lucky to live in southern California, where the nights are warm and tropical and delicious. But even though Jessica had gotten me to the club in body, she couldn't do anything about my spirits. I was totally depressed. Seeing all the happy couples dancing together reminded me of all the times I'd been there with Todd. He'd hold me tight in his arms during the slow songs, whisper in my ear, kiss me tenderly. He'd make me feel as if I were the luckiest girl in the world, the only girl for him. *Had he been thinking about Michelle the whole time?* I wondered now, tormented by the possibility. *Was he pretending I was someone else?*

A few of the guys asked me to dance—Aaron, Winston, Barry—they're really a sweet bunch. But Jessica's platform sandals were so uncomfortable and I was in such a rotten mood that finally I just kicked off my shoes and walked away from the dance floor onto the dark, deserted beach.

When you're sad, nothing is as soothing as the sound of the ocean waves pounding on the shore. The ceaseless rhythm takes you out of yourself, out of time, and the immensity of the ocean makes all your problems seem trivial. I walked toward the Pacific, my dress billowing in the night wind, the sand cold and damp under my toes, waiting for the weight of sorrow to lift from my shoulders. It didn't happen. My heart stayed as heavy as a stone.

Oh, Todd, I thought, tears stinging my eyes. *How could you love someone else?*

At that moment I missed Todd so much, I wanted so much to see him running down the beach toward me, that when I saw a shadowy figure in the distance, I thought I was dreaming. No—he was real. My heart skipped a beat, and I held my breath as the boy drew nearer. In the moonless gloom I couldn't see his face, but I could tell he was tall and well built. *Todd!* I nearly cried out.

The boy stepped closer. I saw that his hair was blond, not brown. It wasn't Todd. It was . . .

"Jeffrey?" I called, my voice quavering. "Is that you?"

Jeffrey French hurried up to me. "I saw you come out here," he explained, lightly touching my arm. "You looked upset. Is anything wrong?"

I shook my head, but my denial wasn't very convincing.

"Liz, what is it?" Jeffrey asked.

The note of concern in Jeffrey's low, warm voice triggered something buried deep inside me. I burst into tears.

Jeffrey's hand slid up my arm to my shoulder. I tried to halt the flow of tears, but it was impossible. "Elizabeth." One more step, and Jeffrey was close enough for me to smell the spice of his aftershave. Close enough to wrap his arms around me. Which he did. "Ssh. Don't cry," he murmured, stroking my hair.

Just a minute before, I'd been wondering how Todd could love another girl. Now I remembered how deeply I'd loved Jeffrey, and how much it had hurt when Todd moved back to Sweet Valley and I had to choose between the two of them. The first time Jeffrey held me in his arms was at a beach party, and the last time . . .

"The last time you held me like this was the night we broke up," I whispered, hardly even aware of what I was saying. "All those months ago . . ."

Jeffrey gazed down into my face, his green eyes alive with emotion. "It doesn't feel like that long ago to me. Because I never stopped loving you."

"No, Jeffrey. Don't say that," I begged.

"It's the truth," he said hoarsely. "I know you don't think about me anymore, Elizabeth, but I've never been able to get you out of my mind. There's no one else."

He pulled me closer, and even though I knew it

wasn't the right thing to do, I tightened my arms around his waist. Lifting my face to his, I met him halfway. Our lips met, and like a tidal wave, his warm, wonderful, wildly unexpected kiss washed away my sorrow and my fear, my loneliness and my disappointment. I was in over my head, but I didn't care. It felt too good letting myself drown in Jeffrey's eyes, his arms, his steadfast love.

Late that night I tiptoed in and out of the bathroom, careful not to wake Jessica, who was sound asleep in her room on the other side of our adjoining bathroom. I didn't want to explain where I'd disappeared to at the Beach Disco and why I'd stayed out so late.

My lips still burned from Jeffrey's kisses. Undressing in the dark, I dropped my clothes heedlessly on the floor.

My mind whirled from what had happened. As we'd walked on the beach and then sat in his car and talked—and hugged and kissed—some more, it had all rushed back to me: what fun times Jeffrey and I had had together, how caring and supportive he'd always been, how nuts I'd been about him. Now I was home, though, about to crawl into the bed I'd been lying on earlier that evening, crying my eyes out over Todd. What was going on with me?

The horrible thing was, I'd been in this place before—split in two between Todd and Jeffrey. That time I'd chosen Todd. It ended up feeling inevitable. He was my first love, my only real love.

Or so I thought. Jeffrey was there for me tonight, I reflected. *He's never stopped loving me, being true to me. Whereas Todd . . .*

I started crying again, dizzy with confusion. Todd and Jeffrey. Todd *or* Jeffrey. Yes, I made a choice before. But was it the right choice?

I switched on my desk lamp, hoping the bright light would chase this nightmare away. The problem was, I wasn't asleep. It wasn't a nightmare; it was real.

My eyes blurry with tears, I stared unseeingly at my bookshelf. Gradually, I focused on a row of small clothbound volumes. My diary. Years and years of my most secret thoughts and feelings were recorded on those pages. I'd turned to my journal in times of joy and heartache. It was all there.

My life . . . I lifted a volume at random from the shelf. What might I learn from these pages?

Sitting down at my desk, I opened the book and began to read.

Part 1

Friday, 11:00 P.M.

Dear Diary,

I can hardly bear to write this down. Putting words on the page will make it seem real, and I want so much for it to turn out to be a mistake, a dream, a joke.

But it is real. Todd is moving away— far away. He told me tonight during the talent show. . . .

There's nothing like the feeling of satisfaction you get from working really hard on a project and then seeing it all come together. For weeks I'd spent all my spare time planning the Sweet Valley High Talent Show; now, as I sat in the back of the packed auditorium with the rest of the judges, I could hardly believe what a success it was turning out to be. DeeDee Gordon's sets were fabulous, and the acts were all

12

fantastic. Everyone got teary when Olivia Davidson played a sad love ballad on her guitar; all laughed hysterically at Winston Egbert and Ken Matthews's comic magician routine. Patty Gilbert astonished us with her graceful dance, and then . . .

It was Todd's turn. I held my breath as my boyfriend stepped up to the microphone, wondering why he looked so solemn. He'd been incredibly secretive about his routine, but I'd just assumed he was planning to do comedy. So why the long face?

"Originally, I was going to stand up here and tell jokes," Todd began quietly, "but since I don't feel like laughing myself, I don't think I'd have much luck getting you to laugh. Instead I'd like to read a sonnet by the nineteenth-century poet Christina Rossetti. It's called 'Remember,' and it has a special meaning for me tonight."

Before Todd began reading, he glanced around the auditorium. I knew instinctively that he was looking for me. "Remember" was one of my favorite poems, and I'd shared it with him. *Why is he reading it now?* I wondered, my eyes fixed on his face. What was the "special meaning"?

Todd's deep, husky voice filled the auditorium. I focused on each word, searching for a clue.

"Remember me when I am gone away,
Gone far away into the silent land;
When you can no more hold me by the hand,
Nor I half turn to go yet turning stay.
Remember me when no more day by day

13

You tell me of our future that you planned:
Only remember me: you understand
It will be late to counsel then or pray.
Yet if you should forget me for a while
And afterwards remember, do not grieve:
For if the darkness and corruption leave
A vestige of the thoughts that once I had,
Better by far you should forget and smile
Than that you should remember and be sad."

Todd spoke the last line of the poem and then stood for a moment longer. Even from the back row I could see tears glitter in his eyes. He still hadn't located me; I was sitting too far back. Without another word he turned and left the stage.

There was a brief hush, and then the audience, puzzled by this somber performance, clapped dutifully. As the lights dimmed briefly for a set change, I sprang to my feet. I had no idea why Todd had chosen to read the poem, but something was wrong—that much was clear. I had to find him—I had to find out what it was.

Backstage was chaotic with excited performers and stage crew milling about. Just as I was about to give up, I spotted Todd by the exit, preparing to step out alone into the night. "Todd!" I cried, hurrying after him. "Wait up!"

When he turned to face me, his expression was so sorrowful, I stopped dead in my tracks. "Todd," I said, my heart in my throat. "What's wrong?"

I saw him swallow; he was making a massive effort

to keep his emotions under control. "I just found out for certain the other day," he replied brokenly. "I didn't want to believe it was true. God, I've been praying. . . ."

"You didn't want to believe *what* was true?" I asked, my mouth dry with dread.

"My dad's getting transferred." The words fell like stones into a pond, sending out ripples of shock. "We're moving to Vermont."

"Vermont?"

My knees turned to mush; Todd reached out for me and I fell into his arms. "Dad doesn't want to go, but his job is hanging in the balance," Todd explained.

"When?" I asked, praying he'd say a month, two months.

"We're leaving a week from Sunday."

Todd's shoulders slumped; tears started rolling down his cheeks. The horrible reality sank into my brain, and my own eyes brimmed and spilled over. "Todd!" I cried, burying my face in his chest.

I've always loved poetry because of how much emotion a writer can squeeze into just a few well-chosen words. When you read a good poem, the images and feelings just sort of explode inside of you; it's like magic. I never imagined a poem could have the power to break my heart, though. Now I know those words will be burned in my brain forever. I can hear them right now. "When you can no

15

more hold me by the hand . . ." I can hear Todd's voice breaking with emotion as he stands on stage and reads "Remember" in front of the entire Sweet Valley High student body. Just a few days ago we were so happy. The world was perfect. How could this happen? What am I going to do without him?

Sunday, 11:30 P.M.

Dear Diary,

One more week is all we have left. One lousy week. I swear I can hear the clock ticking; it sounds so heartless. If only I could make time stand still! But of course I can't. Every hour that passes is an hour that will never come again. That's why Todd and I are spending as much time together as possible.

He stopped by tonight before dinner, just for a few minutes on his way home from doing some errands for his dad. I keep praying that there will be some way out of this, but I know there's not. If Mr. Wilkins doesn't accept this transfer to Burlington, he'll lose his job—that's the bottom line. So obviously Todd and his mother have to be supportive. Todd's trying really hard to be a good sport, so I'm trying, too. I don't want to make it worse for him. But it's hard!

I have to pour it all out here on these pages, Diary. I don't want to cry all the time when I'm with Todd—I've been bot-

16

tling up my tears tight. Here they come. . . .

I'm going to miss him so much! He's just the best, sweetest, most adorable guy, and I can't even remember what my life was like before we started going out. I mean, before I met Todd, I'd dated other boys but I'd never been in love. I'd only dreamed about it. With Todd, being in love turned out to be even more wonderful than my dreams. He's my best friend, first of all. I can talk to him about anything, and he's always there for me. Sure, we've had our ups and downs, our fights and misunderstandings—every couple does, right? Things like that either break you up or make you stronger. It's the latter with us—we just keep growing closer and closer. Todd's like a rock I can always lean on, the person who makes me laugh when I'm down, who helps me come up with solutions to my problems, the person I want to share every secret with.

So I'm not just crushed at the prospect of not having a date to Lila Fowler's next party. It's a lot more than that. It's the little things all through the day: meeting at my locker before the first bell, walking to class together with our arms around each other, cheering him on at basketball games, getting his opinion on my latest Oracle *article, going for walks on the beach, gabbing on the phone every night before we go to bed. I'll tell you a secret, Diary. I've never talked to anyone* about this—not Jessica, not Enid—even Todd wouldn't guess. They'd think I was so silly, totally nuts. But sometimes when I think about the future, I see me and Todd married, living in Sweet Valley or maybe some place totally different—San Francisco, New York, Denver, who knows!—with a house and kids and careers. And still, after years and years, I picture us having so much fun together, finding new things to love about each other every day. Is that corny or what??

It doesn't matter, though. Instead of years, it turns out we have only seven days. We won't even be alone his last night in Sweet Valley because Enid's throwing a big going-away party for him at the Beach Disco. She's the sweetest person—I know she means well. But I don't see how I'll be able to bear having all our friends witness our goodbye. I don't know how I'll hold myself together. It's going to hurt so much.

Saturday, midnight

I just got home from Enid's farewell party for Todd, and since there's no way I'll be able to fall asleep, I might as well write about what happened between me and Todd tonight. I'm still so incredibly sad about his moving, but there's hope in my heart now. I feel a little bit stronger. . . .

18

The Beach Disco is the perfect setting for just about any kind of party. The outdoor dance floor is lit only by strings of tiny lights and the moon and stars above. Between songs you can hear the Pacific Ocean waves crashing on the shore; if dancing cheek to cheek isn't romantic enough for you and your date, you can always sneak off for a stroll by the water.

Enid lived up to her promise to make Todd's last night in Sweet Valley one he'd never forget: Every single friend of his was there. We were all dressed up, and a lot of people brought going-away gifts: boxes of stationery so Todd could write letters, picture frames with photos from great times he'd had with his friends in the past, California souvenirs like wacky sunglasses and surf shorts so he wouldn't forget his hometown once he was living in northern New England.

Of course, everybody wanted to talk to him, shake his hand, give him a hug. A lot of people are going to miss him; I'm not the only one. But finally I had to be selfish. "Let's sit the next one out," I whispered in his ear when the song we'd been dancing to ended. "We haven't had a chance to talk all night."

Hand in hand, we slipped away from the dance floor. The night breeze was cool, and when I took off my shoes, the sand felt cold under my feet. But the only sensation I was really aware of was the warmth of Todd's hand squeezing mine. How were we ever going to be able to let go?

As soon as we were out of sight of the Beach Disco, we reached for each other, holding on tight as if we were drowning. He crushed me in his arms, his mouth searching for mine, and we kissed hungrily. We were like two people discovering one another for the first time, but it wasn't the pleasure and promise of a first kiss that swept us away; it was the inexpressible sorrow and longing of a last.

"I love you, Todd," I sobbed, pressing kisses all over his face, which like mine was wet with tears. "I love you so much. There will never be anyone else for me, ever."

He cupped my chin in his hands, gazing deep into my eyes. "I love you, too," he said hoarsely. "My heart belongs to you—it's yours forever. That's why I want you to have this."

He fumbled in the breast pocket of his jacket, pulling out something small wrapped in tissue paper. My hands trembling, I unfolded the paper. "It's beautiful," I gasped, lifting the tiny gold locket by its chain. It twinkled in the moonlight. "Oh, Todd."

"It isn't much," he mumbled. "You don't have to put a picture of me in it, either. But promise you'll wear it, close to your heart."

We embraced again. I felt his heart beating against mine, and it was as if we had one heart between the two of us. "How can I live without you?" I whispered.

"You'll manage," said Todd, stroking my hair. "We'll both manage. And . . ." He cleared his throat. "I want you to know it's OK if you decide to date other guys."

I looked up at him, startled. "It is?"

"It's not fair to expect you to waste your life waiting around for me," he reasoned. "I mean, I'll visit whenever I can, and who knows, maybe Dad'll get transferred back. But in the meantime . . ."

"But I don't *want* to date other guys!" I protested.

Todd looked incredibly relieved. "You don't?"

I squeezed him tightly around the waist. "I bet everybody's giving you the same advice they're giving me. Long-distance relationships never work, it's best if we give each other our freedom, get on with our lives. Well, I'm not giving up on us," I said fiercely. "I don't care what other people think. We *can* keep our relationship alive if we try. I really believe that."

"Me, too," Todd said earnestly. "And I'm ready to work hard. I'll write to you every day and get an after-school job to pay for phone calls and plane tickets. You can count on me, Liz, just like you always have."

I buried my face against his chest. "But what about the girls you'll meet in Burlington?" I asked.

"I hope I'll make some new friends. But I'll never hold another girl in my arms like this." He wrapped his arms around my shoulders, cradling me gently. "And I'll never kiss another girl like this. . . ."

Our lips met in the most incredibly tender kiss. It was salty from our tears, but sweet, too. Because it was a pledge, a vow. "I'll be true to you, Elizabeth Wakefield," Todd whispered. "We'll make the best of the situation—we'll make it work. And someday . . ."

I clung to that word like a lifeline. "Someday," I repeated, "we'll be together again."

*   *   *

21

It happened. He's gone. I didn't think it would be so painful; after our talk on the beach last night, I thought I'd be able to keep my chin up, act brave. But when the moment actually came to say good-bye, it was like being run over by a train. . . .

It was horrible, standing around in Todd's front yard watching him help his father load suitcases into the car. At first I tried to pretend the Wilkinses were just going away on a trip. *He'll be back,* I told myself. *They're not really moving.*

I must have looked pretty pathetic, because finally Todd's father told him to spend the last ten minutes with me instead of with the luggage. Todd practically carried me around the side of the house to the backyard, where we could have some privacy. The minute we were out of sight, I burst into tears.

"Don't leave," I begged, pounding my fists helplessly against his chest. "Oh, Todd, please don't leave me."

"Stop, Liz. Don't make me cry." It was too late; tears were streaming down his face, as well. "I didn't want to do this," he choked out. "I wanted to be strong for your sake. But I feel like I'm falling off the earth into space or something. I'm scared, Liz. I'm going to be so lost without you."

I flung my arms around his neck. "You'll be fine,"

I sobbed. "You'll make new friends. Burlington will feel like home in no time."

"No." He shook his head. "It could never be home. Not if you're not there."

We stood holding each other, rocking back and forth and crying. Too soon we heard his father shout, "Todd, time to go!"

Todd stepped back from me so he could look into my eyes. "We'll be OK, Liz," he whispered, kissing me tenderly. "I'll call as soon as I get to Vermont."

I nodded dumbly. Taking my hand, Todd led me back around the house.

We stood in the driveway a few yards from the station wagon. "So this is good-bye," I said, trying to sound casual. I waved to his parents, who were already in the car. "Have a nice flight, Mr. and Mrs. Wilkins."

Todd kissed me again. "Go on home," he said gruffly. "I can't leave if you're still here."

"Sure. See ya, Todd."

Turning my back, I strolled down the driveway. I heard the car engine start. One step, two, three . . . Then my knees crumbled. *This is it,* I realized, my throat aching with sorrow. *He's really going.*

Whirling, I sprinted blindly back to the car. Todd, still standing there, grabbed me, hugging me with all his might. "I'll never love anyone like I love you, Todd Wilkins," I cried.

He kissed me one last time and then climbed into the backseat, his eyes still locked on mine. I kept my eyes glued to his face as the station wagon rolled out of the driveway. "Good-bye, Todd," I whispered.

The car disappeared from sight and my vision blurred. I couldn't see for the tears—the whole world melted like a watercolor in the rain. Sinking down onto the pavement, I buried my face in my hands and sobbed.

Monday, 4:00 P.M.

Dear Diary,

It's been a week since Todd left—the longest, loneliest week of my life. I just tried to write a short story, thinking that might make me feel better, but all I came up with was this sad little poem:

The woman waits in the house by the water
A wide-brimmed hat shadows her face
Shielding her eyes from the glare of sun on sea
The sea empty day after day
Empty of sail, empty of hope, as she paces
The widow's walk.

Isn't that depressing? I thought I wasn't writing about myself—I was writing about an imaginary woman who lived hundreds of years ago, thousands of miles away, on Nantucket or someplace like that. But she is me, waiting day after day for someone to come home . . . someone who's never coming home again.

I know Todd's lonely, too, but it can't

be as bad for him. At least he has a new town to explore, a new school to get used to. Meanwhile, everything I do, everywhere I go, reminds me of him. When I walk down the halls at SVH, I keep expecting to see him around the next corner. At lunch I find myself looking around the cafeteria for him. Heading to the newspaper office after school, I consciously have to stop myself from swinging by the gym first to watch a few minutes of basketball practice. Everybody's being really nice and trying to distract me, especially Jessica, but nothing helps. The only time I don't miss Todd is when I'm writing him a letter— that's all that keeps me going. I tell him everything that's in my heart, pour myself onto the page, and somehow it makes me feel close to him. I've been writing to him a lot, a couple times a day. Which means I'm kind of letting everything else slide— homework, my newspaper column, even you, Diary. But you understand, don't you? Nothing's any fun anymore without Todd to share it with. I don't even want to leave the house because I might miss a phone call. So far he's called three times— three bright, tiny stars in a week that's felt like one long, black night. How will I make it until he visits, when I don't even know when that will be?

Nicholas Morrow called tonight—kind of a surprise. Kind of a disappointment, too, since when I heard a guy's voice on the line, I thought for a millisecond that it might be Todd. You remember Nicholas, right? He's my good friend Regina's older brother—he graduated from SVH last June, and he's working at his dad's computer company for a year before going to college. He had a pretty serious crush on me at one time. . . . Anyway, it turned out Nicholas had heard—how, I wonder?—that I'm covering the annual Sweet Valley Boat Club Regatta this weekend for The Oracle. *He's racing his family's yacht, and he asked if I'd give him a lift to the marina.*

I was sort of flustered—I mean, it seemed like a strange request—but I said yes. Could Nicholas still like me? Is he hoping we can start something now that Todd's moved away? No, he must know that nothing's changed. I still love Todd—I'm definitely not available. Jessica is making a really big deal out of this, of course, as if it's a date or something. Maybe Nicholas does *have an ulterior motive. Oh, well. I'll deal with that when and if I have to.*

Back to Jessica, I know she thinks I'm moping. She wants me to put Todd behind me and start dating other guys. But frankly,

26

she just doesn't understand. She's never had a relationship that lasted more than a couple of days; she doesn't know what it's like to really love someone, to belong to him heart and soul. She's my sister and I adore her, but sometimes she can be so . . . shallow. Forgive me, Diary, but it's true.

Saturday, 10:30 P.M.

Dear Diary,

I was kind of annoyed the other day when Mr. Collins, the newspaper adviser, pressured me into covering the sailing races. I wasn't that into it, and it seemed as if there had to be other kids on the staff who'd be psyched for the assignment. But I ended up having a blast at the regatta today. It was impossible not to get caught up in the excitement—the boats are so beautiful, and it was a close, thrilling race. At the very last second Nicholas and the Seabird edged out Bruce Patman's boat for the blue ribbon—I screamed myself silly. I got great material for the story, too, interviewing the contestants and talking to spectators—finding out who they were cheering for and why. After he won, Nicholas invited me and Jessica to a victory party on the boat. It was fabulous—a catered lunch, champagne, and the most gorgeous, breezy, sunny day for a sail. Nicholas treated me like a princess. I had so much fun, I almost feel guilty. . . .

All of a sudden I noticed that Nicholas and I were alone on the starboard deck of the *Seabird*. Nicholas noticed, too, or maybe he'd planned it that way. Before I could steer us away from a personal conversation, he launched into a speech about how happy he was that I'd spent time with him before the race that morning and then stayed after to help him celebrate.

"We've never really talked about what happened between us a couple months ago," he said, dropping his eyes and flushing slightly. "But I just want you to know—"

Any other girl in Sweet Valley would have killed to be in my Keds at that moment. Nicholas is a hunk: tall and muscular and ruggedly handsome with glossy dark hair and deep-green eyes. He's also smart, witty, and sweet. But I knew he was about to say he was still interested in dating me, and I didn't want him to. It would be better if the words weren't spoken—they'd only make it hard for us just to be friends. "Nicholas, can we just let this subject lie?" I broke in. "I don't feel comfortable talking about it."

"The last thing I want is to make you uncomfortable," he swore. "And I'd never force myself on you, Liz—I'm not trying to jump into Todd's shoes or anything like that. I'd like us to be friends, that's all. I'd like you to come to me if you ever need someone to talk to, a shoulder to cry on." He flashed me a sheepish, appealing grin. "No strings attached. OK?"

I smiled back, happy and relieved. I genuinely

like Nicholas; we could have a lot of fun if I wasn't worrying that he hoped something romantic would develop. "Thanks for the offer," I said. "I'm sure I'll take you up on it."

"So how about tomorrow afternoon? Are you busy? If not, you and Jess should stop by my house— we're having a barbecue. It'll be fun—I'd enjoy your company."

My smile faltered. Doing things occasionally with Nicholas, as a friend, was fine. But two days in a row? What would Todd think? I wondered. We'd decided to hold on to each other despite the distance, and not to date other people. But here I was, practically the minute he left town, spending the better part of a weekend with another guy—a guy I *knew* had the hots for me.

But if Nicholas said being friends was enough for him, he meant it. Besides, I liked hanging out with him. Why should I deprive myself? I was lonely without Todd—I needed all the friends I could get. And Jessica would be psyched to see me get out of the house for a change.

"Sure," I said lightly. "If Jess doesn't have other plans, we'll stop by."

"Great," said Nicholas, a pleased sparkle in his emerald-green eyes.

I guess I have to trust Nicholas, Diary. Did I mention what he said his special, private name for the Seabird is? My Favorite Twin.

Dear Diary,

I got a wonderful letter from Todd yesterday, and I've been curled up in bed this morning reading it over and over. Not that I could ever forget why I fell wildly in love with him, but he reminds me all the time by being so caring and perceptive. I'm going to copy down part of the letter here in case I ever lose it, which would be impossible, since I plan to sleep with it under my pillow from now until the day that may never come but which I'll keep praying for—the day Todd moves back to Sweet Valley. . . .

"This is confusing, isn't it, Liz? I feel far apart from you, but at the same time I feel as if you're with me all the time, no matter what I'm doing. I'll see something that I think would make you laugh, and I laugh as if you're right there by my side. A lot of times I find myself kind of writing a letter in my head—there are just so many things I want to tell you. Maybe that's weird, but it keeps me from going crazy with loneliness for you. One thing I'm sure of, though— this is probably even harder for you. At least I have the excitement of a new school and town to keep my mind off things. Whereas you . . . The only thing that keeps me going is knowing how strong you are, Liz. But there are times when you won't

*feel strong, and when that happens, just re-
member how much I love you. . . ."*

*I feel pretty strong right now, Diary. As
if I'm going to be able to keep things in perspective. I have faith in myself and in Todd
and in what we have together. It's exactly as
he says, we're together in spirit even
though we're three thousand miles apart—
he's close beside me right now. Hmm . . .
and I'm in bed in my nightgown! Pretty
naughty—I'll have to write and tell him all
about it!*

Sunday, 8:15 P.M.

*So much for being strong and in control. I
can't believe I boasted about that just this
morning. Jessica and I went to the Morrows'
barbecue this afternoon—a big mistake.
Nicholas was so attentive, fetching me things
to eat and drink, stealing me away for a private walk and talk. . . . He can insist he's content with a platonic relationship until he's
blue in the face, but I'm pretty sure he's still
infatuated with me. I know the signs. . . .*

"So, Elizabeth, did you and Todd discuss dating
other people?" Nicholas asked.

I'd been hoping to avoid a repeat of yesterday's
tête-à-tête on the yacht, but when Nicholas suggested a stroll around the estate grounds, I couldn't

31

say no without seeming rude. Now I stared at him, taken aback. He might as well have added "In other words, how about going out with me?"

Hadn't we gotten this out of the way yesterday? *Guess I'd better set Nicholas straight once and for all!* "Actually, we did," I said, aware that my face was now the same magenta-pink as my polo shirt. "We decided not to date other people. Neither of us wants to. We're still totally committed to our relationship."

It was pretty blunt, but I couldn't dance around the subject if Nicholas was going to keep misinterpreting me and hoping we might become a couple.

He sighed, visibly disappointed. Immediately, though, a hopeful, boyish smile brightened his face. "Does that mean we can't see the new James Bond movie some night this week?"

The early show on a school night didn't sound too dangerous. "Of course not. I'd love to," I said, smiling.

"Good. Then I *do* stand a chance with you!"

Before I could respond, Nicholas placed both hands on my shoulders and kissed the tip of my nose. When he touched me, I jumped, so for all I know, he was aiming for my mouth but missed. One thing is for sure. *I* keep missing the target when I try to get across the idea that I only want to be friends!

I realized right away that I shouldn't have said yes about the movie. Nicholas wants more than I can give, and it looks as if nothing's going to change that. Just now I told Jessica what happened. I was about to call Nicholas and cancel the date, but she made me hang up the phone. She chewed me out big time—she's fed up with me "wasting" my time on a long-distance romance. "Any other girl in Sweet Valley, including me, would be delirious about going to a movie with Nicholas," she said. "Don't be a fool. Go out with him, relax, have a good time. You'll forget about Todd, and then who knows what will happen?"

So I didn't call Nicholas tonight, but that doesn't mean I won't find some excuse between now and Wednesday to break the date. I called Enid instead, and she said pretty much the same thing as Jess, but in a nicer way, of course. She thinks it's fine for me and Todd to want to stay faithful to each other, but I shouldn't cut off all my other options. I should be "open" to something new if it comes along. "Just do what feels natural," she advised. What would feel natural right now would be lying on a blanket under the stars at the beach with my arms around Todd. . . .

Wednesday, 6:30 P.M.

Dear Diary,

I feel like a boat cut loose from its mooring. A bird that's fallen out of the nest before it's learned how to fly. I haven't heard from Todd all week.

He phoned Monday when I wasn't home

33

and Jess spoke to him. Since then I've left three messages, but he hasn't called back. I know he's busy—he told me that he has to do extra work in some of his classes to get up to speed, and he's started practicing with the basketball team. I hope he's made some friends, but could he really be going out every night? I'm not worried. At least I don't think I am. No, I'm not. Jessica thinks it's highly suspicious, though. It's true, Todd's so cute, he probably has to fight off the girls at his new school. But we have an understanding, right? We're still a couple. OK, so it's settled: I'm not "worried," but I do feel kind of let down. Does this have anything to do with why I didn't call off my date with Nicholas tonight?

Wednesday night, late

I'm a horrible girlfriend. I don't deserve Todd—I never did. He's been gone less than two weeks, and already I've thrown myself into the arms of another boy. I kissed Nicholas Morrow good night after the movie. Really kissed him. What is wrong with me?

As we stood on the front steps of my house, I realized I should have jumped out of the car before Nicholas could offer to walk me to the door. But it was too late.

"Thanks for spending the evening with me," said Nicholas, his voice low and husky.

He lifted a hand, cupping my face gently. A shiver raced up my spine, infusing my body with the electric warmth of anticipation. He was going to kiss me. What's more, I *wanted* him to kiss me.

Instantly, I saw that I'd been fooling myself. Letting Nicholas put his arm around me at the movie to "comfort" me, pretending he was the only one with expectations while of course *I* only wanted friendship. The fact was, Nicholas Morrow was thoughtful, charming, sophisticated, gorgeous, and incredibly sexy. The physical attraction was mutual, and I could feel it pulling our bodies together like magnets.

He slipped his arm around my shoulders. A brief image of Todd flickered through my brain, only to be erased by the tentative touch of Nicholas's mouth on mine. I knew I should pull away, but instead I responded passionately. It felt so good to be kissed, to be held. My hands moved to the back of his neck, pressing him closer. The kiss grew deeper, warmer. . . .

If Nicholas hadn't stopped when he did, would I have stopped? Luckily, he's a gentleman he didn't take advantage of catching me off guard. Or maybe I wasn't really off guard. . . . I'm so confused, Diary. I like being with Nicholas. I liked kissing Nicholas—I can't deny that! But does that mean I like Nicholas? Or am I just trying to fill that big empty space inside me any way I can?

35

I don't know how I got myself into this situation. Nicholas isn't pressuring me—he wants me to take all the time I need to think things over. But what good will thinking do when my head is in such a whirl? Todd was right. I won't always be strong. Tonight I was weak, weak, weak. I failed the first test of our long-distance relationship. The locket Todd gave me feels heavy around my neck . . . or maybe that's just my heart, weighted down with guilt. Oh, Todd, why did you go away and leave me all alone?

Friday, 4:30 P.M.

Dear Diary,

I thought the week before Todd moved to Vermont was the worst week of my life, but this one is giving it a run for its money. I haven't heard a single word from Todd. Whenever I call, his parents tell me he's out or "busy," and he never calls back. The letters have stopped coming, too, the letters I've been living for, reading over and over until I know them by heart. I haven't stopped writing to him, but now I have this horrible picture of my letters lying on Todd's old desk in his new bedroom, unopened. I just don't understand it. What happened? How could he change his mind about wanting to stay in touch? Just like that, without even telling me? Did I say or do something wrong? He couldn't know about Nicholas; no one knows about Nicholas, and there's not that much to know, anyway. Todd must have . . . I don't even want to write this. I don't want it to be true. But there's no other explanation. He must have met another girl. I'm crying too hard to write anymore.

Friday, 6:00 P.M.

Speaking of Nicholas, he just stopped by. He was so sweet—he apologized for kissing me the other night. And you know what I did, Diary? Boy, did I suprise him, and myself, too! I hope I don't regret being so impulsive. I asked him out to dinner tonight, and I made it pretty clear I'm ready to put the whole "let's just be friends" chapter of our relationship behind us. I flirted like crazy. Or maybe you couldn't even call it flirting—I came right out and told him I was glad we kissed!

I could tell he was completely floored by my change in attitude, but also pretty psyched. He's picking me up in an hour to take me to a very classy and romantic Italian restaurant. And you know, Diary, I'm psyched, too. Jessica is right. I've been a fool to think Todd and I could stay faithful to each other. He's dumping me—he doesn't want anything to do with me. And Nicholas does. So it's not even a question of making a choice—Todd did that for me. Nicholas is so wonderful, much better looking than Todd when you get right down to it, and tons more mature. Older guys are definitely the way to go! Nicholas is ready to treat me like a princess—what more could a girl ask? I think we'll have a memorable evening, and this is only the beginning. I'm not going to wait around pining for Todd Wilkins, that's for sure. Well, maybe I'll still pine. It doesn't matter that he's broken my heart—I still love him and miss him. But I won't call or write to him anymore. I won't wait around. It's time to move on. I'll throw myself into this new romance with Nicholas and count on my stupid heart to catch up as fast as it can.

Saturday, 3:30 P.M.

I really laughed for the first time in ages this afternoon. Did I tell you about Jessica's new part-time receptionist job at the Perfect Match Computer Dating Agency? Talk about a disaster waiting to happen! You know how obsessed she is with matchmaking; she's always trying to set up her friends, or her sister or brother, with someone totally unsuitable. Although actually, now that I think about it, she's been pushing me in Nicholas's direction, so maybe she's not always off base. That's the exception that proves the rule, though.

Lately she's been after Steven to start dating again, even though he's still grieving for Tricia Martin, his girlfriend who died of leukemia. Today Steven and I were sitting out back by the pool when the doorbell rang. We called out for whoever it was to come back, and this creature dressed totally in black leather with about ten pierces in each ear and a cigarette glued to her lip sauntered around the corner. Can you picture a girl less likely to appeal to my wholesome, all-American brother?? She acted as if Steven had invited her over, when in fact he'd never laid eyes on her in his life. I just about choked trying to control my laughter. Steven did his best to convince her that she had the wrong guy, but she just plunked herself down, on his lap practically, and started ranting about Plato's philosophy of ideal love—how our souls all wander around searching for our perfect match. "Perfect match"—those were her exact words. Finally Steven and I clued in. Yep, you guessed it: Jessica strikes again! She's been using the computer at work to hunt up dates for Steven, without his blessing, of course. Boy, did he chew her out! She won't pull that stunt again in a hurry.

Tuesday, 9:00 P.M.

Dear Diary,

Enid and I went to the beach after school today—we haven't done that in a while. I

39

didn't realize it, but I've been kind of blowing her off. I'm seeing a lot of Nicholas: dinner and movie dates, horseback riding, sailing . . . Enid and I talked about that. She's pretty surprised at how quickly the whole thing is developing, and she didn't exactly criticize me—you know how tactful she is. But she recalled how she felt when her old boyfriend George broke up with her to go out with Robin Wilson. Enid plunged right back into the dating scene, assuming that would make her feel better, but of course it didn't. It was too soon. She wasn't over George yet, and it only made the pain worse trying to find some guy to act as a substitute for him. It just reminded her of how irreplaceable he was.

So she thinks I'm too much on the rebound for Nicholas. Steven said pretty much the same thing a few days ago. They're two of the smartest, most sensitive people I know. Are they right? I feel as if I'm falling in love with Nicholas, that he could be the one. Am I misleading myself? Would this have happened if Todd hadn't dropped me like a stone?

Friday, 4:30 P.M.

Walking home from school this afternoon, I started thinking about Todd. What else is new?? Maybe it was the warm sun on my skin, the soft breeze—anyway, something reminded me of the first time he kissed me. And all at once I saw things clearly for the first time in weeks. It happens that way sometimes, you know? There's no earth-shattering event, no big argument. You're quiet and alone and thoughtful, and suddenly your eyes just open wide and you see the world around you for what it is. You see into your own heart. This is it, Diary: I'm still wildly, deeply, forever in love with Todd Wilkins. I can't just transfer those feelings to another guy, even someone as wonderful as Nicholas. Maybe it could have worked for Nicholas and me if I'd kept him at arm's length until I was really over Todd, but what's going on between us now is all wrong. I didn't mean to use him, but that's basically what it amounts to. I ricocheted from missing Todd so much, I couldn't think of anything else but trying to forget him completely, and poor Nicholas got caught in the crossfire.

I'll have to explain this to him as soon as possible. I'm not looking forward to it! He'll be so hurt—he really cares for me. Why did I have to learn this lesson at his expense? Unfortunately, I won't see him until tomorrow night—Lila's having a party, and we were planning to go together. It's not ideal, but I'll have to tell him at the party, or on the way over.

That gives me a whole night and day to write a letter to Todd. I should have done this *a week ago! Maybe while it's fresh in my mind, I should jot down some of my feelings and questions. . . .*

"Dear Todd, I haven't heard from you in a couple of weeks, and I guess you can imagine how hurt and worried I am. Have you decided it doesn't make sense for us to hold on to our relationship now that we live so far apart? Have you met someone new? Maybe we were crazy to think it would work. I need to know what's going on, though. If it's over, please tell me. Give us a chance to say good-bye properly. It's the only way I'll be able to get on with my life, to learn to live without you."

I can't mail that now that I've cried all over it and the ink is all runny and blotchy. Oh, Diary, as hard as it is not knowing, I'm just not ready for it to be final. I'm not ready for Todd to say good-bye.

Saturday night, late

Dear Diary,

Where can I possibly begin? This has been the most wrenching, emotional night of my life. . . .

Lila Fowler has never been and will never be my favorite person, but you have to give credit where it's due: she throws a fabulous party. At least a hundred people mingled by the pool and on the lawn behind Fowler Crest. There was great live music to dance to, colorful Japanese lanterns, tall glasses of tropical punch garnished with fresh fruit and little paper umbrellas, and table after table of food.

I'd resolved to get my talk with Nicholas over with right away, preferably in the car on the way to Lila's. Then if he didn't feel like hanging out with me—and I assumed he'd never want to see me again—he could just drop me off at the party or take me back home. But when he rang the doorbell and I saw him standing on the front step, dressed in white linen pants and a striped cotton sweater, a broad smile on his suntanned face, he looked so sweet and handsome. . . . And then I couldn't get a word in edgewise during the ride; Nicholas was bursting with stories about his regatta that day. *This isn't the right moment,* I decided as we parked the car in the drive at Fowler Crest. What a chicken.

It was weird walking into a party with someone other than Todd. Everybody stared pretty blatantly; it was the first time Nicholas and I had been out in public as a "couple." *The first and last time,* I thought, fighting the urge to turn on my heel and run.

Nicholas put his arm around me and steered me toward the dance floor. A slow song was playing—one of my favorites. Correction: one of Todd's and my favorites. Nicholas cradled me in his arms and we started swaying to the music. I rested my head on his shoulder. With my eyes closed I could almost pretend he was Todd. He wore a different cologne, but they were about the same height and build.

What a terrible thing to do, to dance in one boy's

43

arms while you're daydreaming about another! It was the only way I could keep from falling to pieces, though. I was about to break up with Nicholas, and it would be terribly awkward. After that I'd be on my own dealing with losing Todd. That was what I had to look forward to. But just for a moment I could hide from reality, safe in a dreamlike bubble.

Still enfolded in Nicholas's arms, I opened my eyes. Slowly, I focused on a dark-haired boy in a navy blazer and corduroy trousers standing on the edge of the patio staring at me and Nicholas. For a long, awful, disbelieving moment my heart literally stopped beating. *It couldn't be,* I thought. *He can't be here!* But he was.

"Todd!" I cried, shoving Nicholas away from me. The color had drained from Todd's face; his eyes were wide with surprise and the pain of betrayal. "Todd!" I cried again as he spun around and raced away into the night.

> *I started shaking as if I would never stop. It was so horrible, so humiliating. I wanted to sink into a heap on the floor and sob, but all my friends were watching.*
>
> *Nicholas took me home, and finally we had a totally honest conversation about what's been going on between us. I'm so lucky—he was incredibly understanding. Talk about a one-in-a-million guy. . . .*

The minute we were alone in Nicholas's Jeep, I fell apart. "I'm sorry, Nicholas," I sobbed, burying my

44

face in my hands. "I've ruined everything. For me and Todd, and for me and you."

"If there's still a 'you and Todd,' Liz," he said quietly, "then there's never *been* a 'you and me.'"

It was true, and I couldn't lie to him anymore. "I still care too much for Todd to start a relationship with anyone else," I confessed, the tears flowing faster. I thought I was ready, but I'm not. Seeing him again just now, like that, when I was with you, made it crystal clear. My heart isn't free."

Looking away from me, Nicholas turned the key in the ignition. His profile was stony and hard, but only because he was trying not to show how much I'd hurt him. "I'm sorry," I repeated.

His jaw clenched, he smiled stiffly. "So am I, Elizabeth."

"I was planning to tell you even before I saw Todd," I said. "I never meant to lead you on, Nicholas. You've been such a good friend to me. Oh, you must hate me!"

As we drove slowly toward my neighborhood, Nicholas laughed, a bitter, sad sound. "No, I don't hate you," he assured me. "How could I? I've been in love with you since the day we met. Nothing can change that."

"Then we—we can't just be friends?" I stuttered.

Gripping the steering wheel tight, Nicholas took a deep breath. "We can be friends," he said with an effort. "I'll take what I can get. But you can't keep treating me like a yo-yo. You have to decide, once and for all."

Once and for all . . . It was so scary, so final. With Nicholas I always felt secure. A shoulder to cry on, arms to hold me, words of love and encouragement— I'd be giving all that up. I didn't want to let go. But he was right. It wasn't fair to expect him to be my boyfriend one minute and the next minute step aside for someone else. I was cheating him, and cheating myself. I had to learn to stand on my own two feet. I couldn't use a relationship like a crutch.

"Please forgive me, Nicholas," I whispered. "And please be my friend."

The instant he stopped the car in front of my house, I jumped out and ran up the driveway. It was so hard, leaving him there staring after me. He'd accepted my decision gracefully, but I knew I'd hurt him deeply. How many hearts, including my own, would I break tonight?

At home I changed my clothes, splashed cold water on my face, and got ready to head back out to look for Todd. Then Jessica burst in and dropped a bombshell that would've flattened me if I hadn't already felt crushed. . . .

"This is all my fault!" my sister wailed as I pulled a sweater on over my head. "If I hadn't interfered, if I hadn't told Todd that you . . . that you . . ."

I stared at her. "Interfered?" The word was like a red flag in front of a bull. I felt my breath quicken with anger. "What did you tell Todd, and when?"

46

"The last time he called, a couple weeks ago," Jessica said, chewing her lip nervously. "You weren't home and I told him . . . I told him . . . oh, Liz, I was only trying to help!"

I grabbed her shoulders and shook her hard. "What did you tell him?"

"I told him he was ruining your life by tying you to a long-distance relationship," Jessica confessed. "I said if he really loved you, really wanted the best for you, he'd give you the freedom to date other people, to just plain enjoy your life. I really laid on the guilt. I told him that as it was, you'd lost interest in everything and were moping all the time. Because you *were*, Liz!"

"So that's why I haven't heard from him," I said, dazed.

"I didn't tell him just to blow you off," Jessica defended herself. "He came to that conclusion on his own. I'm sorry, Liz. I know I shouldn't have meddled, but I was worried about you and—"

I waved at her to shut up. I couldn't listen anymore, and I didn't have the energy to yell at her. I could focus on only one thing: I needed to see Todd more than I'd ever needed anything in my life.

Jessica was still trying to explain as I ran into the garage and revved up the Fiat. For an hour I drove all over town looking for Todd—I tried the Dairi Burger, Miller's Point, the school parking lot. I was desperate; I was crazy. If I didn't find him and tell him

47

*how much I still loved him, tell him that
Nicholas didn't mean anything to me and
that he was the only one, I knew I'd never get
over it. I'd just give up. There'd be nothing
left to live for. . . .*

° ° °

The hope ebbed from my heart as I cruised
through downtown Sweet Valley. Todd's car wasn't at
the pizza palace or the ice-cream parlor; it wasn't
anywhere. Should I start checking hotels? Was Todd
traveling with his parents? Maybe he was staying with
the Egberts. Maybe he'd left Lila's and headed
straight for the airport to fly back to Vermont!

That thought was too terrible to contemplate. Not
knowing what else to do, I turned onto the street
where Todd used to live. I'd driven over to his house
so many times in the past, I could do it in my sleep,
which was just as well because I was crying. Parking
the car in his old driveway, I climbed out and walked
across the lawn toward the dark house. "Todd," I
whispered into the night. Only the sigh of the breeze
in the trees answered me.

The house was locked up tight; it didn't make any
sense for Todd to be there. But for some reason I
couldn't turn and walk away. Some force seemed to
pull me around the side of the house into the backyard. It was where Todd and I had stolen those last
moments together as his father readied the car for
the trip to the airport, where we'd hugged and talked
and cried. Where we'd made promises that neither of
us had managed to keep. . . .

The shadows around me seemed to stir with re-membered emotions, as if the ghost of our lost love still hovered there. Then with a start I realized that it wasn't a ghost keeping me company. I wasn't alone; a dark figure sat, head bowed, on the back step.

"Todd!" I cried, stumbling forward.

He leaped to his feet, and an instant later we were in each other's arms, crying with relief and kiss-ing each other over and over. "Oh, Todd," I sobbed, holding him as tightly as I could. "I thought I'd lost you forever."

"I thought I'd lost *you*," he said, his voice crack-ing. "To Nicholas Morrow."

I shook my head. "No. I'm still yours. Oh, Todd . . ."

My whole body trembled violently with the effort to hold back another onslaught of tears. Todd stroked my hair, rocking me gently. "Ssh. It's OK now. We found each other again. It'll be all right."

We sat on the back step for more than an hour, unburdening our hearts. "I didn't know what to do when I hung up the phone with Jessica that day," Todd confessed. "She was right—it was selfish of me to hold on to you. But I knew you wouldn't see it that way. If I asked you point-blank if you were unhappy, you'd deny it because you wouldn't want to hurt me. So I decided to just go ahead and give you your free-dom whether you wanted it or not. You'd be mad and hurt, but you'd get over it and it would be the best thing in the end. When I got to town this morning—Dad was supposed to fly out to take care of some business, but at the last minute he couldn't make it so I came instead—I started to drive over to your house to beg you to forgive me, but I chickened out. So I went to Lila's and . . ."

"We should have talked it over together," I said, remembering my mental anguish during the last two weeks. "When you didn't write or return my calls, I was so scared and confused. I thought you'd met someone else."

"No way." Wrapping an arm around me, Todd pulled me to him for a kiss. "You've been on my mind constantly. I have absolutely no interest in dating other people."

I bit my lip. After what he'd witnessed on the dance floor at Lila's, I couldn't exactly make the same claim. "I have to explain about Nicholas. There's nothing between us—I mean, he'd like there to be, but I finally told him it's just not going to happen. I want to be with *you*, Todd." Tears spilled down my cheeks. "I don't *want* my freedom."

Todd brushed the tears gently from my face. "You didn't do anything wrong, Liz. Don't feel guilty. I think we've got to admit that even though we want to strangle her for being such a busybody, Jess had the right instinct about all of this. We weren't being realistic."

I nodded, sniffling. "We can't pretend that nothing's changed. We need to learn to be strong without each other, to be independent."

"Exactly," Todd said, his dark eyes earnest. "The Elizabeth Wakefield I know and love lives life to the fullest. She's always looking for new experiences, making new friends. I want to stay part of your world—that's all I ask."

"Oh, Todd!" I flung my arms around his neck, showering him with kisses. "You'll always be the most important part. I'll always love you."

He laughed into my hair. "Well, if you welcome me home like this every time I make it back for a visit, it's not such a bad deal!"

Before Todd went back over to Winston's, he said to remember that the locket he gave me is a token of friendship, not a chain. I feel so, so much better, Diary! I know I'll be sad when Todd flies back to Burlington tomorrow afternoon, but it won't be as bad as when he left the first time. We know what we're dealing with now. Our love is strong enough to survive good-byes.

I'd be perfectly content at this moment except for one thing. Jess and I were hanging out in the kitchen eating a midnight snack when Steven got home, and he seemed pretty upset. Apparently Betsy Martin, Tricia's sister, said some really harsh things to him when he was dancing with Cara Walker at Lila's. "How could you forget my sister so soon? Did you ever really love her?"—that sort of thing. I can't believe it—just when Steven's finally getting over his mourning and enjoying life again! Boy, wouldn't I like to give that girl a piece of my mind. I'm really worried about Steven. I hope he doesn't let this stand in his way, take it too much to heart. If there's one thing I've learned in the past couple weeks, it's that you can't put your life on hold no matter what you've lost.

Saturday night, really late!

Or should I say Sunday morning, early??? The most romantic thing in the world just happened, Diary! I was trying to fall asleep, weaving in and out of dreams of Todd, when I heard something at my window. I thought it was just a tree branch scratching, so I started to doze off again. Then I heard another sound outside. I peeked out and there was Todd, standing on the lawn in the moonlight looking up at me! It was just like a scene from a movie. Dad had been fixing a rain gutter, and the extension ladder was still leaning up against the house. Todd actually climbed up it. . . .

"What are you doing?" I whispered, stifling a giggle. In the shadows below I saw Todd moving around in the bushes; then there was a scraping sound, and the ladder jolted closer to my window. "Todd! Are you crazy?"

He started up the ladder and I held my breath, expecting one of my parents to knock on my door at any moment and demand to know what was going

52

on. How could anyone sleep through all that racket? Or maybe Todd wasn't really making much noise—it was just my guilty conscience. I mean, it was two o'clock in the morning, and there I was in my short, skimpy nightgown waiting for my boyfriend to climb through my bedroom window!

I pushed the window up as far as it would go. Todd got to the top of the ladder and placed his hands on the sill. Leaning out, I planted a big kiss on his grinning mouth. "Congratulations!" I whispered. "You've just become the first man to successfully scale Mount Wakefield!"

I was trying so hard not to laugh that I was pretty much useless to help Todd inside. He made it halfway through and then caught his foot on the sill. With a big thump we fell on the floor on top of each other, giggling like crazy.

"You're going to get me in so much trouble," I whispered as we took advantage of the mishap to hug each other tightly.

"I just had to kiss you good night one more time," Todd explained, his warm brown eyes full of love. "Since I won't have another chance for so long."

"You're absolutely nuts," I said, gazing at him adoringly through my tousled hair.

Rising, Todd offered me a hand and pulled me to my feet. Then he led me to the bed. "Todd," I chastised him, laughing. "If you think for one second that just because we may not see each other for months and months we should—"

He chuckled, putting a finger to my lips. "Ssh.

53

Just sit down. It's more comfortable than the floor! I won't try anything, I promise."

We sat on the edge of the bed, and Todd took me into his arms. I snuggled close, my bare arms and legs suddenly feeling cold. Maybe it wouldn't hurt to crawl under the covers just to warm up, just for a minute. . . . I laughed out loud. Who was I kidding!

"What's so funny?" Todd wondered, nuzzling my neck.

"I was just thinking that I need one of your very best kisses to stop me from shivering. . . ."

And he gave me one of his very best kisses right then and there.

I'll never be able to fall back to sleep now, Diary. Can you blame me??

Part 2

Dear Diary,

I didn't get much sleep last night (and you know why), so I was pretty bleary-eyed at breakfast just now, but I was also grinning ear to ear (and you know why), so maybe the two canceled each other out and I looked normal. No one said anything about hearing ladders banging against the house in the middle of the night, anyway!

Besides, a zombie would have looked glamorous compared to my brother. Steven slouched into the kitchen with such dark circles under his eyes, it looked as if someone had played a prank and drawn on him with a felt-tipped pen. I guess he didn't sleep well last night, either. He just took off somewhere with Betsy Martin—she came by to pick him up just a few minutes ago. Jessica is furious at Betsy and really gave her the cold shoulder—it was kind of embarrassing. I must say, though, having heard what happened at the party last night, I was surprised Steven didn't seem annoyed with Betsy, too. But he wasn't in the least. He looked happy to see her—obviously he prefers hanging out with her to hanging out with us. Where do those two go? What do they talk about? I worry that all they do when they're together is reminisce about Tricia. After all, their love for Tricia is basically all they have in common— not the healthiest basis for a friendship, if you ask me. I mean, I loved Tricia, too. But she's gone. Her hold on Steven shouldn't be even stronger in death than it was in life.

Brrr. Enough morbid stuff. Time to get dressed and go over to Winston's to get Todd! We only have a few hours together—I don't want to waste a minute.

Sunday, 10:00 P.M.

It was hard saying good-bye to Todd this afternoon. Not as bad as the first good-bye, but still. I tagged along while he took care of some family business, and then we took a long walk on the beach. It was such a beautiful, golden California day! I could tell he didn't want to leave. At the airport I stayed with him at the gate until he had to board. And I didn't cry . . . well, not until I was by myself in the car. I guess I'm getting resigned to this situation. We'll make the best of it—that's all we can do. At least now I can look forward to letters and phone calls again! It will seem like such a treat after those weeks of horrible, mystifying silence.

I drove straight over to Enid's from the airport, and we went shopping at the mall. I'm not usually the type to cheer myself up by spending money on clothes—that's Jessica's bag!—but I have to admit, it was good therapy. Not that I could get totally pumped about picking out a dress for the dance this Friday night after the charity volleyball match with Big Mesa. It's the first dance since Todd moved, and it will be so depressing to go by myself. Going with some random date might be even more depressing, though. It would only make me wish even more that I was with Todd.

The strangest thing happened when Enid and I were sitting in Howard's Deli drinking a soda after I made my big purchase of the day at the Designer Shop. I thought I saw Todd coming out of a shoe store! Enid told me I was hallucinating—at that very moment Todd was in an airplane thirty-five-thousand feet in the air over Iowa or someplace—but I really thought it was him, so we ran all over the mall searching for him. Of course, it turned out to be a wild-goose chase. I guess it was like when you see a mirage in the desert—you want something so much, you conjure it up. I've got to face facts: Todd's back in Vermont, and once more the entire continental U.S. stretches between us. The only way to cross it is by dialing a telephone number or writing a letter . . . and since it's too late to call the East Coast, I think I'll start a letter right now.

Monday, 7:15 P.M.

Dear Diary,

I need your opinion on something. Do you think I'm losing my mind?? Seriously! At the end of study hall today I was walking to Coach Schultz's office to pick up the volleyball-team rosters for my Oracle article. Suddenly this guy who I could swear was Todd strolls out of Coach Schultz's office! The bell had just rung, so people were pouring into the hallway, but that didn't stop me from shouting "Todd!" at the top of my lungs. Maybe you don't think I'm crazy, but virtually everybody else at school does. The guy didn't stop, so I chased him all the way to the lobby, where I got a pretty good look at him through the glass as he hopped into a little blue convertible and took off. By then, of course, I realized it wasn't Todd. But the re-

58

semblance is incredible—they could be twins.
Same height, same build, same broad shoul-
ders, same athletic stride, same wavy brown
hair . . . Geez, listen to me! I sound infatu-
ated or something. I have to confess, I did
sort of find him attractive. What can I say?
He's my type! So now I have a mystery to
solve. Who is this guy?

Monday, 7:45 P.M.

Todd called half an hour ago. As soon as I
hung up the phone, I burst into tears. . . .

"Todd!" I exclaimed happily, settling onto my bed
with the phone pressed close to my face. "I didn't expect to hear from you so soon."

"I was going to wait a day or two to call, but I
couldn't hold out—I miss you so much," he said, his
voice husky. "I can't believe yesterday I was in Sweet
Valley, holding you and kissing you. Now all we've got
is the darned telephone. It's really rotten."

"It's not fair," I agreed softly. "But it's better than
nothing. I love the sound of your voice."

"Yours sounds pretty good, too. So what's up?"

There wasn't much news. I filled him in on my
day's activities, without mentioning his mysterious
look-alike. "The volleyball match will be fun, but I'm
not looking forward to the dance that much," I confessed. "Even though Enid *dragged* me to the mall
and *made* me buy a new dress!"

Todd laughed. "Well, wear it and have a good time. And if you want to take a date, or someone asks you, it's OK with me. Remember what we decided."

I sighed. "We'll see. How about you? What's happening in Burlington?"

I expected him to sigh and moan, kind of the way I had. Go on and on about how lonely he was, how much he missed me. Instead he perked up immediately, sounding downright animated. "Actually, there's something fun on the calendar for the weekend," he told me. "My friend Gina—did I tell you about Gina?"

"Uh, no."

"There was so much to talk about last weekend, I guess I didn't get around to telling you about her and the rest of the gang," he remarked breezily. "Well, Gina's in a couple of my classes, and she's one of those incredibly outgoing people—you know, the cheerleader type—who just walks right up and introduces herself and then hauls you off to meet all her friends."

The cheerleader type? The "gang"? "She sounds nice," I said, gritting my teeth at the picture of some peppy, miniskirted bimbo pouncing on my boyfriend.

"She's a fun person to know," Todd agreed. "She's really involved at school and she knows absolutely everyone. She's friends with a bunch of the guys on the basketball team."

I'll bet she is! I thought grimly. "So what's the deal with this weekend?"

"Her parents have a ski cabin in the mountains at

60

Stowe, and she's throwing a party. Fifteen or twenty people—we'll all bring sleeping bags and stuff. I think Joe's going, and Mario and Evan. They're all on the team with me. And some of the other cheerleaders: Cassie, Donna, Ming, Kimberly. And probably Russell, and Gail, and Derek, and—"

As Todd prattled on about his new friends in Burlington, my insides tied themselves into knots as complicated as the ones Nicholas had taught me during a recent sailing lesson. "That will be a blast," I said, struggling to muster some enthusiasm. Of course I wanted Todd to fit in. It figured that eventually he'd be as popular in Burlington as he'd been at SVH. After all, he was a terrific guy. But did he have to fit in so well, so *fast*?

What if he ends up liking Vermont better than here? I wondered anxiously. *What if he likes it so much he doesn't want to come back, even for visits? What if he likes Gina or one of the other girls better than me?*

"We should probably say good night," Todd suggested a few minutes later. "My phone bill's going to be astronomical."

I hadn't gotten a word in edgewise, but then again, I didn't have much to say. "My turn next time."

"Just don't call over the weekend," he reminded me cheerfully. "'Bye, Liz. I love you."

"I love you, too, Todd."

The line between us went dead. As I hung up the phone, I could feel every single mile that stretched between us.

Last week I'd been the one to falter, to turn to someone else. Would it be Todd's turn now? A weekend at a mountain cabin . . . talk about the perfect setting for romance. Would he end up in the arms of another girl?

There, I've dried my eyes, Diary. It's silly to be so paranoid. I should be happy for Todd, and grateful to Gina—it's hard to be the new kid in town. Grateful to Gina? Who am I kidding?? I'm not that much of a saint! She'd better keep her paws off him!

Tuesday, 10:30 P.M.

OK, Diary, I know this is goofy, but I can't help being a little excited. I found out who the mystery man is, the one who looks like Todd! His name is Michael Sellers, and he plays on Big Mesa's volleyball team. Penny had a bunch of photos at the newspaper office, and there he was, smiling up at me, almost as gorgeous in black and white as he is in the flesh. Michael Sellers . . . a nice name, don't you think? Really strong sounding. Anyway, I'll see him Friday night at the volleyball match! I'm totally intrigued. He looks so much like Todd . . . what if the resemblance is more than skin-deep? What if he has Todd's personality, too? Wouldn't that be wild?? Gosh, I'd fall for him like a ton of bricks. Well, it's something to look forward to—something to think about on Friday instead of dwelling on Todd and Gina and the cabin at Stowe.

On a more serious note, Jess and I walked in on Dad and Steven having a heavy-duty talk in the den tonight. Dad shooed us out, but I knew what it was about without having to listen. Mom and Dad are worried because Steven's started to spend a lot of time at home again—cutting classes at the university and blowing off homework and sports in order to hang out with Betsy. I think I understand why Steven doesn't want to let go. There wasn't anything he could do to prevent Tricia from dying—he was totally helpless. But he does have the power to keep her memory alive. I really feel for him, but he has to get past this mourning thing.

I wonder what kind of fatherly advice Dad gave him. Jessica thinks going out with Cara Walker is the answer to all Steven's problems. Fixing them up is now her mission in life—that and flirting with Winston Egbert for some unfathomable reason. Personally, I think it's ridiculous. The last thing Steven needs is to get involved with someone as self-centered and shallow as Cara. She's a gossip and a snob. (Only you, Diary, know my mean streak!) Jessica swears Cara's changed since her parents split up and her dad and younger brother moved to Chicago, though. Can a leopard change its spots? Who knows. I suppose anything is better for Steven than moping around with Betsy Martin.

Friday, 11:30 P.M.

Dear Diary,

What an incredibly bizarre and hilarious night! I'm kind of embarrassed even to put it down on paper. I mean, I've always considered myself to be pretty levelheaded and down-to-earth. Jessica's the one who gets herself into ridiculous situations. But since Todd moved, I swear I'm starting to lose my grip on reality! First of all, getting dressed before the volleyball match, I was more concerned about how I looked than Jessica was. I changed in and out of about ten pairs of shorts and twenty shirts, and I spent a solid half hour wrestling my hair into a perfect French braid. All this to play volleyball. But you know the real reason, don't you? Yep. Michael Sellers from Big Mesa. I was so hyped at the prospect of seeing him! I'd worked myself up into having a total crush on him even though we'd never actually met. It was a good distraction—kept me from having to think about Todd at the mountain cabin with that horrible cheerleader and the rest of the Burlington High cheerleading squad!

So I was pretty nervous and excited driving over to the high school. I got even more nervous when I saw the setup: the volleyball court was right in the middle of the football field, and the bleachers were packed. Ken was our team captain, and he and Coach Schultz led me, Jessica, Lila, Bruce, and John in warm-up exercises and gave us pep talks, but I was basically out of it. I was too busy scoping out the other team!

Close up, Michael was even more adorable than I'd imagined. Everybody else was commenting on how much he looked like Todd, but I don't think they could tell I was in a total state about it. My heart was pounding and my palms were sweating as if I'd already been playing hard-core volleyball for an hour or so. I really wanted him to notice me. Well, he noticed me all right—because I was so wrapped up in noticing him, I played like dirt!

The volleyball hit the ground right at my feet, and the crowd on the Sweet Valley High side of the bleachers let out a collective groan. "Sorry," I muttered to my teammates, scooping up the ball and lobbing it back over the net to Big Mesa.

"Don't worry about it," Ken said cheerfully, patting me on the arm. "We're all bound to miss a few."

Yeah, but I missed that one because Michael Sellers hit it! I could have told him. Instead of confessing this, I clapped my hands and did a couple of little jumps in place. "Get your act together, Wakefield!" I said under my breath. "Don't blow it!"

The first game against Big Mesa continued. For someone who appears to spend all her time at the makeup counter at the mall, Lila is a pretty fine athlete. She nailed a wicked spike against Big Mesa, regaining the serve for us.

For *me*. Taking up position in the service corner, I took a deep breath. Tossing the ball into the air, I hit a smashing overhand serve, the whole time thinking, *Wow, is he ever gorgeous!*

The ball sailed way out of bounds. There was applause from some of the Big Mesa fans, and a few catcalls from the home section.

My face turned as red as Jessica's shorts. "What's your problem, Liz?" my sister hissed. "Did you forget how to play overnight?"

"I guess I'm not warmed up yet," I answered, shrugging. "Give me a break, OK?"

John Pfeifer and Bruce Patman gave me encouraging smiles, but I could tell my teammates were starting to wonder what my problem was. Lucky for everyone, the ball didn't come anywhere near me for most of the game. Then, when it was all tied up 13–13, Michael Sellers rotated into serving position. I could hardly breathe, watching him wind up for the serve. *What a body,* I thought, spellbound with admiration. *And what style!*

Michael Sellers had style, all right. He served the ball right to me. My reflexes were a little slow, to put it kindly, and I dived for the ball a half beat too late, bobbling it out of bounds instead of over the net. It was game point. Obviously thinking he'd found a sure way to score against us, Michael aimed the ball in my direction again. This time, before I could even set myself up for a return, John lunged in front of me to poach the shot.

Under any other circumstances I would have been furious, but I couldn't deny that John saved the point and kept us in the game. For what it was worth, we ended up losing, 15–13.

Bouncing with victorious confidence, the Big Mesa squad formed a huddle on their side of the net to plan strategy for the second game. I could almost hear their captain's—Michael Sellers's—advice. "Just keep hitting it to the girl with the blond braid and navy-blue shorts!"

The Sweet Valley High team huddled, too. They were all pretty nice to me, considering the fact that I'd just single-handedly lost the game for us. "Let's motivate, folks. We can all play better," Ken said generously. "Just relax, Liz, OK? You can do it."

As we took up positions on the court, Jessica whispered to me, *"Don't* tell me the fact that you've totally crumbled has anything to do with that Big Mesa guy who looks like Todd."

My cheeks flushed hot. "I'm obsessed with him," I confessed.

"Save it for the dance later," Jessica advised.

"But what if he's not interested? What if I can't get his attention?"

"Start playing better and maybe you'll have a chance with him!" Jessica countered.

She was right. So far he probably thought I was a bumbling fool. If he thought anything, that is. I wanted to shine in his eyes. *You can do it,* I thought, repeating Ken's encouraging words in my brain. *You can do it.*

We won the second game, no thanks to me. I continued to be blinded by the glory of Michael Sellers, missing every other shot that came my way. Jessica, John, Lila, Ken, and Bruce were panting with exhaustion from the extra effort of having to cover for my lapses.

When we were five points down in the third and deciding game, Ken called a time-out. "This isn't working," he admitted, sounding discouraged despite himself. "We need a new game plan. Ideas?"

Bruce had a couple of suggestions, and then Jessica spoke up. "Liz and I worked out a great play in a beach tournament once," she remembered. "I volley to her, and she pretends she's going to hit it back to me, set me up for a spike or something, but instead she nails it over the net. It's pretty effective."

Not surprisingly, the others looked skeptical. A great play involving me? Ken shrugged. "It's worth a try," he grunted. "OK, let's turn this thing around!"

We shouted and high-fived each other, making a good show of enthusiasm. And then a miracle happened. Jessica set me up for our trick shot, and we pulled it off. We pulled it off once, twice, three times.

The fans roared their approval. Sweet Valley High was back in the game!

Big Mesa was onto me and Jessica now, so we had to start varying our shots. I'd regained my confidence and was playing pretty much up to my usual speed. We tied the game and pulled ahead, only because when Michael served to me, I managed to block out the image of his face and slam the ball right into an opening on the Big Mesa side. Finally we were serving for the game. Ken punched the ball over the net, and an intense, fast-paced volley ensued. Back and forth, back and forth . . .

It almost seemed to happen in slow motion. Jessica popped the ball straight up in the air with her fingertips, and it hovered just over my head. Clenching my fingers in a tight, hard fist, I pulled back my right arm and swung with all my might. My aim was perfect—all the Big Mesa players dived for the ball, but no one reached it. It hit the ground and the fans erupted in the bleachers. We'd won the match!

Bruce flung his arms around me and twirled me around. Our team jumped around like bunny rabbits, in total joy and disbelief. As students poured down from the stands to congratulate and commiserate with their respective teams, the Sweet Valley High players stepped over to shake hands with their rivals. Michael was talking to Ken, and I decided it was time to make my move. I'd shake his hand, ask casually if he was planning to go to the dance. . . .

As it turned out, I didn't need to make a move. I

stopped for a moment to talk to Jessica, and when I turned back around, there he was. Michael Sellers in the flesh, standing about a foot away from me and gazing straight into my eyes. "Can I give you a ride to the Caravan?" he offered in a warm, deep voice that turned my bones to Jell-O.

I told Michael I'd meet him there since Jessica and I had to drive home first to change. I wore the new dress Enid helped me pick out at the Designer Shop the other day, and I could tell he thought I looked pretty hot—the minute I walked into the club, he swept me onto the dance floor without even saying a word. It was like a dream come true, dancing in his arms. He looked like Todd, he felt like Todd . . . I could almost believe he was Todd. Suddenly I was overcome by this flood of feeling. I didn't even know the guy, but I was ready to give myself to him, body and soul. It was like fate—we were meant to be.

Yeah, right! Thank God I figured out pretty quickly what a major misjudgment I was making. Let me put it this way: Michael Sellers is absolutely nothing like Todd Wilkins in the ways that really matter. Once I saw beyond his looks . . .

We took a break from dancing and headed for the refreshment table. Michael eyed the cold buffet disdainfully. "This is the best they could do, after we worked so hard on the volleyball court?" he complained.

Winston was in charge of refreshments, and I thought he'd done a pretty nice job. "My friend went to a lot of trouble to put this together for us," I said, bristling slightly.

"Well, you can tell him or her from me, it's pretty lame."

I blinked at Michael, unable to reconcile this snotty remark with his sweet, handsome face. *Todd would never be so rude,* I thought. "I think it looks yummy," I said weakly, noticing that Michael's complaints hadn't stopped him from filling his plate. *Low blood sugar—that's it,* I told myself. *Everybody gets a little cranky when they're hungry.*

We sat down, and Michael focused on me in a very flattering manner, his mouth curved in a heart-stopping smile. "So tell me all about yourself, Miss Wakefield," he invited. "How come you played so poorly the first couple of games?"

My own smile faltered. "Uh, well, I guess I was having an off night."

"Can't let that happen," he declared, chomping into a sandwich. "That's what separates us men from the boys—we never have off nights. Take football. I'm varsity offense on the Big Mesa team, by the way," he informed me. "Top scorer last season, and I couldn't do that if . . ."

Michael launched into a detailed and self-congratulatory account of how he'd single-handedly led Big Mesa to countless gridiron victories. *What hap-*

71

pened to "tell me about yourself, Miss Wakefield"? I wondered.

"Let's dance some more," he said abruptly, grabbing my arm and yanking me to my feet when the band returned from their break a few minutes later.

This time, it was a little harder to pretend Michael was Todd. I made a valiant effort, though. As we slow-danced, I closed my eyes and rested my cheek against his shoulder. He ran his hand up and down my back, electrifying my skin with his gentle touch. *Yes,* I thought. *This is the way it's supposed to feel. Just like when I'm dancing with Todd.*

I sighed happily just as Michael barked, "Got a problem, bud?"

My eyes popped open. Winston stood next to us, one hand raised to tap me politely on the shoulder. "I just wanted to line up Elizabeth for the next dance," Winston explained, taken aback by Michael's tone.

"She's busy," Michael snapped. "Bug off."

"Michael!" I exclaimed, pushing him away from me.

He dropped his arms, glaring. "What's *your* problem?"

"You're being rude," I replied. "I'll dance with Winston if I want to."

"Yeah? Then you won't be dancing any more with me," he retorted.

"You're right," I said, stepping closer to Winston. "I won't be."

As Michael stared after us in disgust and disbelief, Winston whirled me away from my foolish fantasy. "What a loser!" he proclaimed, dipping me tango

72

style. "I thought he looked a little like Wilkins at first, but now that I know what a jerk he is, I don't see the resemblance at all."

"Neither do I," I agreed wholeheartedly.

I had a good long talk with Enid after the Michael fiasco. We commiserated about how hard, how really wrenching it is, to let go of the past. She knows exactly what I'm going through. When George broke up with her, for the longest time she clung to the hope that he'd come back and things would be like they were in the old days. She just couldn't bring herself to acknowledge that George had started something new with Robin, and his relationship with Enid was history.

I've been doing the same thing, clinging to the past. I admit it: guilty as charged. And I know I need to snap out of it. Todd's gone, and there's a hole in my life, but I can't expect Nicholas Morrow or Michael Sellers— definitely not Michael Sellers!—or anyone else to fill it. It's up to me to make my life complete. And I will. Just give me a little time.

Saturday, 4:00 P.M.

There's someone I'm more worried about than myself, Diary. Steven. At the Caravan last night instead of dancing with

73

Cara or some other girl, he spent the whole time with Betsy reminiscing about Tricia, and just now, washing his car in the driveway, he broke down and sobbed thinking about her. My heart just breaks for him. All I could do was give him a big hug and tell him it would get easier with time, but what if I'm wrong? Jessica said something to me this afternoon when we were laughing about what a creep Michael Sellers turned out to be, and it really stuck in my mind. "Welcome back to the land of the living, Liz," she said. I do feel as if I've taken a big step toward being my old, independent self. I want the same thing to happen for Steven. He has to take that step himself, though— no one can take it for him. And right now he's still madly in love with a ghost. I can only hope and pray that he'll come back to the land of the living. I can only hold out my hand.

Saturday, 11:00 P.M.

Dear Diary,

Jessica and I aren't exactly doing a brilliant job of cheering Steven up. Mom and Dad went out to a dinner party, so the three of us ordered a Guido's deluxe pizza and rented a movie—it seemed like a fun night, all of us being single and just hanging out together. We blew it, though. Jessica just had to

*open her big mouth and bring up the subject
of Cara, at which point the evening went
downhill faster than an Olympic skier. . . .*

"You know," Jessica said, darting a glance at Steven as she reached for a slice of pizza, "Cara wasn't that psyched about going out with Artie Western tonight. He's not really her type."

I was getting pretty tired of Jessica dropping endless hints to Steven about Cara, and I was sure he was sick of it, too. "Why don't you just drop the Cara campaign?" I asked her. "*She's* not *Steven's* type."

"You have no right to say that," Jessica declared.

I twirled a strand of gooey cheese around my fork. "I'll say whatever I want," I countered, "and anyone in Sweet Valley would agree with me. Cara's snobby and two-faced. She hasn't changed."

"That's totally unfair. You're the snobby one, Liz!"

"I'm not snobby, I'm honest," I protested, "and you'd agree with me if you weren't so fixated on playing matchmaker!"

"Would you two shut up?" Steven pounded his fist on the table. Jessica jumped, startled. I dropped my fork. "Would you quit talking about me as if I weren't even here?"

"I was only—" Jessica began.

"We didn't mean to—" I started.

"I'm fed up with you trying to tell me who to go out with," Steven said to Jessica. Then he turned the full blaze of his eyes on me. "And you're out of line, too, Liz. How can you be so ungenerous toward

Cara? Are you so perfect? You've never made any mistakes? Give Cara a little credit—she's learning from her experiences, growing."

I sank down in my chair, feeling completely rotten and ashamed. Jessica pounced on Steven's praise of Cara. "Then you *do* like her!" she declared triumphantly.

"I said butt out, and I meant it," Steven threatened. "I'm not going to date Cara Walker, and that's final."

"You're a coward," Jessica said, shaking her head. "It's not that you don't want to—you're *afraid* to date her. Why don't you admit it?"

Steven glowered. "I'm not afraid of Cara."

"I didn't say you were afraid of Cara," said Jessica. "You're afraid of everybody else, what they'll think and what they'll say. You're afraid Betsy Martin will get mad at you and make you feel guilty."

I held my breath, astounded by Jessica's gall. Steven's face grew dark with anger. "I'm not afraid of Betsy," he said hoarsely.

"You are," Jessica insisted. "If you weren't, you'd be out with Cara right now instead of palming her off on Artie."

"Drop it, Jess, once and for all!" Steven thundered.

But Jessica had one last parting shot. "I'll drop it, but that doesn't mean it's going to go away. The choice is still there, Steven, and you've got to make it. Tricia's dead and Cara's alive. Take your pick."

Flinging back his chair, Steven leaped to his feet. His face contorted with pain, he stormed out the door to the patio.

I stared at Jessica in disbelief. "How could you say that?" I demanded. "How could you be so mean?"

To my surprise Jessica's stern face dissolved into tears. "Do you think I want to hurt him, Liz? Sometimes you have to be cruel to be kind. Steven's off the deep end with this grief thing. We've tried throwing him a life ring, but it's like he just wants to drown. It's time someone shocked him into saving himself."

Through the sliding glass doors I could see Steven sitting on the edge of the pool, his feet in the water and his head in his hands. "Off the deep end—you're right about that," I said glumly. "But I don't know about the shock treatment, Jess. You may just have pushed him further under."

Monday, 11:20 P.M.

Todd called tonight to give me a blow-by-blow account of the ski weekend. Sounds as if they all had a blast skiing, splashing around in the hot tub, having snowball fights, and eating pizza and hot-fudge sundaes in front of the fireplace. I was pretty relieved that he was so eager to tell me all about it—that means he doesn't have anything to hide. He picked up on a little something in my voice, though, because at the end of the conversation he said, "Hey, Liz, you're not worried about competition from any of these girls, are you?" I said not really (lying through my teeth), and he said I didn't need to be—he and Gina are just good pals. So I feel better. Somewhat.

It's unbelievable, but Jessica may have hit on something Saturday night when she yelled at Steven, trying to jolt him back to reality. She has an amazing way of being right sometimes, almost in spite of herself.

Steven was out all day yesterday, and he came home last night looking happier and more relaxed than I've seen him in ages. I found out why from Jessica today at lunch. It turns out he spent the day with Cara! Can you believe that? Supposedly, Jessica begged Cara for details, but Cara wouldn't say anything except that she and Steven went to the zoo for a picnic and had a nice time. Now, the old Cara would never have kept her lips zipped like that. She was Miss Kiss and Tell. I think it was really tactful of her not to dish the details—it proves that she's concerned about Steven's feelings, protecting his privacy. Jess said there's one thing Cara couldn't hide, though: the fact that she really likes Steven.

So Jessica made me admit that it's starting to look as if she had the right idea being so blunt with Steven. He could have gone over to Betsy's as he usually does on Sunday, but instead he took Cara on a picnic. It's so much healthier.

Which brings me to my lousy attitude. Both Steven and Jessica came down hard on me for saying nasty things about Cara, and they were totally justified. I feel terrible that I've been so close-minded—it looks like Cara really has changed. Somehow she's been transformed into the kind of girl who can make my brother smile. I've been feeling pretty ashamed of myself, so after lunch with Jessica I did something that made me feel much better. I went looking for Cara. . . .

I caught Cara just as she was leaving the cafeteria. "Cara, wait!" I called after her.

She turned, her face registering her surprise. "Liz, hi," she said cautiously. "What's up?"

"Can we talk for a minute?" I asked.

She ducked her head, hiding her face behind a curtain of glossy chestnut hair. "Actually, I'm, um, on my way to the library."

"I'll walk with you," I offered.

She shrugged. "Sure."

As we strolled down the hall side by side, I could tell she was uncomfortable. "Cara, I know you and Steven agreed not to talk about your date yesterday, and that's fine," I hurried to assure her. "I don't want to get into that, at least not directly. I just want to apologize."

She glanced at me, her slender eyebrows lifted. "Apologize? For what?"

Now it was my turn to drop my eyes. "I—for a

79

while I've been after Steven to start dating again, to try to make a new start. But I didn't think he should date *you*. Jessica and I argued about it a lot, and I even came right out and told Steven what I thought," I admitted, my cheeks burning. "I was wrong, Cara." Lifting my eyes again, I met her gaze. "It wasn't for me to say. And when I saw Steven last night, I realized that he's a much better judge of character than I am. He was like a new person—you did that for him."

Cara smiled tentatively. "Thanks, Liz. I don't know what's going to happen between me and Steven, but . . . thanks."

I returned the smile with heartfelt warmth. "Thank *you*, Cara, for giving my brother such a lift. I hope we'll be seeing you around. I'd like us to be friends," I added shyly.

We stopped at the door to my classroom. Cara nodded, looking embarrassed but grateful. "Then we will be, Liz," she said, and darted off toward the library.

Saturday, 5:30 P.M.

Poor Steven. He just can't get a break— it's as if he's under a curse or something. I was meeting Jess at the Dairi Burger this afternoon, and he drove me over so he could tell me about his date with Cara last night— talk about a disaster. It was her birthday, and he wanted to make it special for her, so he asked her to choose a restaurant for dinner, someplace romantic. Well, they ended

80

up at the Valley Inn, which is incredibly romantic . . . but it also happens to be the last restaurant Steven went to with Tricia before she died. Isn't that the most gruesome coincidence? He probably should've told Cara right away—it would have saved both of them a lot of agony and embarrassment—but he didn't want to spoil her birthday. Luckily the maître d' seated them on the opposite side of the dining room from where he'd sat with Tricia, and as the meal went along, Steven started to think he'd be able to pull it off. They were talking and laughing and really enjoying each other's company; he forgot all about Tricia . . . until they stepped onto the dance floor and the band started playing the exact same sentimental old song he'd danced to with Tricia, "Always." He felt so guilty betraying Tricia's memory, he freaked out—ditched Cara on the dance floor, threw some money on the table, and split. She had to take a taxi home! Needless to say, she was kind of icy when he phoned her later—who wouldn't be? But she understood when he explained. It sounds as if it's over between them, though, before it even really began. Cara was pretty firm—she told him she couldn't compete with a ghost. They couldn't have a relationship if he was still tied to Tricia, and Steven had to admit deep in his heart he's still not ready.

I'm so disappointed, for Cara and Steven both. He seemed so much happier! Now it's as if he's backpedaling—he's completely downhearted. When we talked, he was on his way to the Martins' to look at old photo albums with Betsy—Tricia's baby pictures. I gently tried to suggest that maybe this wasn't the greatest idea in the world, for him or Betsy, but nothing I said made any impression. I got the feeling I could have been hitting him over the head and he still wouldn't have blinked. I'm more worried about him than ever, but what can I do that I haven't tried already? What can anyone do?

OK, Diary, I realize I'm totally depressing you. It so happens that I have some comic relief—you guessed it, the latest Jessica Wakefield escapade, which I heard all about at the Dairi Burger!

I'd been wondering about Jessica's sudden interest in Winston Egbert. Usually she doesn't give him the time of day, but lately she's been acting as if she has a crush on him—eating lunch with him, asking him to dance at parties, signing up to do a report on F. Scott Fitzgerald in English so they could be partners. I smelled something fishy. Well, it turns out a couple weeks ago Jessica overheard Mom on the phone with Mrs. Egbert talking about how Mrs. Egbert's brother, who's a famous movie director, was coming to town and the Ebgerts were going to have a cocktail party in his honor. Not surprisingly, Jessica decided then and there that the most important thing in the world was to get invited to that cocktail party so Mrs. Egbert's brother could "discover" her and cast her in his next Hollywood blockbuster.

So this is what happened: the day before the party Jessica's over at the Egberts' and she runs into Mrs. Egbert's brother Marty—what a coincidence, huh?? Jess says something about having "career aspirations" in his field, and he's kind of surprised, but pleased, and he promises they can talk more about it at the cocktail party—he'll even bring some material for her to look over. Jessica is thrilled, walking on air, thinking he's going to bring the script of his next movie and audition her on the spot for the starring role. That's our Jessica. So at the party she rushes right up to him, and sure enough, he's brought along a big fat notebook. The script! What I wouldn't give to have seen Jessica's face when she opened it up and read the title of the "movie": Strategies for Waste Disposal in Los Angeles County. She said she just about died when she discovered that Mrs. Egbert's brother Marty is a civil engineer—her other brother, Phil, who couldn't make it to the party at the last minute because he's on location in

London, is the movie director! What a great blooper. I laughed until my sides hurt—I couldn't eat my burger and fries. Jessica's like a tennis ball, though—she always bounces back. She figures all her efforts to butter up Winston won't go to waste—Phil is bound to visit someday!

Saturday, 11:00 P.M.

Sometimes we're not as helpless as we think. I like to believe that, anyway.

I went to talk to Betsy Martin today. It was scary, but I knew I had to try it—there was nothing to lose and everything to gain. Parked in front of her house on Wentworth Avenue, I almost chickened out, but finally I dragged myself out of the car and walked right up to the door, and I'm so, so glad I did. . . .

The doorbell didn't work, and I wasn't surprised. The neighborhood was shabby, and the Martins' house was the most dilapidated on the street: badly in need of paint, with dead shaggy grass in the front yard and a sagging porch. I rapped on the door, lightly at first and then with more force. You can't just knock so quietly no one will hear and then run away, I told myself. Don't be a wimp. This is for Steven.

After a moment Betsy opened the door, her hazel eyes widening when she saw who it was. She'd stayed

84

with my family for a while after her sister's death—
the two girls had lived alone with their widowed, al-
coholic father—and we'd become friends during that
time. Since then, though, we hadn't seen much of
each other, and she had to know that I disapproved of
her influence over Steven. "Betsy, can I come in?" I
asked boldly. "I need to talk to you."

She hesitated, her expression becoming blank.
"Sure," she said, gesturing me into the living room.

Inside, the house was neat and clean, though the
furniture was battered and the wallpaper faded.
Somebody—Betsy, I guessed—was doing the best
she could with what she had to work with.

We sat down on adjacent chairs, and Betsy
waited, her arms folded and her jaw tight, for me to
say something. I cleared my throat. "Betsy, I'm here
because we're friends, so I know I can be open with
you about this. I know we both care about Steven—
we both want the best for him."

"And you don't think he should be hanging out
with me," Betsy interjected.

"I think it's fine for you to hang out together," I
assured her. "It's the fact that all you do when you're
together is talk about Tricia that troubles me."

Two spots of indignant color rose in Betsy's fair
cheeks. "We *loved* Tricia," she said, her voice quavering with barely suppressed emotion. "Why shouldn't
we talk about her, remember her? She meant the
world to us!"

I sighed. This was going to be harder than I
thought. "I know, Betsy," I said gently. "I know how

much you two loved Tricia, and how much you both still miss her. I understand."

Tears sprang to Betsy's eyes; she bit her lip. "Then why are you here?"

"Because . . . I wanted to tell you something you don't know about Tricia, something that was just between her and me. A promise she asked of me, early in her illness."

"A promise she asked of *you*?"

I nodded. "Remember what she did when she first found out she had leukemia, and that the prognosis was pretty poor—she probably wouldn't live? Remember what she did to Steven?"

"She broke up with him without even giving him a reason," Betsy recalled, playing with the fringe on a threadbare throw pillow. "She didn't tell him about the leukemia."

"That's right. She thought it would be easier for him. It hurt her terribly to let him go when she needed him most, but she figured if she cut the emotional ties, he'd have a head start getting over his loss. He'd still be devastated when she died, but it wouldn't hurt in quite the same way."

"Steven found out, though," said Betsy.

"Because *I* found out, and I told him, even though Tricia asked me not to," I admitted. "That was the promise, and I broke it."

"That was the right thing to do," Betsy said fervently. "They were together for Tricia's last weeks, and it meant the world to both of them."

"That's what I thought at the time," I agreed, my

expression somber. "But now I'm not so sure. Maybe Tricia's first instinct was right. She was unselfishly thinking about Steven, what was best for him. If I'd kept my promise, maybe he *would* be over her by now—he'd be suffering less as time passes, instead of more."

Betsy stared at me, her eyes brimming. A solitary tear stole down her freckled cheek. "He *is* suffering, isn't he?" she whispered. "And you think it's my fault."

"I don't think you'd ever hurt Steven on purpose," I hurried to assure her. "I know you love him like a brother. But the fact is, in some ways it's like he died, too. He's given up on life—he's afraid to be happy. He's afraid that loving again means being unfaithful to Tricia, and you've fed that fear."

Betsy rubbed her damp eyes. "It's because I'm afraid, too. I feel like it's up to us to keep her memory alive. So often I wasn't there for her when she was alive—this seems like my last chance to do something for her, and I don't want to let her down. Can't you understand that?"

My own eyes sparkled with tears. I couldn't imagine losing *my* sister. How would I survive without Jessica? "Of course I understand, Betsy. You just have to see that there's a difference between you and Steven. For you the past and present can coexist. You can be devoted to Tricia's memory and have a relationship with Jason at the same time. There's no conflict there. But for Steven, moving on to a new relationship brings a lot of guilt."

"And I've been making it worse." Remorse shadowed Betsy's face. "I've really been coming down hard on him about Cara. Oh, Liz, I didn't even realize I was doing that. I feel terrible."

"Does that mean you'll help?" I asked hopefully. "Will you help me grant Tricia's last wish? Will you help set Steven free?"

Reaching out, Betsy took my hand. I squeezed her hand tightly, feeling the love and commitment—Tricia's legacy—flowing between us. "I'll help," Betsy declared, her eyes glowing.

It was a pretty big victory, getting Betsy to recognize the role she's played in holding Steven back from a full emotional recovery. We really had a terrific talk, but I still felt discouraged about Steven and Cara—there didn't seem to be any way to repair the damage that had been done there. But believe it or not, Betsy of all people came up with a scheme to get those two together, and it worked! Steven told me all about it tonight when he got home. He looked so happy, I started crying, and we gave each other the biggest hug.

It turned out he'd gotten this mysterious note earlier this evening, supposedly from Mom, saying the rest of us had gone out to dinner and reminding him to meet "his friend" under the clock at Sweet Valley High at seven P.M. He couldn't remember making a date with anybody, but he's been pretty spacey lately, so he went, and who should show up at seven but Cara! She'd gotten the same mysterious message from her mother! Just as they were figuring out that someone had set them up, Mr. Collins's little boy Teddy rode up on his bicycle with two packages, one labeled "Cara" and the other "Steven." Inside were pencil drawings: for Steven a beautiful portrait of Cara, and for Cara a picture of Steven. Right away Steven knew who had drawn them, and he knew what it meant. Betsy is an artist, and she'd given them her blessing, and it was as if they had Tricia's blessing as well. He said it was like a door opening . . . and the best part was, Cara was on the other side waiting for him, ready to give him one more chance. He didn't tell me all the juicy details, but I could tell by his dreamy smile that something pretty romantic happened!

Betsy enclosed a note to Steven with the drawing of Cara, which he showed to me. Here is what it said:

Dear Steve,

I have finally come to realize what Tricia knew long ago: a wonderful person like you should be looking toward his future, not his past. You made my sister so happy while she was alive. Now it's time for you to bring your kindness and affection to someone else. Do *what Trish wanted, Steve: embrace life and all the beautiful things it has to offer.*

Fondly, Betsy.

Isn't that remarkable? I'm so happy for my big brother, I could burst. After all he's suffered, he deserves a happy ending, and a new beginning. Meanwhile, Todd wasn't home just now when I called. He's been out a lot lately. . . . What's around the corner for me?

I walk forward.

"Life goes on"—that's what everyone says.

I walk forward, my steps slow,
Looking over my shoulder into the past.
Waiting by phones and at airports,
My steps halt.
Frozen in time.

Part 3

Dear Diary,

Jessica and I ate lunch together today so we could start planning for Grandma and Grandpa Wakefield's visit—they're coming tonight, for three whole weeks! Isn't that fantastic? We haven't seen them in more than a year—I can't wait to give them both a gigantic hug.

Anyway, Jess had this idea to decorate the house with streamers and balloons, "Welcome, Gram and Gramps," that sort of thing, and she was blabbing on and on about it. It was hard to pay attention to her, though, because I was totally distracted by an argument Dana Larson and Emily Mayer were having at the next table. You know, of course, that Dana is the lead singer for The

91

Droids and Emily plays drums—they're best
friends as well as bandmates. Well, Emily is
usually the sweetest, quietest, most easygoing
girl, but I've noticed that she's been really
tense lately, and the other day she told me
she'd overheard her dad talking with her
stepmother Karen about sending her away to
boarding school. Isn't that awful? She was so
upset, and I don't blame her. It seems to have
something to do with her little half sister,
Karrie. That's what she and Dana were ar-
guing about in the cafeteria. Dana was say-
ing Emily's lucky to have a new baby at
home; Emily told her she just didn't under-
stand. Suddenly they dragged me into the
discussion and it went from bad to worse. . . .

"Hey, Liz!" Dana Larson waved a hand to get my
attention. "Help me talk some sense into Em. She's
acting like having a cute little baby sister is such a
drag, just because she has to change a dirty diaper
now and then."

I twisted in my chair to face them. I didn't really
want to butt into the conversation, which seemed
kind of personal; Emily's cheeks were pink with embarrassment. But I couldn't exactly ignore Dana.
"Well . . ." I began.

"You know, Dana," Emily broke in, pushing back
her wavy brown hair, "I do more than change a few
dirty diapers. I baby-sit all the time, whenever Karen
wants me to, whether I have other plans already or

not. My whole life has changed since Karrie was born."

"So try to see the bright side," Dana said cheerfully. "You have an adorable baby sister to love. I'd *adore* a baby sister, wouldn't you, Liz?"

"A new baby is a big adjustment for a family," I pointed out with an encouraging smile for Emily. "I bet it throws everybody off balance—everybody has a new role to play."

"That's the problem," Emily said, twisting the stem off an apple. "Karen doesn't want me to have *any* role. She just wants to eject me from the family."

"I don't believe it," Dana declared. "Karen's a doll! Whenever I come over, she's so nice to me." Dana turned to me for confirmation. "She's always baking chocolate-chip cookies or something—hardly the wicked stepmother, wouldn't you say?"

"You don't know, Dana," Emily burst out before I could answer. "You don't *live* with her. It started way before Karrie was born, but it's worse now. She wants to be a family with just my dad and Karrie. I'm a reminder of Dad's first marriage—I get in the way. She doesn't want me around, and she's making my life miserable!"

I reached out to touch Emily's arm, but she'd already jumped to her feet. Tears spilling down her face, she grabbed her tray and dashed off.

Dana pushed back her chair, her brown eyes concerned. "God, I didn't mean to be so insensitive," she murmured. "I didn't realize it was that bad at home for her. Poor Em!"

I watched as Dana, her cropped blond hair

bouncing, hurried through the cafeteria after Emily. Jessica whistled. "Do you think her stepmother is really that horrible?" she asked.

I shook my head. "How can we know? We only have one side of the story." But Emily didn't strike me as the sort of person to exaggerate, and she certainly wasn't a liar. I couldn't help thinking about the boarding-school story. What was going on at the Mayers' house these days?

After school I met up with Emily at the Oracle *office. Mr. Collins told me she was dropping by because she wanted to join the editorial staff, which kind of surprised me. I hadn't realized she was interested in writing—I thought music took up all her time. Well, I got the whole scoop from Emily, and now I'm really worried about her. . . .*

"So you want to find out what's involved in writing for the newspaper!" I greeted Emily cheerfully. "I didn't know you had journalistic aspirations."

Emily dumped her books on a table and flopped into a chair. "To tell you the truth, Liz, I don't," she confessed. "This whole writing thing is a shot in the dark for me."

I tipped my head to one side, puzzled. "So . . . you're just looking for something to help you keep busy," I suggested delicately. *In other words, something to keep you out of the house so your stepmother doesn't drive you crazy!*

Emily inched her chair closer to mine. "Sort of. Liz, can I talk to you about something? I really need some advice—I mean, I'm *desperate*—and you're the smartest, most considerate, most *stable* person I know."

I smiled wryly. "Don't give me too much credit," I warned her. "My life falls apart on me at regular intervals. But I'm always happy to lend an ear. What's on your mind?"

"Well, you got the gist of it at lunch today," said Emily. "And remember what I said to you the other day, about boarding school?" I nodded. "Well, it's not just a vague possibility," she continued. "Karen really wants to send me away, and she's bearing down hard on my dad about it."

"That's terrible!" I exclaimed. "He'd never go along with it, though . . . would he?"

"In the old days, no," Karen said sadly. "When it was just him and me after my mom died, we had a really special relationship. We were really close and he was totally supportive of everything I did. Like my music. He was the one who bought me the drum set, because *he'd* played drums when he was a kid. It would never have occurred to him to send me away! But since he married Karen . . ."

"Things have changed."

Emily threw up her hands. "I've tried so hard to get along with her, and it's been an uphill battle because all the effort's on my side. I wanted it to work, though, because I knew it would make Dad happy. He's madly in love with her and she's his wife and

95

that's just the way it is. But nothing I do ever pleases her. Even before she got pregnant, she was constantly picking on me, criticizing my friends, ragging about my grades, complaining about the drums—'that fiendish racket,' she calls it."

It was as if a dam had broken; the words poured out of Emily in an unstoppable flood. "It got worse when Karen was pregnant," she went on. "She was so fussy about keeping the house clean, about noise, meals, everything. Dad and I had to tiptoe around; it was like we needed her permission just to draw a breath. And since the baby was born . . ." Emily heaved a deep sigh. "It's like Karen has two missions now: to be a perfect mother to Karrie, her precious, adorable *real* daughter, and to get *me*, her stepdaughter, out of her house."

"Oh, Emily," I commiserated. "I'm sure it won't come to that. She's a new mother. Maybe she's just stressed out, blowing off steam."

"No, it's a cold-blooded campaign," Emily swore. "Every chance she gets, she bad-mouths me to my father. Her latest thing is The Droids. She's always been negative about that, about the noise when I practice, about the hours I keep. Dad always understood when I had to be out late because of a gig, but now Karen claims that all this disrupts little Karrie's routine and *her* peace of mind. It's anti-intellectual, and the other kids in the band are wild, a bad influence—she doesn't come right out and say she thinks they're a bunch of drug-dealing social outcasts, but that's the message she manages to get across."

"Wow," I breathed.

"So once she's got *that* picture in Dad's head, it's not a big step convincing him I need the discipline of boarding school," Emily concluded, her whole body limp with despair. She gestured around the *Oracle* office. "This is my last hope. She'd just *have* to approve of my being on the newspaper staff. I'll give up the drums, if that's what it takes."

"Oh, no, Emily!" I cried. "You couldn't give up the drums, the band. You love music, it's your life!"

"I love music, but I love my dad and Sweet Valley more," Emily said simply.

"Do you really think it's going to come down to a choice, a sacrifice like that?" I asked.

Emily nodded glumly. "And even that might not be enough. Karen's not going to let up until she gets her way. She's going to make *Dad* choose. Her and Karrie against me. How can I get him to take my side?"

Isn't that a heartbreaking story, Diary? I feel so sorry for Emily . . . and so lucky, in comparison, to have two loving, supportive parents who think the world of me. Anyway, I'd better put you away and run downstairs. I can smell something burning in the kitchen— Jessica must be cooking!—and Grandma and Grandpa Wakefield will be here any minute!

Monday, 10:30 P.M.

Hi again, Diary,
We had the most wonderful evening with Grandma and Grandpa—it is so fabulous to

see them! They get younger all the time, I swear. They are so active and happy and interested in a million things. Grandma's in school getting her Ph.D. in American history at the University of Michigan—isn't that the coolest? I love thinking about her walking around campus with a backpack, looking just like a kid except for the fact that she has silver hair. She's such an inspiring role model— I hope I'm still learning new things and having adventures when I'm her age.

Anyway, Mom cooked a marvelous dinner—teriyaki steak and mushroom rice and fresh fruit salad—and as usual Grandpa had us cracking up the whole time with his hilarious stories. We made a million plans for this week—Thursday after school we'll go to Hampshire Place, the new mall, and Grandma wants to take us to a museum an hour's drive up the coast. It's going to feel like a holiday every day. I wish they lived closer so we could see them more often, but I guess that's part of the reason their visits are so special. We have to make the most of them once a year. Grandma's in Jessica's room right now, helping her with Mr. Jaworski's history paper! It's going to be a great three weeks.

One cloud in an otherwise bright sky . . . I talked to Todd tonight. Why a cloud? you ask. Usually he's the one who puts stars in my eyes. Well, not tonight. After we hung up,

I just sat on my bedroom floor and cried. It was a fairly ordinary conversation. He blabbed about a basketball game his team won the other night, a big test he has tomorrow, that sort of thing. I don't know what it was exactly that got to me. Maybe that he could have been talking to any of his old friends from Sweet Valley—he would've told the same stories, in the same way, to Ken or Winston. There was no special feeling there for me. Oh, Diary, I wish I didn't care so much if he sounds distant or doesn't tell me he loves me before we say good-bye. I wish I could feel like just another old friend. I'll get over this . . . won't I?

Tuesday, 10:15 P.M.

Grandma, Grandpa, Jess, and I had a ferocious card game after supper tonight. Grandma invented the game—it's a wacky variation on poker that involves a lot of cards flying around and people shouting. We really made a racket! And I swear, Grandpa cheats—I told him so and we all started laughing hysterically. They are really a riot, more fun than a lot of my Sweet Valley High friends!

Too bad Mom didn't want to play cards with us. Maybe it would've cheered her up— she seemed a little down tonight. Probably she's just tired from working so hard. It's tough having a demanding career and also taking care of a house and kids, although of course Dad helps as much as he can, and so do Jess and I. I admire Mom a lot—she's a great role model, too, just like Grandma. Hmm . . . have I ever told her that I think so?

Wednesday, 4:00 P.M.

Dear Diary,
I learned something absolutely unbeliev-able about Emily Mayer today. Her mother isn't dead!

"Hi, Em," I said brightly, looking up from the computer I was typing on as Emily strolled into the *Oracle* office. "How's that trial article about the marching-band competition coming along?"

Emily wrinkled her nose. "It's not," she confessed, slipping off her jacket and straddling a chair. "I struggled with it all last night, but I have absolutely no idea how to pull all the facts together into a story."

"It's tough," I agreed, tilting back in my chair. "You'll get the hang of it with some time and practice, though. The best thing to do is just go for it—whip something off."

"What if it's crummy?"

I laughed. "Then Penny will make you rewrite it, or maybe she'll decide not to include it in the paper at all. You won't know until you try."

"I don't know, Liz." Emily sighed tiredly. "I might not have the energy for this."

I tapped a pencil thoughtfully on the table. "It *does* take a lot of energy, and a fair amount of time," I agreed. "You have to really love it. Are you sure you want to trade drum practice"—I held up the rough draft of the article I was working on—"for this?"

"No, I'm not," Emily admitted, "but I told you what was going on at home. Things are getting hairier all the time. Last night Dad and I had a big talk about my curfew—Karen wants me in at ten on weeknights so I don't wake up the baby, which basically chops band practice in half. He always used to trust me—I didn't even have a curfew. Now he says I'm not trying hard enough to accommodate Karen. I'm really getting scared, Liz." Emily's eyes were wide. "I have to prove to them that I *am* trying to do things the way they want me to. Maybe if I become an editor for the newspaper . . ."

"I want to help you, but I can't guarantee that you will," I said frankly. "And I also can't guarantee that it will make a difference for you at home if Penny and Mr. Collins *do* make you an editor."

Emily looked as if she were about to burst into tears. I racked my brain to think of something to say that would comfort her. *There's bound to be another side to this story,* I speculated. Karen Mayer could be a witch . . . or she could just be an ordinary woman, frazzled from taking care of an infant and doing her best to build a stepfamily. *Maybe Emily's biased against Karen because she thinks Karen's trying to take her mom's place. That would sure make it impossible to keep things in perspective!*

"I'm sure your father would feel terrible if he knew you were this unhappy," I began slowly. "He hasn't stopped loving you just because he now has Karen and Karrie to love, too. It's hard to make a stepfamily work, hard for everybody involved. Do you . . ." I searched for a tactful way to ask a nosy, personal question. "Do you still think a lot about— how old were you when your mother died?"

Emily's face flushed bright red, and I wanted to kick myself. What a mean thing to do, to bring up that painful subject! How could I be so nosy and insensitive?

"Can you keep a secret, Liz?" Emily asked to my surprise.

Her manner was urgent, confiding. I blinked. "A secret? Of course."

I waited. Emily took a deep breath. "My mother . . . isn't dead."

I practically fell off my chair. "She *isn't?* Then what . . . why . . . ?" I stuttered.

Emily's shoulders slumped; she's a petite girl, and all of a sudden she looked as tiny as a child. "One day when I was in second grade, I came home from school and she was gone," Emily related quietly. "She'd left a note for my dad and me—no explanation, really, just an announcement. She was going to Chicago, and she didn't plan to come back." Her face crumpled.

"Oh, Emily," I said softly, shifting my chair so I could slip an arm around her shoulders.

102

Emily sniffled. "What a thing to do, huh? She was true to her word—she never did come back. Dad divorced her, and after that we didn't hear from her much. She was pretty messed up back then—he decided it wasn't healthy for me to talk to her, and I was happier when we stopped the phone calls. It was so confusing for me—it really tore me up. I have no idea whether she ever got her life together."

"So you made up a story," I said.

"I was ashamed," Emily explained. "It seemed so weird. What did it say about me and Dad? It was easier to pretend to the world that she'd died. That way I didn't have to explain to other people something I didn't even understand myself."

I clucked my tongue sympathetically. Emily straightened her shoulders. "I just don't know how much more I can take," she said, making a visible effort to sound matter-of-fact. "My family fell apart once before, and now it may happen again. Dad's my whole world, but now he's leaving me, in a different way than Mom did, maybe, but it feels the same."

I squeezed Emily's hand. "I wish I could help."

Emily smiled bravely. "You do, just by listening. And you won't tell anyone about my mother, will you?"

"Not a soul," I promised.

"I knew I could trust you." Emily hopped to her feet. "I guess I should head over to the library and take another crack at my trial article."

"Don't do it if it's not fun for you, Em. Your time's too valuable. And you know," I mused, "if Karen *is* looking for reasons to find fault with you, changing

103

your extracurricular activities probably isn't a long-term solution to the problem. She'll just get after you about something else."

"Good point." Emily shouldered her backpack and started toward the door. "Thanks, Liz," she said, turning back for a moment. "I always seem to feel a lot better after talking to you."

"Then talk to me all you want," I urged her with a smile. "Seriously. Call anytime, or just drop by my house."

"I may take you up on that," she said, waving. "So long."

What a secret, huh, Diary? Poor Emily, having to carry a burden like that around. She seems like a strong person, considering, but there's only so much one sixteen-year-old girl can take. I can't help feeling that that household is heading for a major explosion. . . .

Wednesday, 10:30 P.M.

Grandma and Grandpa took me and Jessica out to this fabulous Chinese restaurant tonight. We had so much fun trying to decipher the menu, and then when the food came, Grandpa pretended he didn't know how to use chopsticks even though of course he does because he and Grandma eat Chinese all the time—they practically live on take-out food now that she's back in school and doesn't have time to cook. The fortune cookies were the funniest part. Grandma's said, "You will set foot on every continent on earth before your days are done." Isn't that a good fortune for an adventurous person like her? And Grandpa's said, "Beware that your jests don't turn back on you," or something like that— good advice for the world's worst practical joker. You wouldn't believe mine—it really gave me the chills. I have it right here in my pocket. "Don't give your heart away— you can't live without it." Doesn't that say it all?

So it was another unforgettable night with Gram and Gramps. I love them so much. Something strange happened right before we left for the restaurant, though. Mom got home from work early—she actually canceled her last client for the day so she could grocery shop for a big cookout. She seemed bummed when Jessica and I told her we'd already made plans with Grandma and Grandpa. She wanted to come along with Dad, but we reminded her that he hates Chinese and that's why we never get to have it. I was worried that we'd hurt her feelings, but Jessica says moms don't get insecure about stuff like that—what difference does it make if

we eat the steaks tomorrow instead of tonight? I hope that's true.

Thursday, 4:15 P.M.
Dear Diary,

I'm lying on a chaise lounge on the patio,
soaking up the warm late-afternoon sun.
Boy, does it feel good! Living in southern
California is the greatest. I hope Todd is
freezing his buns off in Vermont!

Mom's acting stranger and stranger. She keeps
asking me and Jess to do things with her, at really
funny times when it's not convenient for anybody.
Like last night she wanted to go to a movie when
we all got back from the Chinese restaurant, but
Grandma had already suggested a walk, and then
Jess and I had homework. And right after school
today she called from the office—she wanted to go
for a drive along the water. In the middle of a
workday! Can you figure this out? I felt bad
blowing her off, but we already had plans to go
shopping at Hampshire Place with Grandma and
Grandpa. Jessica doesn't think it's anything to
worry about, but I can't help wondering. Did she
and I do something to cause this weird behavior,
and if so, what?

Thursday, 9:30 P.M.

Emily called when I was sitting on the
patio before. I feel so bad for her. Diary, you

106

don't hear me say this often, but her step-mother is a witch. *There's no doubt in my mind now—Emily's not exaggerating the situation, and she's not biased. Wait till you hear this story!*

We couldn't talk on the phone because Emily burst into tears and was totally incoherent, so I invited her over. Poor thing walked the whole way and ended up having to sit at the dinner table with my entire family. I told her we'd talk later, but she was so on the verge—she started to cry right then and there, and of course then everyone got really worried and wanted to know what was wrong. I thought she'd be too embarrassed to say, but I guess she felt at home with us— Grandma gave her a big hug and Mom ran into the kitchen for some food. Before we knew it, all the gory details were spilling out.

It sounds like for once Emily was having a nice, relaxed, happy day. Ordinarily, it's like walking on eggshells trying to stay on her stepmother's good side. She can't do anything without Karen yelling at her or interfering. First Karen tried to restrict Emily by making rules about when she could practice her music and stuff like that, and then she started changing them totally arbitrarily. Whatever Emily does, she's bound to get into trouble for it. Meanwhile, brochures keep coming in the mail from New England boarding schools—really scary. But this afternoon Emily thought she was safe. Karen had taken little Karrie to the pediatrician for a checkup, so Emily figured it was a good time to invite over Dan Scott, the Droids' bass guitarist, to hear her new cymbal set. Now, I happen to know that Emily has a wicked crush on Dan, although she'd never come right out and admit it. Right now they're just good buddies, but the relationship is on its way to something more. So there they are, having a good time, when Karen barges down into the basement holding Karrie, who's squalling up a storm, and lights into Emily, right in front of Dan. Karen yelled at her for making so much noise and for having a boy in the house without permission, and then—this is the worst part—she accused Emily of turning into a tramp like her mother. She revealed Emily's secret, and she called Emily's mother a tramp! Isn't that the meanest thing you've ever heard?

So Karen's hysterical, the baby's screaming, Dan is totally mortified, and Emily's just numb. I get the chills just picturing the scene, and I could tell Mom and Dad and Jess and my grandparents were just as horrified. Emily said she showed Dan out and then called me. She couldn't think of anything else to do. We all felt so bad for her. She wants to stay with us for a while—she doesn't want to go back home, and I don't blame her. Mom and Dad think that's fine, for a night or two anyway, but of course they made her call her father so he'd know where she was and that she was all right. She did, and came back to the table even more shaken. It turned out Karen had told Mr. Mayer a totally skewed version of what happened this afternoon, and he yelled at Emily for being disobedient and uncooperative. I guess I'm not surprised, from what I know of Karen, but isn't that despicable? Emily couldn't bear to tell her dad the truth of what really happened. She just swallowed the lecture, and then he gave her a horrible ultimatum: be back home in one hour, or he'd put her drums out on the street. I can't believe a father would say anything so cruel to his daughter, but I guess he meant it. Gram, Gramps, Jess, and I drove her home, and I've never seen a sadder, more defeated person.

Friday, 4:45 P.M.

Dear Diary,

I looked for Emily all morning, but I didn't see her until lunch period, when she came by the newspaper office. She didn't want to talk about what happened when she got home last night, but I can guess. She asked me about putting an ad in The

Oracle—she's selling her drum and cymbal set! I think her dad and stepmom made some kind of deal—we won't send you to boarding school if you quit The Droids and toe the line around the house. It seems so unfair—music is her heart and soul!

I tried to talk her out of it, but she'd made up her mind. So after school I tracked down Dan Scott. He really, really cares about her. I can tell by the look on his face when he talks about her how worried he is. . . .

"Dan, I want to talk about Emily," I said, stopping next to his locker.

Dan looked up from dialing the combination, his face flushing. "Did you—did she . . . ?"

"She told me about what happened at her house yesterday," I confirmed. "It sounded awful!"

Dan raked a hand through his baby-fine, sun-streaked hair. "It *was* awful. Emily's really private about a lot of things—I had no idea what she was up against at home. That stepmother of hers . . . I wouldn't be in Em's shoes for the world. But what can we do?"

"Has she said anything to you about quitting The Droids?"

He nodded, his gray eyes flashing. "We can't let her do it, Liz. I'm not thinking about the band—I mean, we'll miss her, and it will be tough finding another drummer as good. I'm thinking about her, her happiness and her sanity. What will her life be without music? It's her favorite thing. Why should she have to give it up to please her stepmother?"

"It's not fair," I agreed. "If she sells her drums, she'll regret it for the rest of her life."

"Sells her drums?" Dan repeated, his jaw dropping. Clearly he hadn't heard that part of Emily's plan. "She wants to run an ad in *The Oracle*—that's how serious she is about this."

"I can't believe it." Dan shook his head. "She might as well sell part of her body, an arm or a leg!"

"What do you think I should do?" I asked. "I could pretend I forgot to put the ad in, but next week she'd probably just ask me again—or ask someone else on the staff."

"No, you shouldn't lie to her," said Dan. Suddenly his eyes lit up. "Wait a minute. How much did you say she was asking for the drums?"

"I didn't, but the ad's right here in my purse." I pulled out Emily's neatly folded note. "Two hundred dollars or best offer."

Dan rubbed his chin thoughtfully. "That's a bargain for a drum set of that quality. Someone'll snap them up in no time."

"And Emily will lose them forever," I said, crestfallen.

To my surprise he smiled. "Not if *I* buy them from her."

I gaped. "You?"

"Sure, why not?" His grin widened. "I don't just play bass, you know—I've dabbled with a few other instruments, including drums. So, what if I buy this set, play them for a while . . . and then decide to return them to their rightful owner?"

I resisted the urge to throw my arms around him. It made me so happy to know there were two of us fighting for Emily—the odds didn't seem so stacked against her. "Dan, that's a great scheme, and a real act of love!"

He blushed at the word "love," but he was still smiling. "I'm starting to think that's my motivation," he confessed.

Sunday, 3:30 P.M.

Dear Diary,

It's been more than a week since I last wrote in here. Sorry about that! I've been really busy with school—a French exam, a biology lab report, my Oracle *article about the new Honor Society inductees—and doing things with Grandma and Grandpa. So busy, I haven't even been thinking that much about Todd. That feels really good, to tell you the truth. You don't need a boyfriend to have a full and happy life, you really don't. I've been telling myself that for ages now, but I'm actually starting to believe it. We still talk once a week on the phone, of course, and when I hear his voice, the feelings rush back. Sometimes he's really affectionate and sometimes I am and sometimes we're both pretty casual. All in all, though, I don't even feel* jealous when he talks about his friends, including Gina. It's as if I've finally been able to put my past in a compartment—it's just another part of my life, and not even the biggest part anymore. I feel free, and I hope he does, too.

Mom just proposed a big mother-daughter shopping trip, but Grandma's taking me and Jessica hot-air ballooning in a few minutes. Sounds like fun, huh? Trust Grandma to want to do something so wild and crazy. Mom almost sounded mad when we told her—maybe she doesn't think it's safe. I can't help feeling that there's something bugging her, but if she doesn't tell us what it is, what can we do?

I haven't seen much of Emily Mayer lately. She didn't call me all last week, or even drop by the Oracle office. Dan said he successfully purchased her drum set, for "a friend" supposedly, and he said Emily's spending all her free time baby-sitting for Karrie. He gets the impression that that's the only way Emily can think of at this point to keep the family peace, but Emily won't talk about it. It just can't be healthy, bottling everything up like that. She must really miss her drums and The Droids. But maybe if things are better at home, it was the right choice for her. It still doesn't seem fair to me.

Grandma's shouting for me—time to go ballooning!

Sunday, 10:45 P.M.

Jessica thought hot-air ballooning was the greatest thing ever, and she'd probably go up again tomorrow if she got the chance, but once was enough for me. The fact that I didn't vomit was a major triumph! My stomach's still a little queasy. But what an incredible view! The balloon place was right on the beach, and we lifted up and sailed like a bird high above Sweet Valley, looking down on the sparkling ocean and the rolling green hills. It was so quiet and still up there, nothing like flying in a plane, and it was a smooth ride until the end. The landing was pretty bumpy!

When we got home, Dad took me and Jess aside for a little talk about Mom. I just knew there was something funny going on with her. . . .

"Do you really need to talk to us now, Dad?" Jessica asked. "We're helping Grandpa make soup."

"It'll only take a minute," my father promised.

Taking each of us by an arm, he steered us toward his study. I caught Jessica's eye behind his back. "What did we do?" I mouthed.

114

She lifted her shoulders, saying silently, "I have no idea!"

Dad closed the study door behind us, and my feeling of impending doom deepened. It looked as if we were about to get a major lecture . . . but why, and about what?

"Is something wrong, Dad?" I asked anxiously.

He sat down on the edge of his desk and folded his arms across his chest. It was his courtroom pose, and he looked pretty stern. I automatically felt guilty, even though I didn't know what crime I'd committed.

"Actually, something *is* wrong," he confirmed. "It's your mother. Have you noticed anything odd about her behavior lately?"

I glanced at Jessica, thinking about the conversations we'd had on this topic. "Well, yeah, now that you mention it," I said. "But, Dad, what's the matter? Is she OK?"

Jessica clapped a hand over her mouth and collapsed onto the sofa. "Ohmigod," she wailed. "Mom's sick. She's dying! She only has a few weeks to live, and that's why she keeps asking us to do stuff with her. Ohmi—"

"No, no, no," Dad interjected hurriedly. "Don't panic. It's nothing like that. Physically, she's fine. It's her feelings that are a little bruised these days, that's all."

"Her feelings? What do you mean?" I asked.

"Well, this may seem funny to you. You probably don't think of your parents as being ordinary people with weaknesses and insecurities, but we

115

are. And right now your mother feels left out."

"Left out?" repeated Jessica, baffled.

I nodded slowly, the light dawning. "Grandma and Grandpa," I guessed.

Dad nodded. "That's right. The four of you keep running off to do fun things together, and she never seems to fit into your plans. She's afraid she can't compete with them, that she's boring in comparison. Worst of all, she thinks you kids don't need her anymore, that you've outgrown her. The whole situation has her feeling pretty low."

"Poor Mom!" I exclaimed, overcome with guilt. "We really didn't mean to exclude her. I'd never hurt her feelings on purpose."

"Of course you wouldn't," Dad said soothingly. "And naturally you want to make the most of Grandma and Grandpa's visit. I just thought you should know the score. Now, let's put our heads together and come up with a plan to cheer her up!"

Needless to say, Jessica the world-champion schemer came up with a perfect plan immediately. And Mom totally fell for it!

We went up to my parents' room and found her sorting through old baby pictures of us and Steven, looking totally depressed. She looked even sadder when we asked permission to throw a surprise farewell party for Gram and Gramps before they leave next weekend. I could read her mind—she thought she was being left out in the cold once again. But then we said we really needed some help. Should we make it a small party, just the family, or invite some of our friends? Have a sit-down dinner, or a buffet? You should have seen her—she was so cute. She lit up like a Christmas tree—she started tossing out suggestions and giving advice about menus and decorations, and it was just like the old days. It obviously made her feel good to be consulted, and it made me and Jess feel good, too. Dad was right—you never think of your parents needing attention, but they really do!

Thursday, 11:00 P.M.

What a day—and night—this has been! I finally heard from Emily again, but it wasn't the way I might have hoped. She called me from the Box Tree Cafe around seven thirty, in tears. I buzzed over in the Fiat, worrying the whole time that the reason she was upset was because her dad and stepmom had decided to send her to boarding school. The true story was even worse.

According to Emily, the trouble started at home with a new doll Karen gave Karrie to play with. Emily noticed that one of the doll's button eyes was loose and suggested that they should stitch it on more tightly, but Karen brushed Emily off and gave the doll to the

117

baby anyway. Then the phone rang. Karen was on the line arguing with her mother, when Emily saw Karrie pop the button into her mouth. The baby started to choke—she turned blue, she couldn't breathe. Karen dropped the phone and started screeching hysterically. She was utterly useless—clearly she didn't have the faintest idea what to do to help her own choking baby! Thank God Emily remembered learning the Heimlich maneuver in a first-aid class, and she grabbed little Karrie and pressed down on her diaphragm and the button popped up. Emily saved Karrie's life!

That should've been a happy ending, right? But right at that minute Mr. Mayer burst into the room. He saw Karrie bright red and screaming, and Karen clutching the baby and sobbing, and the room basically turned upside down, with the phone dangling and Karen's mother probably still yakking on the other end. Instantly he assumed that Emily had done something wrong—that she'd tried to hurt the baby! Isn't that insane? But this is the most unbelievable part. While Mr. Mayer's demanding to know what's going on and accusing Emily, Karen doesn't say a word. She didn't tell him what had really happened: that Emily had prevented their little daughter from choking to death. When Emily tried to speak up in her own defense, her father just shouted at her to get out of the house.

I was really speechless when I heard this. I wanted to help Emily and give her advice, but a situation like that is just so far out of the realm of my experience. When she told me she planned to take the money she got for her drum set and run away to Chicago to find her mother, I really went blank. I know she needs to be part of a family, but she hasn't heard from her mother in four or five years. What are the chances that she'll be able to track her down, or that her mother will even want her?

I didn't know what else to do, so I brought Emily home so my parents could help. Mom saw that Emily was completely drained and hustled her upstairs to lie down for a while in my room, then we all pow-wowed in the kitchen. I gave them the whole scoop, including the fact that Emily wanted to stay overnight with us and then catch a train for Chicago in the morning. It seemed pretty obvious to me and Jess why Emily refused to call her father and tell him where she was, but Mom insisted that someone had to call Mr. Mayer. She thought it should be me, and finally I saw her point. I didn't feel too good going behind Emily's back like that, especially with Jessica calling me a rat fink, but I didn't really have an option.

My hand was shaking as I dialed the Mayers' number, let me tell you. I ended up being pretty glad I made that phone call, though. They came right over—Mr. Mayer, Karen, and the baby—and you'll never believe what happened. . . .

The doorbell rang and my heart leaped into my throat. My phone call with Mr. Mayer had been brief—he'd demanded to know where his daughter was and then hung up before I could tell him that Emily wanted to spend the night. *It's going to be like last time,* I thought anxiously, *when he threatened to put her drum set on the street if she didn't come home. He's going to drag her back by the hair, just so he can make her pack her bags and send her off to boarding school.*

Practically my whole family had gathered in the front hall: Mom, Dad, Grandpa, and Jessica. They were behind me; what's more important, they were behind Emily. Taking a deep breath, I opened the door.

Mr. Mayer stood on the step, and to my surprise Karen and the baby were with him. "Hi," I said weakly. "Come on in."

We all stepped into the living room, but before anyone could say anything, Karen started calling out, "Emily. Where's Emily?"

Karen Mayer looked as if she'd been spun around by a tornado. Her hair was tousled, her eyes wide and red-rimmed, and her complexion was blotchy from crying. Little Karrie looked unhappy about how tightly her mother was clutching her. "Emily!" Karen repeated, her voice shrill. "Where are you?"

120

"I'm right here," said a clear, calm voice.

We all whirled to look at the speaker. Emily descended the staircase, Grandma Wakefield at her side.

She looks so brave, so composed, I marveled. I could tell Emily felt stronger, just having my grandmother's arm wrapped supportively around her waist. But would she be strong enough to face what might be coming?

I waited, trembling, for Karen or Mr. Mayer to start yelling at Emily. Then my mother broke the pregnant, explosive silence. "Maybe we should give the Mayers some privacy," she suggested to me and the rest of my family. "Why don't we—"

"No," Karen interrupted fiercely. "What I'm about to say needs to be said in front of everybody—in front of all Emily's friends. Emily . . ." Karen's voice cracked. Tears spilled from her eyes like a fountain, streaming down her cheeks and splashing onto the baby's downy head. "Emily, I . . . I owe you an apology."

My jaw dropped. On the other side of the room, staring blankly at her stepmother, Emily looked as stunned as I felt.

"I'm so sorry," Karen continued brokenly. "You saved my baby's life just now, and I didn't even thank you. I didn't speak up to defend you to your father—I let him think something else entirely had taken place."

Karen dropped her head, pressing her face against little Karrie's. For a moment we all stood in silence, watching Karen's shoulders shake with sobs. No one knew what to do or say.

121

Then Karen lifted her face again. She took a deep, ragged breath, clearly struggling to get her emotions under control. "That's only half of my apology, though," she said, her eyes traveling around the circle of expectant, sympathetic faces. "I'm sorry, Emily, for being unfair to you from the very first day I moved into the house. I was just so jealous! You were the apple of Ron's eye, and I didn't know how I could ever compete with his love for you. I felt so inept and insecure. You were better at everything: cooking, running the house, helping your dad with things, even taking care of little Karrie. You just had a way with her, you were so natural and comfortable, whereas I couldn't seem to do anything right. She'd start to cry and I wouldn't know how to comfort her. I was sure that I was going to be a terrible mother, and I didn't even want to *try* to be a stepmother to a teenaged girl. That seemed absolutely impossible."

Karen's face crumpled.

"Can you ever forgive me, Emily?" she whispered. "Will you give us another chance to become a family?"

I looked at Emily; we all looked at Emily. When Karen first started talking, Emily's expression had been stony and unreadable. Then she'd appeared shocked. But now . . .

Emily's face softened; a light of hope, compassion, and love brightened her eyes even as they filled with tears. In a few strides she'd crossed the living room to throw her arms around Karen and little Karrie.

My own eyes grew misty as Mr. Mayer hurried

forward to embrace his wife and two daughters. I hugged my own mother, my heart bursting with thankfulness. I thought about the little trauma we Wakefields had just been through, when we had to remind my mom how much we loved and needed her. It takes a lot of work to hold a family together, but it's worth it. I knew Emily had envied me and Jessica because of our wonderful, close-knit family, and now it looked as if her own dearest wish was going to be granted: she was going to be part of a family of her own.

All's well that ends well. The Mayers drove off, and we Wakefields collapsed from emotional exhaustion. Gram and Gramps went straight to bed, Mom plunged into a steaming-hot bubble bath, and Jessica ran for the telephone—that's always the best therapy for her. I got a sweet, friendly letter from Todd today, and I read it over a couple of times. Hearing from him really made a difficult day a lot nicer. This long-distance-relationship thing has its up and downs, but in general one thing hasn't changed: he's still my best friend, and the fact that he thinks about me and wants to share things with me gives me a good feeling deep down inside.

Saturday, 11:45 P.M.

What an awesome farewell party for Gram and Gramps! The Mayers came over,

123

*and Steven was home from school, and my
father made the most wonderful toast. . . .*

A couple of days ago I never would have believed
this scene could take place. My whole family was
gathered in the living room for cocktails and hors
d'oeuvres, and Emily Mayer was with us, and her father and stepmother, too. And everyone was smiling
and laughing, relaxed and happy! Emily hadn't run
away to Chicago; her parents weren't going to send
her to boarding school. They were a family, and families stick together.

My dad must have been on the same wavelength,
because all at once he lifted his glass. "To families,"
he said.

Mr. Mayer wrapped an arm around Emily's shoulders, dropping a kiss on top of her head. "To families," he echoed, his voice vibrant with emotion.

Now Karen raised her glass. "To mothers and
daughters," she toasted, smiling warmly at Emily.

My mom laughed happily. "I'll drink to that!"

We couldn't forget why we were all there in the
first place. "To grandparents," I said, beaming at
Grandma and Grandpa. "And to many more fun-
filled visits like this one."

"Next time we'll try hang gliding, or maybe
bungee jumping," Gram promised, her eyes twinkling merrily.

It was kind of a misty moment, but Jessica
brought me back to earth. "Let's go put the finishing
touches on the buffet, Liz," she said meaningfully.

"Of course. The *buffet*," I repeated.

She darted into the kitchen with me on her heels. We were just in time to hear the sound of someone tapping on the sliding glass door that led out to the patio.

I slid open the door. Dan Scott, Dana Larson, Guy Chesney, and Max Dellon stood outside, surrounded by all their band equipment . . . including Emily's drums!

"Come on in, guys," I whispered, beckoning. "Let's set up in the dining room."

Five minutes later The Droids were ready to rock and roll. By pushing the table toward one end of the dining room, we'd cleared space for the drums, guitars, and microphone. Jessica dimmed the lights and I stepped out into the hall.

"Come on, everybody!" I shouted. "Dinner's served."

Our guests spilled from the living room. Taking Emily's arm, I steered her forward. "Somebody has to be first in line at the buffet," I said cheerfully. "Why don't you lead the way, Em?"

Emily looked a little puzzled as I shoved her into the dark dining room, but she didn't protest. Then all of a sudden the lights came on, and simultaneously, The Droids burst into the opening notes of one of their most popular songs, "Let's Get it Together."

I have never seen anyone so surprised. Emily stood like a statue, her eyes practically popping out of her head. "Dan!" she squeaked. "Dana!" Then her eyes focused and a look of pure joy transformed her face. "My drums!"

125

The band paused in midsong so Dan could explain. "My friend changed his mind," he told Emily. "So if you want them back . . ."

"If I want them back!" Rapturously, Emily ran a hand over her beloved drums. "Do I ever . . . hey!" She turned to Dan, and his affectionate, mischievous smile gave him away. Emily flung her arms around his neck. "Dan Scott, you adorable boy! You planned it this way all along."

Grinning, Dan hugged Emily back. It was hard to tell at that moment which of the two was happier.

Untangling herself from Dan's embrace, Emily quickly took up her position behind the drums. The Droids, whole once again, launched into another irresistible tune. Grandma and Grandpa started dancing; Steven twirled Jessica in a circle; even Mr. Mayer and Karen were snapping their fingers. I saw Dan lean over to whisper something in Emily's ear that made her smile and blush. The song really said it all. *When people get it together,* I thought, *what beautiful music we can make!*

Sunday, 2:30 P.M.

Dear Diary,

Something really weird is going on. The other day I talked to Eddie Strong at the Thrift Mart convenience store where he works and he said he made a delivery to the Morrows' house and saw Regina. I was really surprised—I thought Regina and her parents were in Switzerland! She's been at a clinic in

126

Bern for a while, getting this radical therapy—she's been nearly deaf all her life, but soon her hearing may be back to normal. So how could she be home in Sweet Valley? We're good friends—we've been writing letters back and forth regularly. Wouldn't she have gotten in touch with me?

There seemed one easy way to find out. I drove over to her house, but I saw absolutely no sign of life there—the iron gate was padlocked tight. My next stop was Bruce Patman's house—if anyone knew what was up with Regina, it would be her boyfriend. But he was just as surprised as I was. According to Bruce it's a really unlikely time for Regina to come home, as she's in the middle of a new round of treatments. Not a man to waste time, Bruce picked up the phone and dialed the Morrows' number. A strange woman answered. She identified herself as Regina's aunt and said Regina wasn't there, then hung up before Bruce could ask any more questions.

Which means we have a mystery on our hands. Because, according to Bruce, Mr. and Mrs. Morrow are both only children. Regina Morrow doesn't have an aunt! What on earth is going on at the Morrows'?

Part 4

Dear Diary,

I can't stop thinking about Regina Morrow. Eddie said he saw her—he was pretty definite about it. But the woman who answered the phone when Bruce called—Regina's aunt, supposedly, even though Bruce swears she doesn't have an aunt—said Regina wasn't there. Is she or isn't she? And if she is home, why hasn't she called me? Why hasn't she called Bruce? Somebody's there—Eddie made a grocery delivery, after all! So why is the mansion locked up tight? Who is that strange, creepy woman who answered the phone?

Jessica thinks I'm being totally batty about this. She calls it my "Nancy Drew complex"—trying to make a mystery where there

128

isn't one. She laughed her head off, imagining me and Bruce prowling around in the bushes outside the mansion, with flashlights and magnifying glasses. Not that we've done any prowling . . . yet.

Jessica also points out that I'm kind of hypersensitive on the subject of kidnapping because of my own horrible experience. For as long as I live, I'll never forget the two days I spent tied up in that crazy man's cabin. . . . He didn't harm me physically, but I've never been so scared. I didn't know if I'd see the light of day—see my family, my friends— ever again. So it comes down to this: is my imagination acting up on me, or is something really wrong at the Morrows'? I wish I could get the scoop from Nicholas, but he's vacationing in San Francisco, and I have no way of reaching him. What if Regina's being held prisoner in her own home?

Tuesday, 6:30 P.M.

Dear Diary,

A really freaky, scary thing happened today. I couldn't stand not doing anything any longer, so I drove over to Regina's house after school to see if I could find out what was going on. Now I'm more sure than ever that she's in serious trouble and that Bruce and I need to find a way to help, and fast. . . .

The road had been climbing steadily for a few minutes. As I rounded a bend in the Fiat, a breathtaking vista of emerald valley and sparkling blue ocean appeared before me. On an ordinary day I would have paused to savor it—the Morrows lived in the ritziest, most spectacular part of town, and usually I loved having an excuse to cruise around there. But this wasn't an ordinary day. I wasn't paying a social call—I was sleuthing.

When I reached Regina's driveway, I caught my breath. I'd expected to find the gate closed and padlocked like the last time. Instead, it stood wide open.

Wide open . . . but somehow not very inviting. I gulped, my sweaty palms slip-sliding on the steering wheel. *Go ahead, Liz,* I urged myself. *Turn in. Drive right up to the front door. This is your big chance!*

Slowly, apprehensively, I coasted down the long, winding driveway. The beautiful house came into view, framed by draping cypress trees and a wild tangle of blooming shrubbery. There was something foreboding about it. The windows looked like blank, unseeing eyes. *Or maybe they* do *see,* I thought, clenching my teeth to keep them from chattering. *Maybe someone's watching me. . . .*

Jessica's right, I concluded as I parked the car and hopped out. My imagination did tend to work overtime. I hadn't actually *seen* anything, but I was ready to expect ghosts and burglars and monsters. It was selfish to be scared; I needed to be alert and brave and ingenious, for Regina.

Climbing the steps to the porch, I pressed hard

on the doorbell. Ten seconds passed, then twenty, thirty. . . . I'd been standing on the porch for a full two minutes and was about to turn away, when I heard a bolt slide back. On the other side of the heavy wood door, a few more locks clicked, and then the door inched open.

A woman with gray-streaked auburn hair, pale skin, and cold gray eyes stared out at me suspiciously. "Yes? What do you want?" she snapped.

Not the most hospitable greeting, I thought. And she was gripping the edge of the door so tightly, her knuckles were white; clearly she was ready to slam it in my face.

"I'm . . . I'm here to see Regina." My voice came out in a nervous croak. "I'm a classmate of hers from Sweet Valley High. Somebody mentioned that she was home from Switzerland, and I thought I'd just drop by, because it's been ages since I—"

"Regina isn't here," the woman interrupted, glancing over her shoulder. She started to push the door shut.

Quickly, I stuck out my foot. I knew a lie when I heard one, and suddenly my courage returned. "She's not here? Are you sure?" I asked, craning my neck to see beyond her into the foyer. "A mutual friend of ours very distinctly said that—"

"She isn't here," the woman repeated. "Your friend was mistaken. Now would you please—"

Just then I glimpsed a movement at the far end of the hall—a shift in the pattern of shadow and light. A figure emerged . . . Regina!

131

"Regina!" I cried. "You *are* here! Bruce and I have been trying to call you for days!"

Startled, the woman turned to look, momentarily dropping her hand from the door. Taking advantage of her lapse, I kicked the door wide.

Regina hurried forward, her big blue eyes glued to mine. She opened her mouth as if to speak, visibly distressed.

"What are you doing down here?" the woman barked. "I told you to stay upstairs!"

Regina froze, biting back any words she'd been about to utter. The woman continued to stare hard at her, and as I watched, Regina backed up in the direction of the staircase. "Regina," I said again. "What's going on?"

Regina's only answer was a frightened, imploring glance. Then she turned around and walked back up the stairs.

I repeated the question to the woman. "What's going on?" I demanded, hands on my hips.

"She's sick," the woman explained curtly, pushing against the door. "She can't have company—she should be lying down."

"But why . . . who . . . ?"

I was talking to myself. Despite my effort to prop the door open with my toe, the woman succeeded in slamming it shut. On the other side the bolt thudded into place with a sound of ominous finality.

I considered ringing the bell again, but there didn't seem to be any point. Regina's "aunt" would just keep insisting that Regina was too ill to see me . . . if she bothered to answer the door at all, that is. If she really *was* a member of the Morrow family, I didn't have a right to harass her or try to force my way past her into the house.

I walked back to the Fiat, a troubled frown creasing my forehead. As I slid into the driver's seat, I glanced once more at the house. For the first time I noticed that the second-floor windows were shuttered. They really *were* like blind eyes. *Regina's up there and she can't see out,* I realized, the anxious knot in my stomach pulling tighter.

I started the engine and stepped on the gas. All at once I couldn't wait to get home and share this story with Jessica and Bruce. My sister couldn't kid me about a Nancy Drew complex any longer. Because one thing seemed certain. Regina hadn't looked sick. She'd looked scared . . . to death.

Jessica had to agree that this was a very strange and creepy encounter. Now she's worried about Regina, too. So we did something kind of drastic—we called the police and told them we thought there was a problem at our friend's house. They said they'd send someone over to check it out, and about an hour later Sergeant O'Brien called back. He was pretty brisk with us—said there didn't appear to be anything out of order. The woman identified herself as Skye Morrow's stepsister, Claire Davis, visiting from out of town. In the future, Sergeant

O'Brien advised us, we should keep our noses out of other people's business and not bother the police with trivial, misplaced concerns.

Skye Morrow's stepsister . . . Bruce had to admit it was plausible. He's been dating Regina for a while, but that doesn't mean he knows every single detail of her family history. But he got pretty upset when I described my glimpse of Regina. We're both shaken up, and desperate to do something. I wish I knew how to get in touch with Nicholas! Whoever this Claire Davis person is, she's mean and maybe even dangerous. No matter what the police think, there's no question in my mind at this point that Regina is being held prisoner against her will. But why? What's going on? Bruce, Jess, and I have got to get to the bottom of this before harm comes to Regina!

Wednesday, midnight

Too nervous to sleep. I have to write this story down, otherwise I'll never believe it happened, that we're really in the middle of something this crazy.

Jessica's the one who got the ball rolling, and I have to hand it to her—her scheming mind can really be useful at times. We made contact with Regina today in the most daring, incredible way. . . .

134

"It's really important that we get the note just right," said Bruce as he steered the black Porsche up the long, winding hill road leading to the Morrows' estate. "Run it by us one more time, Liz."

It was Wednesday after school, and Bruce, Jessica, and I were driving to the Morrows'. I sat up front with Bruce; Jessica was squeezed in the sports car's tiny backseat with a box of Thrift Mart groceries: a carton of milk, a dozen eggs, orange juice, English muffins, two boxes of cereal, and a six-pack of diet soda. I smoothed my hand across the sheet of notebook paper. "'Dear Regina,'" I read out loud. "'We know you're home and we're worried about you. Are you OK? If you can, write us a note. If you wrap it around something heavy and drop it out your window, we'll pick it up tonight. Tell us everything— what we can do to help and who we should go to. And promise us you'll be careful! Love, Bruce, Liz, and Jessica.'"

My voice had been shaking as I read the letter. I was so scared for Regina!

"I guess that says it all," Bruce said, his own voice grim. "All we can do is pray Claire Davis doesn't read the note by mistake." His jaw tightened convulsively. "What if she . . . *punishes* Regina?"

"Claire Davis won't see the note," Jessica declared with supreme confidence. "Chill out, Bruce. Our plan is perfect in every detail—there's no way it can misfire!"

Jessica could be a little too casual about serious things sometimes, but she was right about the plan, which she'd dreamed up herself. "We've thought this out pretty carefully," I reassured Bruce. "You make the weekly Thrift Mart delivery in Eddie's place; the note is tucked inside a copy of *Ingenue* magazine, which would never in a million years interest that horrible Claire Davis! She gives the magazine to Regina, who finds the message. It's foolproof."

"Let's hope so," Bruce muttered.

"The *Ingenue* magazine bit is an especially brilliant touch, if I may say so myself," Jessica remarked with satisfaction. "Remember when Regina first moved to Sweet Valley and the local modeling agency 'discovered' her and she ended up as an *Ingenue* cover girl? The magazine is bound to catch her eye, and as soon as she flips it open . . . *voilà!*"

We'd reached the Morrows' driveway. Bruce braked to a stop just short of the gate. "OK," he said, his intense blue eyes glued to my face. "Let's review this one more time, step by step."

"We'll park out of sight of the house so Claire doesn't see your car and get suspicious," I recited. "You'll go ahead with the box of groceries and ring the bell."

"And if I run into trouble, I'll whistle twice," said Bruce.

"That's our cue to drive back to your house and wait for you there," Jessica chimed in.

"I don't like that part," I confessed, biting my lip. "I don't like the idea of just ditching you."

"If something goes wrong, the two of you have to get out of here fast," Bruce insisted. "I'll be right be-

136

hind you, I promise. It's less than a mile to my house—I'll jog. And if I don't turn up in half an hour, call the police."

As the Porsche started down the driveway, my heart began to hammer just as it had the day before when I stopped by the Morrows' on my own. About fifty yards from the mansion, Bruce did a U-turn and parked the car with its nose pointing back toward the street. He killed the engine, then placed the keys in my palm. "Don't forget," he said. "If you hear me whistle, get back in the car and drive. Don't look back."

Jessica and I both nodded, our eyes wide as saucers.

Hoisting the box of groceries, Bruce strode off. Jessica and I paced back and forth alongside the car. "Bruce is really brave, isn't he?" I remarked, my eyes following his tall, broad-shouldered figure until he disappeared around a bend in the drive.

"I didn't think he had it in him," Jessica acknowledged. "But I guess love can transform anyone, even somebody as spoiled and egotistical as Bruce!"

"He really does care for Regina," I confirmed. "He'd do anything for her—run any risk."

A minute passed, and then another. I looked at my watch. Shading her eyes, Jessica peered down the driveway. "All he had to do was ring the doorbell and hand over the box of groceries. What's taking him so long?" she wondered.

I jingled the car keys nervously. "You don't think . . ." Horrible possibilities flickered through my brain. Claire Davis had somehow overpowered

137

Bruce—maybe she had a burly male accomplice, or a gun! Perhaps at that very moment they were tying Bruce up . . . or perhaps he was lying unconscious . . . or even . . .

We both stood stock-still, listening for the dreaded double whistle. "Maybe we should sneak up to the house and see what's going on," Jessica whispered. "Maybe we should—"

At that instant Bruce sprinted into sight, his hair whipped back and his arms pumping. Jessica let out a startled cry.

I leaped into the driver's seat and stuck the key into the ignition. The Porsche's engine roared to life. Shifting into neutral, I scrambled into the passenger seat just as Bruce reached the car.

Jessica dived into the backseat and Bruce dived into the front seat, and a split second later we were tearing out the driveway, a cloud of dust in our wake. "What happened?" Jessica yelped. "Did Claire Davis see through your disguise? Did she find the note? Did we get Regina in even worse trouble?"

"No, no, no," Bruce replied, wiping the sweat from his forehead. "I think it went off OK. I was just running because . . . I wanted to get out of there. That woman really gives me the creeps!"

I shivered in sympathy. She'd given *me* the creeps, too. *And Regina's in her power.* . . . "Was it Claire Davis?" I asked.

"Thin, maybe thirty-five, graying hair, ice-cold eyes?"

I nodded. "That's her."

"She's the one who answered the door," Bruce related. "She looked pretty mean, but she didn't seem to suspect me. She took the groceries without a word." He laughed dryly. "Oh, and I got a fifty-cent tip. If she's after the Morrows' money, she doesn't have her hands on it yet."

"Did you see Regina?" I asked.

Bruce shook his head. "I didn't see anyone else. That woman probably has her locked up." He pounded his fist on the steering wheel. "I'm more worried than ever," he declared. "There's no way that woman's a relative of the Morrows. Something is really, really wrong."

I sank back in my seat, fidgeting with my gold lavaliere necklace. "And now all we can do is wait," I said.

"Until nightfall," Bruce agreed.

At nine o'clock this evening, Jess and I swung by Bruce's in the Fiat. A few minutes later the three of us had shimmied over the wrought-iron fence—the gate was locked—and were prowling around in the shrubbery outside the Morrows' house, searching for a message from Regina. It was pitch-black—no outside lights on—and I don't mind telling you, we were scared witless. We kept bumping into each other, and I nearly screamed about ten times. It occurred to me that if Claire had intercepted the note, we might be am-

bushed—we could all end up being prisoners with Regina.

We were about to give up when I spotted something shiny in the grass. Regina's silver compact, with a letter inside! Bruce grabbed the compact, and you have never seen three people run so fast. If anyone had a stopwatch on us, we could have qualified for the Olympics. As soon as we were safe in the car, Bruce read the letter out loud to us. We were worried before, a little scared, but now we're terrified. Regina, and her parents, too, are in even more serious trouble than we ever could have guessed—this really is like a James Bond movie!

I'm going to copy her letter here, so in case something happens to the original, we have it for evidence:

Dear Bruce, Liz, and Jessica,

I got your note in the magazine, and I've never been so happy to hear from anyone. I do need your help—I'm being held hostage, and so are my parents! Claire Davis, the woman who's posing as my aunt, kidnapped me in Bern and brought me here. Mom and Dad are being held someplace else, I have no idea where. But they're safe—at least they're alive. For now.

This is as much as I know of what's going on. Claire and her accomplices want to steal the prototype for the revolutionary computer microchip Dad's plant has designed. Years of research went into this chip—the prototype is priceless. I think they're going to use me somehow to get the chip—I figured out that much the other day, eavesdropping on a phone conversation of Claire's. I don't know the details, though—for example, when this is supposed to take place. They made my father call the servants and tell them to take a vacation, but I don't know for how long. Claire said one thing to the person on the other end that seemed especially mysterious: "Money is heaven." Maybe it's code—a clue? I wish I knew more! But I have to be very careful. Claire says they'll kill my parents if I try to contact the police or anyone else, if I make one false move, and I believe her. I'm completely in her power—that's why I didn't speak to you the other day, Liz.

So I do need your help, but you must be very careful. Please. These people are really dangerous. You've got to find out where they're holding my parents and rescue all of us at the same time, or someone will end up dead. And whatever you do, don't call the police. A patrol car came over the night before last, and "Aunt" Claire was so mad, she locked me in my room and threatened to tie me up and gag me.

Nicholas is staying with a friend in San Francisco for two weeks, Buddy Ames, who

141

lives on Delaney Street. Please call Nicholas and tell him what's going on—together I know you can save me and Mom and Dad. Promise me, though, that you'll be extremely careful. I wouldn't be able to bear it if something happened to you guys, too. I am so frightened. If I never see you again, I love you all very much. Regina.

The letter pretty much devastated us. I thought Bruce was going to burst into tears, or maybe put his fist through a window or something. He was so upset, and so frustrated at his powerlessness. We felt a little bit better after we called Nicholas, but still incredibly tense. Nicholas is driving down from San Francisco at this very moment—he should be in Sweet Valley by breakfast time. He'll go directly to the Patmans'—Bruce's parents are out of town, so Bruce is going to play hooky. Jessica and I will race over there right after school— no Oracle for me, no cheerleading for Jess, no centennial-committee meeting for Bruce. We're working against the clock— nothing matters now but Regina and her parents.

I almost wish we hadn't had to call Nicholas—he's worried sick and probably driving like a maniac. Poor guy. And poor, poor Regina. But we'll figure something out, the four of us. We just have to.

Dear Diary,

Another insane day. I'm almost too tired to write. Everything's happening so fast and furious . . . where should I begin? I guess the most important thing is that Nicholas is home. Jessica and I broke all the speed limits driving over to Bruce's after school, and when I saw Nicholas out back by the Patmans' swimming pool, I just about burst into tears of relief. He's so smart and strong and brave. I felt braver, too, just because he was there with us—now it's a lot easier to believe that we'll be able to brainstorm a way out of this mess.

But, boy, was he ever upset. He couldn't sit still—he'd been talking all day to Bruce, and by the time Jess and I showed up, he was ready to explode. Before we could stop him, he jumped into his car to head over to the estate. I ran after him, and we drove over there together and had a pretty wild close encounter. . . .

We'd nearly reached the driveway to his house. Nicholas was driving; I put a restraining hand on his arm. "Remember Regina's letter," I begged him. "We have to be incredibly careful. One slip, and those horrible people will . . . they'll . . ."

I couldn't bear to say it. *They'll kill her.* But Nicholas got the message. Tapping the brakes, he steered the car onto the shoulder of the road just a few yards from the entrance to his family's estate. "I don't want to do anything stupid to endanger Regina and my folks," he said, his voice hoarse with urgency. "But I have to do *something*, Liz. Don't you see?"

I nodded, my eyes brimming with tears. "Of course."

"I'm going to make a quick scout around the grounds of the estate," he told me. "Don't worry, I'll stay out of sight. I just want to see if I can get a look at that woman, or find out anything else about the people who've hatched this diabolical plot."

I sighed, knowing there was nothing I could say to dissuade him from this course. "I'll wait for you here. But I still think—"

Just then Nicholas gripped my arm and put a finger to my lips. "Ssh. Someone's coming!"

We sat in tense silence. He was right—now I heard the sound of a car engine, too. A second later a blue car came into view, heading down the driveway in our direction.

"What are we going to do?" I gasped, terrified. "We're sitting ducks. Whoever it is might recognize you as a member of the family. We'd better get out of here!"

"It's too late for that," Nicholas pointed out. "We spotted them, so that means they've spotted us." He frowned, thinking hard. Then he slipped an arm around my shoulder. "OK, Liz. We're just a young couple out for a drive, stealing a moment for romance. I'm going to kiss you." Despite the stress of the moment, he managed a mischievous smile. "Try to look like you're enjoying it."

I caught my breath as Nicholas folded me in his arms. His lips met mine in a long, lingering kiss. I knew it was just for cover, but I couldn't help getting caught up in the heat of the moment—the heat pouring from Nicholas's body into mine. Our emotions were so heightened by the fear, the danger. He was holding me closer than was absolutely necessary—it wasn't just a pose. . . .

My heart was pounding so hard, I could hardly focus on the sound of the blue car, closing in, and then retreating into the distance.

We pulled apart, both breathless, just in time to catch a glimpse of the car speeding off down the road. Our ruse had worked—the driver hadn't paid the least bit of attention to us.

"A beat-up blue Dodge," Nicholas observed. "License-plate number . . ."

He rattled off the digits, and I scribbled the number down on the notepad I carried in my purse.

"And that man . . ." Nicholas murmured.

"Claire's accomplice."

Nicholas furrowed his brow. "Must be. But I swear he looked familiar. Who is he? Where could I have seen him?"

We were both stumped. "It'll come to me," Nicholas said at last with an exasperated sigh. "It had *better* come to me!"

He started the car again. "Let's go back to Bruce's," I urged. "We came really close right there to being seen. I think it's taking too much of a chance, roaming around in broad daylight."

Reluctantly, Nicholas agreed with my reasoning. "You're right. There's nothing we can do here. But it makes me crazy, Liz, thinking my sister's so close and I can't reach her—I can't protect her."

I clasped his hand tightly. "We'll reach her," I promised. "I don't know how, I don't know when, but we'll get her out of there."

Back at Bruce's we prodded Nicholas to try to think if his father had any enemies or business competitors who might take such a desperate step to acquire the microchip. We made a big breakthrough! Nicholas remembered a former employee at his dad's Connecticut plant who'd been fired for stealing from the company. According to Nicholas the man was completely bitter and unbalanced. He served some time in prison, then moved to California. Just recalling the story caused Nicholas to remember the man's name—Phillip Denson—and his face. And now Nicholas is almost positive that the man driving the beat-up blue Dodge was Denson! Tomorrow the four of us will see if we can track Denson down. Maybe he's got Mr. and Mrs. Morrow!

In the meantime I have a feeling this is going to be another sleepless night. I'm not just preoccupied with Regina's danger. I'm

146

thinking about Nicholas, too. I know he only kissed me as a cover, Diary. We needed to look as if we had some reason to be parked like that. But did he have to hold me so close or kiss me so long? I don't think so! And the way I responded . . . it really took me by surprise. Was my heart pounding out of fear, or was it something else?

To make it all a hundred times more confusing, Todd called an hour ago. It was a pretty lighthearted conversation, but I felt terribly guilty on two counts—one, because I didn't tell him about what was going on with the Morrows, and two, because of Nicholas and the kiss. How can I be getting mixed up about this subject all over again? Didn't I decide I couldn't be with Nicholas at this time in my life, that he couldn't replace Todd in my heart? Then why did it feel so good to be in his arms? Needless to say, I didn't tell Todd about that kiss. I'm not going to tell anyone—not even Jessica.

Friday, 10:30 P.M.

Big news today, Diary! We found Phillip Denson, and we found Mr. and Mrs. Morrow!

It was really pretty easy. We looked in the phone book, and there was only one Denson listed in the area: P. Denson, 1386 Lakewood Drive, Fort Carroll. So Jess, Bruce, and I cut

147

school and drove over there with Nicholas to investigate. By the way, Diary, you know I wouldn't cut school without a really good reason, but it was justified this time, don't you think?

When we got there, we saw this kind of nice-looking teenaged guy mowing the lawn. The blue Dodge was nowhere in sight. Our secret weapon, Jessica Wakefield, hopped out of the car and went to work on the boy, who turned out to be Denson's son, Mitch. She pretended to be taking a neighborhood census for a school newspaper article and almost managed to charm her way into the house, but Mitch was cautious. She did get a good look in the living-room window, though, while Mitch was inside fetching her a glass of water, and that's when she spotted the Morrows!

The good thing is, the Morrows looked all right. They haven't been harmed . . . yet. They must be so scared, though, and worried sick about Regina. I feel so sorry for them! So now we know who we're dealing with, and we know where all the major players are located. The bad thing is, we don't know what to do next. We can't try to rescue Mr. and Mrs. Morrow, because then Claire might do something to Regina, and we can't go after Regina for the same reason—it might spur Denson to harm her parents. Nicholas is *frantic, nearly out of his mind. Maybe we should've called the police right off the bat, despite Regina's plea.*

We can talk about that possibility tomorrow. Tomorrow . . . what will it bring?

Saturday 4:00 P.M.
Dear Diary,

Four brains are really better than one. We solved a major clue today and actually put together a plan for rescuing Regina and her parents!

Hanging out at Bruce's this afternoon, we read and reread Regina's note, the one she dropped out the window for us the other day. Remember what she overheard Claire Davis saying on the phone, "Money is heaven"? Well, thanks to Jessica, we've translated it to "Monday at seven." Isn't that brilliant? And it makes sense. Monday at seven: that's when Claire will take Regina to the plant to get the microchip!

And that's our window of opportunity, the only time when we can be sure Claire won't hurt Regina. That's when we're going to make our move. Bruce and Jessica will break in at Denson's to free Mr. and Mrs. Morrow, and Nicholas and I will go to the plant to foil Claire.

This is really dangerous, Diary. I think these heartless criminals would commit mur-

der without a second thought. Our rescue plan is pretty solid, and I think we can pull it off, but . . . so much is at stake! Wish us luck. We'll need it.

Monday, 11:00 P.M.

Oh God, I almost can't believe I'm still alive to record this. Just a few hours ago I was staring down the barrel of a gun. . . . Where should I start? I guess at the beginning, before everything went haywire. At seven P.M. on the dot Nicholas and I were hiding in the bushes outside the MicroTech plant on Route 5. . . .

The foliage rustled and shook as Nicholas rejoined me behind the rhododendron bush. From where we were hidden, we had a good view of the security gate about twenty yards away, and the main entrance to the plant.

Nicholas had been at the pay phone calling Bruce and Jessica, who'd driven Nicholas's Jeep to Fort Carroll. "I reached Bruce on the Jeep's car phone," Nicholas whispered, crouching next to me. "I told him we just saw Claire Davis and Regina enter the plant, so he and Jess have a green light to go in after Mr. and Mrs. Morrow."

My whole body began trembling at this announcement. At that very moment, then, Jessica and Bruce were charging into Phillip Denson's house to rescue

150

the Morrows. *Maybe Jess will be able to sweet-talk Mitch again, and it will all go off like clockwork*, I thought hopefully. *Maybe Mitch's father won't even be around.* But another scenario insisted on rearing its ugly head. What if Phillip Denson *was* home? What if he thwarted the rescue attempt? What if he pulled a gun? *My sister*, I thought, choking back a sob. *Oh, if anything happens to my sister . . .*

I glanced at Nicholas. I could tell by the tense set of his handsome jaw that he was thinking the very same thing—he was worried about *his* beloved sister, still in the clutches of a cruel and desperate kidnapper.

I opened my mouth to say something comforting just as Nicholas shot out a hand and gripped my arm. "Liz, look! They're coming out!"

We both stared eagerly at the entrance to the plant. Sure enough, Claire Davis and Regina had reappeared, in the company of a silver-haired man. "Walter Frank, the plant manager," said Nicholas. "They're shaking hands. He's giving Regina a package."

"The microchip!" I exclaimed.

Waving good-bye, Walter Frank turned to reenter the building. With one hand Claire Davis seized the package from Regina and with the other steered Regina down the sidewalk toward the security gate.

That was our cue. I had to get to them while they were still in view of the guard—Claire would be afraid to make a fuss and draw attention to herself. Meanwhile, Nicholas would sprint back to the pay phone and summon the police.

We jumped to our feet and Nicholas gave me a

quick hug. "You're the greatest, Liz," he whispered hoarsely, his breath warm against my hair. "I'll never be able to thank you enough for taking this risk to help my family." Did he drop a light kiss on top of my head? I couldn't tell. He was gone; I was on my own. I had a job to do, and lives hung in the balance.

Stepping onto the sidewalk, I walked briskly toward the security gate, flashing the badge Nicholas had managed to dig up for me. My heart was racing like a rabbit's as I intercepted Claire Davis and Regina about halfway between the building and the gate, but I managed a breezy, casual smile. "Excuse me," I said, addressing myself to Claire. Out of the corner of my eye I could see Regina's eyes widen. "It's after hours and there aren't many people around, so I wonder if you can help me. I'm researching an article for the *Sweet Valley News,* and I need to arrange an interview with the plant foreman. Do either of you know him?"

I glanced from Claire to Regina and back again. Regina's hands were clenched in tight fists, but otherwise she gave no sign that she knew me . . . that she knew the crucial moment had arrived.

"We don't know the foreman," Claire Davis snapped, giving Regina a little push forward. "We're not employed here. Now if you'll excuse us, we'll be on our—"

"Oh, you probably work for another high-tech firm in the area," I babbled, improvising wildly. I had to keep them talking—I had to stall them until the police arrived. *Did Nicholas get through to them? Are they on their way?* "You could answer some questions for me, too! What company do you represent?"

Claire Davis glared at me. "We don't represent . . ." Suddenly her flint-gray eyes grew even squintier than usual. "Wait a minute," she spat. "You're not a reporter. You're the girl who came by the house the other day, asking for Regina!"

I'd been wondering how long it would take her to recognize me, and I had a story already concocted. "The girl who . . . ?" I repeated, puzzled. Then I laughed. "Oh, you must be referring to my identical twin sister. Believe me, this happens all the time. Yes, she's friends with Regina Morrow. Are *you* Regina?" I turned to Regina, extending my hand. Regina took it limply. "Nice to meet you. I'll tell my sister I ran into you."

"Thanks," Regina whispered.

Claire Davis's pale complexion had grown blotchy. She tugged impatiently at Regina's arm. "We're in a hurry," she muttered to me, "so if you don't mind . . ."

I was running out of material. *I could ask to borrow a pen or something,* I thought desperately. *Or maybe I should just collapse on the sidewalk in front of them—pretend I swallowed my gum, or that I'm having a heart attack. Do sixteen-year-old girls ever have heart attacks? What's taking the police so long?*

Brushing past me, Claire Davis propelled Regina down the sidewalk. I dashed after them. "Wait a minute," I called. "I think you dropped something."

Claire pivoted, looking back over her shoulder. At that moment I saw Nicholas sprinting at top speed

across the nearly empty parking lot. *What's he doing?*
I wondered, my jaw dropping. *He's supposed to wait
for the police!*

"Regina!" Nicholas hollered.

Claire spun around again. She reached for
Regina, but Nicholas was too fast for her. Grabbing
his sister, Nicholas shoved her behind him, sheltering
her with his body.

"Nicholas, watch out!" I screamed as Claire Davis
fumbled in her handbag and whipped out a small
handgun.

The police were still nowhere in sight. "Help!
Guard!" I shouted, but the security guard had left his
booth and entered the plant, perhaps to lock up for
the night. There was no one to turn to.

I froze, one hand outstretched, my heart stuttering
with terror. Claire raised the gun, pointing it straight
at Nicholas's broad chest. "No," I begged. "No!"

I waited with dread for the sound of a gunshot.
Instead my ears were assaulted by the piercing shriek
of tires squealing. All four of us whirled.

"Bruce!" I cried joyfully as he braked the Jeep
and leaped out, Jessica and Mr. and Mrs. Morrow at
his heels.

But Claire Davis still had the gun, and now as I
stared in horror and disbelief, another car roared into
the parking lot. A beat-up blue Dodge. Denson.

The engine still running, Phillip Denson sprang
from the car, a gun already in his hand. Mitch followed slowly, his eyes downcast. "Don't move!"
Denson barked, waving the gun for emphasis.

154

"Don't anybody move or you're all dead!"

Bruce, Jessica, and the Morrows halted, staring helplessly at me, Nicholas, and Regina. I clutched Nicholas's arm; Regina let out a sob.

They had us surrounded. Our plan had failed.

It was the most terrifying moment of my life, Diary. Two guns pointing right at us— there was no place to run. I really didn't think we'd make it out of there alive, but Mr. Morrow started talking to Denson, and then . . .

"Phil, put down the gun," Mr. Morrow pleaded, stepping forward. "Listen to reason."

"I said don't move!" Denson shouted angrily.

Mr. Morrow stopped. "What do you want, Phil?" he asked, his voice low and calm. "What are you trying to accomplish?"

"I want to see you ruined, the way you ruined me," Denson snarled. "I want to see *your* life in tatters."

"I didn't ruin your life," Mr. Morrow said. "You ruined it. You embezzled from the company—that's a crime. We had to prosecute you, and you had to pay for it."

"But I served my time and I'm *still* paying." Denson's eyes flashed with dangerous madness. "I'm under a cloud I just can't shake. My wife left me, I can't get another job in the industry. What are my options, I ask you?"

"There's always another way out," Mr. Morrow said.

Denson laughed mirthlessly. "Well, I've got a way

155

out now for you and all your friends, boss." He lifted the gun. "Just to make sure none of you try to track me and Mitch and Claire down in Rio. Say good-bye."

Nicholas lurched forward. "You can't kill—"

"Stay back!" Denson warned him, waving the gun. "Or you'll be first!"

My vision grew blurry with fright. Regina and I clung to each other, half fainting.

Then I heard the most beautiful sound in the world. Sirens. "The police," I gasped. "Finally!"

Denson jerked his head in the direction of the sirens, momentarily distracted. Bruce and Nicholas sprang forward simultaneously, knocking Denson to the ground. The gun spun from Denson's grip, clattering across the pavement.

But Claire still had her gun, and now she pointed it at Nicholas's back. "Nicholas!" I screamed. "Watch out!"

Nicholas, Bruce, and Denson wrestled on the ground, cursing and grunting. A shot rang out. Had Nicholas been hit?

The three men continued to struggle. Nicholas was uninjured. "She missed," Regina whispered thankfully. "She missed."

The sirens were upon us. Four police cars whipped to a stop just a few yards away, and an instant later eight officers raced toward us, their guns drawn. Nicholas and Bruce had managed to pin Denson.

"Drop the gun and put your hands in the air!" Sergeant O'Brien commanded Claire Davis.

It was over. Two officers pushed Mitch and Claire against a squad car, frisking them. Denson was already in handcuffs.

"Mom! Daddy!" Regina cried, hurling herself into her parents' arms.

Bruce hugged Jessica, and Nicholas hugged me. "Mom and Dad and Regina are safe," Nicholas whispered, his voice filled with relief and gratitude. "We're all safe."

Back home at the Morrows' we practically collapsed with exhaustion, relief, and joy. Mr. Morrow cracked open some champagne, and we drank toasts and talked and talked. The best part of it was that Regina can hear! The treatments have restored 85 percent of her hearing—it's like a miracle. She doesn't have to go back to Switzerland, either—she can finish the therapy on an outpatient basis in L.A. You should've seen her and Bruce. They sat on the couch with their arms around each other, and they just wouldn't let go.

When Nicholas drove us home, Jessica ran into the house to let us have a moment alone. He pulled me into his arms, and we held each other tight for a long, long time. When he finally released me, there were tears in his eyes. What he must be feeling right now! He came so close to losing everyone who's most dear to him. I can't

*tell you how glad I am that everything
turned out OK!*

Friday, 1:25 A.M.

*I suppose it's Saturday, actually. Another
late night! I just got home from the Morrows'
party, and I have to scribble a few lines before
I go to sleep. What a bash! It was partly a
welcome-home party for Regina, and partly a
thank-you party for the four detectives—yes, I
took a bow—and the Morrows did it in style,
as usual. Live music, a catered buffet . . . I had
the best time—danced until my feet hurt and
stuffed myself with shrimp and cocktail sauce,
which as you know is my absolute favorite.*

*I have a secret, Diary. Nicholas kissed me
again. No excuse this time—we weren't
sleuthing! And I have to admit, it felt wonderful. We were standing on the balcony
overlooking the patio and the party below,
alone in the moonlight. Nicholas is so incredibly gorgeous—those adorable eyes, that luscious black hair, and that body. I'm getting
goose bumps all over again. It just sort of . . .
happened. We turned to each other, and his
arms went around me, and I lifted my face,
and . . . magic. Bliss.*

*But then the moment was over . . . and it
was just a moment, Diary. It was delicious,
sweet and beautiful. I don't regret it. But the*

whole rest of the evening my stomach was churning. I kept thinking about Todd, wondering what he's doing and how he's feeling, if he's spending his Friday night with somebody special. . . .

When I said good night to Nicholas, I gave him a sisterly, "just friends" peck on the cheek, and I could tell he understood. I made a decision a couple of weeks ago, and it was the right one—I'm sticking by it. Nicholas is an absolute dream, but I'm just not ready to have another boyfriend.

It makes me sad. I can't help feeling that I'll never love anyone the way I love (loved?) Todd. Maybe someday. But not now.

Part 5

Dear Diary,

My twin sister is driving me crazy for a
change. I'm still exhausted from what we all
went through last week with Regina and her
parents, and I was looking forward to a few
hours lounging in the sun by the pool in the
backyard. I thought maybe I'd doodle a few
short-story ideas—something thrilling and
scary based on my recent brush with the
criminal element. But who can hear herself
think when Jessica Wakefield is spouting
off?? Her latest crisis is being in charge of
the big Sweet Valley Centennial student picnic. Bruce is president of the student centennial committee, and he appointed Jess and
Lila cochairs of the picnic—don't ask me
why. Talk about a recipe for disaster. (Sorry,

bad pun!) Not surprisingly, Jess has decided that the easiest way to take care of the picnic is to delegate all the work to other people. She's already talked me into designing a poster and manning the kissing booth . . . well, she didn't exactly have to twist my arm about that last part!

It really is going to be a great centennial celebration—hard to believe little old Sweet Valley is one hundred years old! I feel really proud to live in a town with such an interesting history. The picnic is just part of it— there's also going to be a parade, fireworks, and of course the big football game against Palisades High. Sounds like fun, huh? It will be a downer if we lose the game, though, and that could very well happen if Ken Matthews gets benched. He's flunking Mr. Collins's English class—can you believe it? It's hard for me to imagine, since English is my favorite subject. Everybody has a hard time with something, though. Poor Ken—supposedly if he doesn't do well on his next assignment, he'll be on academic probation, which means no football. This isn't general knowledge, by the way—Bruce filled us in (he has the inside scoop, being on the centennial committee). I also got a hint from Todd—Ken calls him every now and then in Burlington, and that's one of the topics that's come up recently. That and Ken's crazed passion for . . .

Suzanne Hanlon! Gag me. Had I mentioned that Ken's dating her? This is even more mystifying to me than a failing grade in English! It's pretty big gossip at school because they're the world's least likely couple: Ken the superjock and Suzanne the supersnob. I just don't get the attraction. Sure, Suzanne is beautiful. She's superrich and sophisticated. But she's so incredibly stuck-up, she's off the meter. She makes Lila Fowler look like a sweetheart. Why would Ken want to date the chief of the local culture police, Miss Season Tickets to the Symphony, I Go to Films Not Movies, Rock and Roll isn't Really "Music"? I mean, she is such a wet blanket, and so supercritical of everything and everybody. I'm not just being catty; it's the truth.

Who can explain love, right? Anyway, it explains why Ken's being so secretive about his problem: he doesn't want Suzanne to find out. For some strange reason she wants to believe that he's just an athlete by accident, and his heart really lies with classical music and art. That's her dream Ken. I don't think she'd care about his getting kicked off the football team, but she's so literary (she thinks she is, anyway!), she'd probably drop him like a stone if she found out he's failing English. It would be too embarrassing for her to have her name linked to such a cretin. Poor Ken!

That's why I decided to call him just a few minutes ago and offer to help him with his next English assignment. We've been buddies for so long—he was Todd's best friend— it seems the least I can do. He was kind of taken aback that I'd heard the whole story, but he said sure, he'd appreciate a few tips. So he's dropping by later this afternoon.

Which gives me forty-five minutes to myself. Back to the pool . . . let's hope Jess has gone elsewhere!

Monday, 9:30 P.M.

Ken and I had a good talk this afternoon—I think I helped him over his writer's block. He's basically a smart guy, he just gets psyched out. For example, his English assignment for Wednesday is to write a short story, and he'd pretty much given up without even trying. He thinks he's not creative, that he doesn't have anything to say. Luckily, I thought of a perfect way to give him a jumpstart. . . .

"I'm just a crummy writer, that's all there is to it," Ken said with a depressed sigh.

I squeezed a wedge of lemon into my iced tea and contemplated him thoughtfully. We were sitting on the patio, and his blond hair looked almost white in the late-afternoon sun. Even frowning, he was re-

163

markably handsome, with sky-blue eyes and chiseled features. And it went without saying the star quarterback of the Sweet Valley High varsity football team would have a phenomonal body.

Ken has brains, too, though, I thought. *Just not a lot of intellectual confidence.*

"You're not a crummy writer," I argued. "I remember your paper on Edgar Allan Poe in English last year—it was terrific."

"That was just a book report," Ken said glumly. "Plot summaries. Mr. Collins wants me to write an *original* short story. How am I supposed to do that?"

"All you need is one good idea," I said. "Have you tried reading some short stories? Sometimes that's a good way to get inspiration."

"It only makes me more convinced I can't do it," Ken confessed. "I read these great stories—like Hemingway, or O. Henry, or whoever—and I can *see* that they're great, but I don't have the first clue why. How the author does it, how they're put together, how they work." He grinned wryly. "I need a play-by-play on the blackboard, like we do in football."

I laughed. "A how-to manual. Yeah, I know what you mean. Hey, wait a minute!" Suddenly I had a brainstorm. "Be right back."

I ran into the house and up to my room. After a minute or two of rifling through my desk drawers, I found the manila folder I was looking for and hurried back down to the patio. Ken was slumped on a lounge chair, his eyes closed wearily.

"Sit up, Matthews," I commanded. "Coach

Wakefield has something to show you!"

I handed him the folder, and he opened it curiously. "It's a short story I wrote, about a kid who moves to Sweet Valley—what that's like for him, how the town looks to someone new," I explained. "All my preliminary notes and outlines are in there, too. Maybe if you look it over, it will give you an idea of how you get from the beginning to the end of a story."

"Liz, this is great!" Ken exclaimed, skimming the first few lines.

I shrugged, suddenly feeling shy. I had to fight back an impulse to grab the folder from him and hide it away again in my desk. "Actually, Ken, you're the first person I've shown this to. I'm really private about my writing—my fiction and my poetry. So I hope you'll—well, I'd appreciate it if you didn't show it to anyone else."

"But it's really good." Ken gave me a puzzled smile. "Why wouldn't you want people to read it? You should be proud that you're so talented at something."

"I guess I just don't feel ready yet with my stories," I reflected. "It's not like writing for *The Oracle*. Someday, maybe. In the meantime . . ."

"You can trust me," Ken promised. "I won't show it to anyone. And, Liz, I really appreciate this." His blue eyes, glowing with sincerity, held mine for a long moment. "Seriously. You're a lifesaver."

I socked him lightly on the shoulder. "What are friends for?"

*   *   *

165

I haven't exactly had second thoughts about giving Ken my story folder, but I can't help feeling just a little bit . . . anxious? Exposed? It's as if he's seeing me naked or something—I mean, not even Jess or Todd or Enid, my very closest friends, have read any of my stories! But I do trust Ken, and it makes me happy to think he'll learn something from my scribblings. I'll be happier, though, when that folder's back in my desk drawer, safe and sound!

Todd called right after dinner and we talked for about ten minutes. Ten minutes, and we'd said just about everything we had to say. How could that be? When he first moved to Vermont, we'd gab for an hour—we'd have to tear ourselves away, thinking about the horrible phone bills we were running up. I guess we just don't have that much to say to each other anymore. We stick to the facts—we don't get deep into our feelings the way we used to. On the one hand, I suppose it's a relief. We don't end up crying every time because we miss each other so much. But mostly, it's sad. When did we start to get casual about the distance between us? When did it start to feel normal?

Tuesday, 8:00 P.M.

I talked to Ken today, and we laughed about how we've both gotten stuck with the

166

kissing booths at the centennial picnic—I'm manning the boys' booth and he's manning the girls', of course. Jessica's not letting anyone off the hook! He said his short story for English is coming along. I'm so relieved. If he'd told me he was still stuck, I don't know what advice I would've been able to come up with. I asked him confidentially what he thought of my story. He hesitated for a second—he scared me, I don't mind saying! "What if he thinks it's junk? What if I can't write?" But then he said he loved it. Phew. I told him I couldn't wait to read his story—I'm sure he'll really surprise us all with how much natural talent he has.

Wednesday, 10:20 P.M.

Dear Diary,

I just got back from the "literary evening" Suzanne Hanlon organized at the school library. About twenty-five people, including yours truly, read original poetry. There were a few really wonderful poems—Olivia's and Winston's especially—but most of the stuff was so pretentious, I couldn't help giggling once or twice. I kept catching Ken's eye, and we'd both practically choke trying not to burst out laughing. He really looked mystified; Suzanne would be applauding her brains out over some truly terrible poem, and Ken would just kind of scratch his head. I'm sorry,

167

Diary, but she is just such a snob. I'm trying to like her because I like Ken, but it's hard. Make that impossible. It seems as if she's trying to change the things that are most wonderful about Ken—that's not what love's all about, in my opinion. First of all, she makes fun of football every chance she gets. I mean, she doesn't have to try out for the cheerleading squad just because she's going out with the quarterback, but there has to be a happy medium. I can tell he feels like a dumb jock when he's around her. He told me about going over to her house for dinner and her whole family was quoting Shakespeare left and right and belittling sports. He must've been so uncomfortable.

Maybe he was uncomfortable tonight, too—maybe that's why he acted a little strange when I asked him about his story. I figured he'd be more relaxed, having handed it in today and all, but I guess he's still insecure. He has to get a pretty good grade on it in order to pass English and play in the game against Palisades, so the pressure's not off until Mr. Collins gives it back. Still . . . It seemed funny that he didn't want to talk about it at all. Maybe it was a really personal story—something autobiographical. Maybe it was about dating Hands-off Hanlon! Ha ha.

Jessica is flipping out more than ever about the picnic. Lila bailed out on her today, which means now Jess has to do all the work herself. She claims she's never going to speak to Lila again for as long as she lives . . . gee, where have I heard that before? She makes the same threat, what, two or three times a week??

Friday, 10:15 P.M.

Something really awful happened today, Diary. I'm so stunned, and mad, and disappointed, I can't see straight. What a betrayal! If I hadn't seen it with my own eyes, I really wouldn't have believed it. . . .

"Stop the presses!" Editor in Chief Penny Ayala declared as she burst through the door of the *Oracle* office after school on Friday. "Wait till you see what I've got in my hand, Liz." She waved a manila folder at me. "I really hope we can find a way to squeeze it into the special centennial issue!"

"What is it, the rough draft of the great American novel?" I joked, swiveling around in my chair.

"Close," she said. "A wonderful short story that ties in with the centennial theme perfectly. And you'll never in a million years guess who wrote it."

I gave her a blank look. I thought about Suzanne and her literary evening and wrinkled my nose. "Not . . . Suzanne."

"Close again!" Penny laughed. "Ken Matthews. Can you believe it?"

169

"Ken!" I exclaimed. "Then it must be the story he turned in to Mr. Collins the other day. So it's good?"

"It's great," Penny confirmed. "Mr. Collins liked it so much, he showed it to me, and I liked it so much, I just ran off ten copies so we can all look it over at the staff meeting in a few minutes."

"Wow," I breathed. "So what did Ken say? This means he got a high grade from Mr. Collins, so he can play in the game against Palisades. He must be thrilled!"

"I'm not sure he even knows yet," said Penny, tossing a copy of the story onto my desk.

"Well, you have to ask his permission to print the story," I reminded her. "I get the feeling from talking to him that he's kind of private about his writing. He might not want everybody reading it."

"I'll track him down after the staff meeting," Penny proposed. "It's a real honor—I'm sure he'll want to be featured in the special issue. Who wouldn't? Go ahead, read it." She waved at the story. "You've got ten minutes before the meeting. See you there!"

Penny disappeared back into the hall. Turning Ken's story right side up, I flipped quickly past the title page. I couldn't wait to read it—I was so proud of him!

The boy walked down the different Main Street, his eyes seeking his reflection in the shop windows; that at least would be familiar when all else was new and strange.

"Wait a minute," I said out loud, blinking at the page. "This can't . . ."

170

I read the sentence again. I read the next sentence, the whole paragraph. It was *my* story, the one I'd let Ken borrow so he could get some ideas!

This has got to be a mistake, I thought, my brow furrowed. *He must have turned in the wrong paper to Mr. Collins. That's it.*

I turned back to the title sheet, and there it was. *My* title, and where my name had been, Ken's name typed in its place. It was so sleazy, so *blatant*—the typefaces didn't even match!

"I can't believe it!" I cried, slamming the paper down on the desk. I felt the blood rush to my face. Ken was my friend. How could he have done this to me? "The thief! I did him a favor, a *huge* favor, and this is how he repays me, by stealing my story?"

Except for me, the newspaper office was empty— by now everybody else was probably gathering in Mr. Collins's classroom for the staff meeting. I jumped to my feet, Ken's plagiarized story clutched in my hand. *I've got to stop Penny,* I thought, seething. The Oracle *can't print this under Ken's name!*

Shoving back my chair, I bolted toward the door. Thirty seconds later I charged, panting, into the classroom.

Mr. Collins, Penny, Olivia Davidson, John Pfeifer, and the rest of the staff all glanced over at me. "Didn't I tell you it was great?" Penny asked, smiling.

"Well, I—"

"I loved it," raved Olivia. "I really didn't think Ken had it in him. Who'd have guessed he's a poet at heart!"

171

"Just goes to show, an athlete can be as well-rounded as the next guy," said John, *The Oracle*'s sports editor.

"I had a hunch Ken could produce something exciting once he set his mind to it." Mr. Collins shook his head ruefully. "Though I have to admit, I would have come down hard on him a lot sooner if I'd suspected he was harboring this kind of secret talent!"

Secret talent? A poet at heart? I stared at Mr. Collins and the others, wondering how they could be so blind, so gullible. "But it's . . ."

My weak protest was drowned out by Penny's announcement. "It's unanimous, then. We clear space for this in the centennial issue, maybe on the front page."

All around the table there were enthusiastic nods of assent. "Great," said Mr. Collins. "Now let's figure out what—"

"Wait a minute," I cut in. "I'm not sure . . ." I cleared my throat, anticipating that this would be an unpopular position to take. I blurted out the words to get it over with. "I don't think we should print the story."

Penny raised her pale-blond eyebrows. "Why on earth not?"

"Well . . ." I racked my brain for a reason. I couldn't just come right out and call Ken a thief and plagiarist in public without confronting him privately first. It didn't seem fair, and even though he'd treated *me* poorly, I wasn't about to sink to that level. "This issue is supposed to focus on the centennial celebration and Sweet Valley's history. Fiction . . . it just doesn't fit in."

"Elizabeth." Mr. Collins laughed. "You know better than anyone that good fiction can give us a truer picture of the world than any fact-filled journalistic piece. Ken's story really gets at the heart and soul of Sweet Valley."

I bit my lip. *Don't I know? I wrote it!* "But we haven't even asked him yet. He's really private about his writing. I bet he won't want—"

Penny brushed off my protest. "Don't worry, I told you I'll talk to him first chance I get." She shook her head, a tiny frown creasing her forehead. "What's the problem, *really*, Liz? Don't you *like* Ken's story?"

"How can she not like it?" John wondered. "Ken's story is the best one that's been submitted to *The Oracle* in ages."

"Yeah," someone else piped in. "Ken's story is . . ."

Ken's story, Ken's story! Everyone stared at me with surprised mistrust, as if they thought I was trying to sabotage "Ken's story" out of professional jealousy. "We just can't print it!" I cried, whirling to race back out the door.

"Hold on, Liz," I heard Mr. Collins call after me. "Let's talk this . . ."

I didn't slow down. I couldn't make sense to anyone else until I'd made sense out of what Ken Matthews had done to me.

I raced full speed to the locker room and then stood outside while Aaron Dallas got Ken

173

for me. I was so mad, steam was probably com-
ing out of my ears, but meanwhile I could hear
some of the guys whistling and teasing Ken.
"Liz Wakefield wants to see you. Oooo . . ." I
pictured Ken smiling, snapping his towel at
them, playing along. He had to know why I
was waiting for him, though. How on earth was
he going to explain this to me?

I stood in the hallway, my arms folded across my
chest, tapping out a fast, angry beat with my right
foot. *How could he use me like this?* I wondered.
He'd probably figured no one would ever find out.
He'd get the grade he needed from Mr. Collins and
give the paper back to me, and that would be that.
What a liar. What a cheat!

A minute or two passed, and then the locker-room
door swung open. Ken ambled out, his hair still wet
from the shower and his Oxford shirt untucked. He'd
stuck his feet into his sneakers without even taking
the time to put on socks. "Liz," he said, not meeting
my gaze.

"I need to talk to you." I whispered so my anger
wouldn't travel back into the locker room. "Now. In
private."

Ken nodded. He glanced around. The corridor
was empty, so he led me to an alcove by one of the
big windows.

We sat down facing each other. Ken still wouldn't
look me in the eye. "I guess you found out about the
story," he mumbled.

When I first stormed over to the locker room, I'd been ready to slug him. Now I felt my fury dissipating. Ken wasn't trying to laugh it off; he looked intensely aware, and ashamed, of his guilt.

"Why?" I asked simply.

Ken rubbed his forehead, grimacing. "I just couldn't do it, Liz," he said tiredly. "I tried, I really did. I sat at my desk for hours, literally. I'd type a line or two and it would be rotten, so I'd throw it out and start again. But nothing was any good. Nothing came close to the stuff *you'd* written. That was what I was shooting for, but I guess I might as well have been shooting for the moon."

"But to turn in my story, with your name on it." I shook my head.

Ken looked as if he felt sick to his stomach. "I didn't plan to. I hope you don't think that. It just . . . happened. I was up against the wall—it was the middle of the night and I still had zilch. I thought maybe if I typed out a few lines from your paper, I'd get a feel for what it's like writing something good. I typed a whole paragraph and I stared at it . . . and it just seemed like proof that I could never write anything of my own. I had to turn something in, though. I couldn't fail English—it would have meant losing everything. Football, Suzanne . . ." He lifted his face to mine, his blue eyes pleading for understanding and forgiveness. "I didn't mean to take advantage of your friendship, Liz. After the game against Palisades, I was going to tell Mr. Collins what I'd done, see if he'd give me one more chance to write a story of my own. I'll go to him now—I'll take the F. I'm sorry, Liz. Really sorry."

I was still hurt and disappointed, but I felt a little better knowing that stealing the paper had been an act of desperation, rather than cold calculation. "It's not just Mr. Collins at this point," I told Ken, relating the scene that had just taken place at the *Oracle* staff meeting.

Ken's face turned chalky under his suntan. "Oh my God."

"I tried to talk them out of printing it, but I couldn't do that without ratting on you," I explained.

"What are we going to do?" he asked.

I shrugged. "It's up to you. Your name is on the title sheet of that short story."

I had to give Ken credit. He shot straight to his feet; he didn't hesitate. "I'll talk to Penny and Mr. Collins right now," he vowed, already striding off down the hall. "It won't go any further than this, Liz."

And you know, Diary, at that moment I really believed him. But he wimped out. I sat in the newspaper office the whole rest of the afternoon waiting for Mr. Collins to come in and pull the story, but he never did. So The Oracle will go to the printer's on Monday with that lie right smack in the middle of the front page.

I really can't believe this has happened. I've known Ken since we were little kids— he's always been a good friend. So it's incred-

ibly sad, because even though I understand why he did what he did, I just don't know if I'll ever feel the same way about him again. He used me and he let me down, just so he could save his own skin. There's no way he could ever make it up to me.

Monday, 9:30 P.M.

Never say never, Diary. It turns out there was one way Ken could make it up to me. Today he did one of the bravest things I've ever seen. . . .

"Hey, Liz. Wait up."

At the sound of Ken's voice I turned slowly on my heel. The final bell had just rung, and I was on my way to the parking lot with the typeset copy of the special centennial edition of *The Oracle*. The printer, Mr. Fulbright, was expecting me in fifteen minutes.

Ken pointed at the bundle in my arms. "Is that the newspaper?"

I nodded without speaking.

"And my . . . your . . . the story's in there."

"On the front page," I said icily.

"Then I'm really glad I caught you." He actually had the gall to smile with relief. "It's not too late, right? You can pull the story out."

I really couldn't believe it. He thought he could just erase his little mistake and no one would ever be the wiser. "Sorry, Ken," I snapped. "You missed your chance. I can't make a major change like that without holding a staff meeting, and besides, at this point we don't have anything to put in its place."

"Yes, we do." Ken fumbled in his backpack, pulling out several typewritten pages. "I spent the whole weekend writing another story."

I glanced at the title page: "Offsides," by Ken Matthews. "Look, Ken," I said, my tone softening somewhat. "We can't just stick in another story. The staff liked the other one because it fit in with the centennial theme. Time's up. We're both going to have to live with this the way it is."

"The stories are exactly the same length," Ken persisted. "And the subject matter . . . it's appropriate, Liz. Just read it. You'll see what I mean."

Shaking my head with a sigh, I started to skim the first few paragraphs of the story. Then I went back to the beginning, reading every line with care. *"The quarterback had lived his life thinking every move he made, on and off the field, was for the best, so it was easy for him to rationalize stealing the paper. But gradually he came to comprehend that if he based a portion of his life on a lie, the rest of his life would be a lie, too."*

I lifted my wide eyes to Ken's. "Ken, this is . . ." I faltered.

"It's the right thing to do," he said simply.

Reaching out, I took his hand and squeezed it tightly. "Are you sure you want everyone to read this story? Because you don't have to do this just to get straight with me. Maybe you should just go to Mr.

Collins and work things out with him and Coach Schultz—"

Ken shook his head emphatically. He was about to do something that would probably lead to being suspended from school and kicked off the football team. What's more, the whole school was going to know every single detail. But I noticed he didn't look depressed anymore—he didn't look worried or ashamed. He looked free. "I can't beg Mr. Collins and Coach Schultz for special favors. I have to face the consequences of what I've done, Liz," Ken declared, his eyes clear. "I need to get straight with myself."

Wednesday, 11:00 P.M.

Remind me, Diary, never to assume anything.

The special centennial issue of the newspaper came out this morning with Ken's story, "Offsides," right there on page one. It took about a millisecond for the kids at school to figure out that it wasn't fiction at all, and then the rumors started flying. In the cafeteria at lunch people were practically taking bets about what was going to happen to Ken: Would he get suspended from school, and for how long? Would they let him play in the exhibition game against Palisades? Things like this don't exactly give you the best impression of human nature. It's as if people enjoy it when someone else gets in trouble. I was sit-

179

ting with Jessica at lunch, and she was just as bloodthirsty as the rest. It really got me steamed. Why weren't people talking about how incredibly brave Ken was for owning up to his mistake that way? Wasn't anyone going to stand up for him, stand by him?

I couldn't even eat my lunch, I felt so bad for him. I felt so bad in fact that I did something I'm ashamed of now. Jess told me Ken had just gotten called to the principal's office. I caught up to him right before he went in, and I offered to cover for him—to lie for him. I was willing to say that "Offsides" was pure fiction—Ken did write the first story, and we switched it just because we liked "Offsides" better. But Ken wouldn't consider it. He told me I was an honest person and should stay that way. He was ready to take whatever Chrome Dome Cooper decided to dish out. The last couple days have been a roller coaster, but no matter what anyone else thinks, I think Ken's coming out of this looking pretty good. I think our friendship is going to survive, maybe even become stronger. Ken Matthews is a pretty cool guy.

It was tough watching him walk into that office—my heart was in my throat. I knew Mr. Cooper was waiting, and probably Mr. Collins and Coach Schultz, too. What would the final verdict be? I worried all afternoon. The whole school was holding its collective *breath. And then I walked out to the football field with Jessica after school, and I saw the greatest thing. . . .*

I'd walked Jessica outside for cheerleading practice so we could talk about the centennial picnic. As we neared the football field, she shaded her eyes with her hand. "Looks like most of the guys are already out there," she remarked, scanning the bench, "but I don't see Ken."

I bit my lip anxiously. "I guess that means he's off the team. Did you see him at all after lunch? God, maybe his detention started right away—maybe they sent him straight home!"

"Poor Ken," said Jessica. "You know, if you hadn't given him that story in the first place . . ."

"I know, I know. Thanks for reminding me that my effort to help out only ended up getting him into deeper trouble. I had good intentions, though. And so did Ken, putting that other story in the paper. I just hope . . ." I heaved a sigh. "I just hope he still feels like he did the right thing, now that the worst-case scenario has come to pass."

Just then our attention was drawn to a lone football player in helmet and pads jogging from the gym toward the field. Jessica stopped in her tracks. "Wait a minute," she gasped. "That looks like . . ."

"Ken!" I exclaimed jubilantly.

"They're letting him play!" Jessica broke into a trot. "C'mon, let's find out what happened!"

We hurried toward the field. Ahead of us we saw

Ken slow to a walk as he neared the bench. His apprehension was evident.

Suddenly I realized what he was facing. He was off the hook somehow—they were letting him play. But everybody knew about his stealing my story. How were the other guys going to react?

Ken stopped a few yards away from the rest of the team. Jessica and I also froze in our tracks. There was a long, horrible moment of silence and stillness and then . . .

Erupting into cheers, Ken's teammates spilled from the bench. Instantly Ken was surrounded by grinning guys trying to hug him and slap him on the back. "You've got a lot of guts, Matthews," I heard Scott Trost tell him. "We're proud to be on your team."

I choked up a little just watching the scene. Ken was back where he belonged.

After cheerleading practice Jessica gave me the whole scoop about what went on in the principal's office. Mr. Collins accepted "Offsides," though he cut the grade from an A to a C because of the circumstances. Enough to maintain a passing grade in English, though, and to keep Ken on the football team. As for stealing my paper, that's a really serious offense, and ordinarily a student would get suspended for a couple days or even a week for something like that. But Mr. Cooper decided that Ken's freely offered

*public confession was appropriate and suffi-
cient penance. Ken didn't need to stay home
from school to think about his mistake—he'd
already taken full responsibility for it. I guess
ol' Chrome Dome's a pretty cool guy, too!*

*So I waited for Ken outside the locker
room and totally pounced on him . . . not to
lecture him this time, but just to give him the
biggest hug ever. One big pimple on the
happy face of the world, though. On my way
to the locker room I'd bumped into Suzanne.
"You must be really proud of Ken," I'd said, a
big, happy smile on my face.*

*"Proud of him for being a dumb jock and
a plagiarist and a thief and humiliating me in
front of all my friends?" she'd snapped. "Are
you kidding?"*

*So much for that romance. I knew
Suzanne was no good for Ken. He deserves
much, much better, and I plan to tell him
that, if he dares to be sad for even thirty seconds about losing her!*

Saturday, 9:15 A.M.
Dear Diary,

*Jessica just burst into my room in tears.
She definitely has reason to cry—it looks as if
she's out-Jessica-ed herself this time! She forgot to confirm the caterers for the picnic
today, so they're not coming. Yes, that's right.
No food at the picnic, and hundreds of peo-*

183

ple have already paid seven dollars apiece for tickets. I wish I could help her out, but I'm covering the centennial celebration for The Oracle, *so I really don't have time. She stomped off determined to cook all the food for the picnic herself. I'd better alert poison control!*

I'll never forget this wonderful day for as long as I live. My hometown turned one hundred years old—what a blast! First there was a parade down Main Street with marching bands and floats depicting events in the history of Sweet Valley. Very exciting. Then I dropped by the Civic Center to see the unveiling of the new mural that Bruce's family donated to the town. It's just beautiful—a sweeping panorama of Sweet Valley then and now. The exhibition football game against Palisades High started at two P.M., and I've never seen so many people packed into the stands. Enid and I had great seats, front and center, and it was possibly the most exciting football game I've ever seen. . . .

"Where's Jessica?" Enid asked as the cheerleaders bounced through a rousing routine.

The Sweet Valley fans responded with a deafening roar. I waved my Gladiators banner energetically, meanwhile picturing Jessica somewhere stewing up vat after vat of some foul, completely inedible concoction. "You really don't want to know," I told Enid. "And by the way, at halftime? Have a couple of hot dogs. Fill up."

"But what about the picnic?"

"Take my word for it," I said. "You won't be sorry."

We were way ahead at the half—21–6. "Ken's having a great game," Enid enthused, munching some popcorn. "Three touchdown passes in a row to Scottie. This is going to be a breeze!"

"They make it look easy," I agreed, slurping a lemonade. "But I wouldn't write off Palisades quite yet. They're division champs—I bet they've got some tricks up their sleeves."

Unfortunately, as it turned out, I was right. Things came together for Palisades in the third quarter— their star Peter Straus ran in two touchdowns in a row. Enid stopped eating popcorn and started chewing her nails. Without even realizing I was doing it, I tore my paper banner into shreds.

When you're behind, the seconds on the clock seem to fly by. "Less than a minute left in the game," Enid muttered. "C'mon, guys. You can do it!"

We were down by three points. It was Sweet Valley's ball on the opponent's seven-yard line, third down. Enid and I stared fixedly at Ken's helmet in the middle of the huddle. "What do you think they'll do?" she asked. "Send in Tim Bradley to kick a field goal and settle for a tie?"

At that moment Coach Schultz took Ken aside.

The coach suggested something; I could see Ken shaking his head. The coach said something else; again Ken replied in the negative, gesturing emphatically.

Then Coach Schultz nodded and patted Ken on the back. Ken jogged back to the huddle. Tim stayed put on the bench.

"Ken's not settling for anything. They're going for the touchdown," I said excitedly. "They're going for the win!"

But could he pull it off? I held my breath, clutching Enid's arm. Ken called the play. The clock started ticking and the imposing Palisades defense rushed forward. Ken dropped back, arm raised to pass to Scottie. But suddenly Scottie slipped. I could see Ken looking quickly around to see if anyone else was open for the pass. There was no one.

"Oh God," Enid moaned, covering her eyes. "I can't look!"

I winced, waiting for Ken to be flattened. Instead, suddenly, he was flying, the ball tucked under his arm. Dodging would-be tacklers, he hurdled over a pile of bodies. Two more strides and he was over the end line. Touchdown!

The crowd surged to its feet in one body, cheering wildly. The instant the buzzer sounded, we all flooded down onto the field to congratulate our victorious team. When I reached Ken, he lifted me in his arms and twirled me around. "You won the big game!" I cried, dizzy and laughing.

He planted a sweaty kiss on my nose. "Yeah, I

won the big game," he agreed, and I knew he wasn't just talking about football now. "Thanks to you, Liz."

Yep, Ken is a winner, all right. It was great to see him in top form on the football field, but I watched another truly gratifying scene outside the gym right afterward. . . ,

Giddy from their triumph, the football players started to stream back toward the locker room to hit the showers. Enid and I waved good-bye to Ken and the others and were about to head in the opposite direction when we saw Suzanne Hanlon approach Ken. "What does *she* want?" I wondered, narrowing my eyes.

Ken stopped in front of her, his helmet in his hand. "Hi, Suzanne," he said, his tone guarded.

To my astonishment Suzanne's pretty face crumpled in tears. "Ken, I'm so sorry," she whimpered. "Can you forgive me for what I said the other day? It was a knee-jerk reaction—I see now that printing that story took a lot of courage. Please." She reached out for his hand. "Say you'll let me make it up to you."

At Suzanne's touch Ken's stiffness melted. He stepped closer, and she met him halfway. "Yeah, I forgive you," he said quietly. They kissed, and I could see Suzanne sigh happily as she rested her face against Ken's chest. "That's better," she murmured. "Now, hurry up in there. As soon as you're dressed, I want to buzz over to the library. There's a special history lecture we simply *can't* miss, and then I was thinking of throwing together a little impromptu dinner party. I want you to meet my friend Mark. You know, the writer? I showed him 'Offsides' and he has some constructive criticism for you. He thinks you should—"

"Sorry, Suzanne," Ken interrupted, stepping back to hold her at arm's length. "How about coming with me to the picnic instead? I promised Jessica I'd man the kissing booth." He tickled Suzanne's waist. "I'll give you a couple freebies. What do you say?"

Suzanne frowned. "A kissing booth? How juvenile. Grow up, Ken. That's just not your scene."

Ken dropped his arms to his sides. For a moment he looked disappointed and confused; then his face cleared and he smiled. "That's where you're wrong, Suzanne," he declared. "It *is* my scene, and a history lecture at the library isn't. In fact, history lectures at libraries bore me to tears, as do literary evenings and foreign film festivals and stuffy dinner parties at the Hanlon mansion."

Suzanne gawked at him, her mouth hanging open. Enid and I had to struggle to keep from jumping up and down and applauding.

"So I guess I'll see you around, Suzanne." Ken bent down to kiss her on the cheek. She was still too stunned to respond. "Have fun at the lecture!"

So Ken and I ended up at the kissing booths, and business was booming. I wonder if his lips are as puffy as mine?? I haven't been doing a lot of kissing in the last few

188

*months, if you know what I mean, and I
thought it would be kind of a kick, but let's
just say I could probably last without kisses
for another few months. A good motivation
to save myself for Todd's next visit!
Meanwhile, Ken kissed even more girls than I
kissed guys—a good way to get over ol'
Suzanne, I'd say!*

*You're probably wondering whatever
happened to Jessica and her food crisis. We
arrived at the picnic to find tables displaying
a gourmet lunch of peanut-butter-and-jelly
sandwiches and potato chips, but no Jessica
anywhere in sight. . . .*

For once there wasn't a line of guys ten deep in
front of the booth waiting to kiss me. Twisting in my
chair, I glanced longingly at the trays of sandwiches,
my stomach rumbling. *I'm pretty hungry,* I thought,
stifling a giggle, *but who'll want to kiss me if I have
peanut-butter breath?*

"Psst, Liz!"

I peered behind the booth. Nothing there but
azalea bushes. Then I heard the voice again. "Liz,
over here!"

I walked around the bushes. "Jess, what are you
doing back here?" I asked. "Bruce has been looking
all over for you."

She rolled her eyes. "Duh, that's why I'm hiding!
If he gets his hands on me, he'll—"

"There you are!" Bruce exclaimed, popping sud-

189

denly into view. Jessica yelped, jumping behind me for cover. Bruce grabbed her arm. "Come on, I want to make this announcement before the crowd starts breaking up."

"Liz, help!" Jessica wailed, looking over her shoulder with pleading eyes as Bruce carted her off.

Bruce didn't slow down until he'd dragged Jessica right up onto the bandstand. Interrupting The Droids in the middle of a song, he commandeered the microphone. Jessica cowered at his side. "Everybody having a good time?" Bruce boomed.

The crowd responded with a hearty cheer. "How about Ken Matthews and the Sweet Valley High football team?" Bruce continued. There was another roar, and Ken stepped out of the girls' kissing booth to take a bow.

Bruce put a hand on Jessica's arm and propelled her forward. She stood with her head hung; I could practically see her teeth chattering. "And I know you're all raving about the food. PB and J always hits the spot, right?"

There were more cheers and quite a bit of laughter. *Poor Jessica!* I thought.

"Well, here's the person we have to thank for the elegant fare," said Bruce, "*and* the person we have to thank for helping the student centennial committee raise even more money than we ever expected. Because of Jessica's frugality—she kept the food budget under seventy-five dollars—I'll have the honor of presenting the Community Fund with a check for nineteen hundred dollars and eighty-seven cents!"

The applause was deafening. Jessica looked up, blinking in surprise. She thought she was public enemy number one, and now it turned out she was a local hero!

Jessica's always been the queen of the quick recovery. Now, tossing back her hair, she stepped up to the microphone and smiled broadly. "Thanks," she said, acknowledging the cheers with a casual wave. "I felt it was the least I could do, and I knew you'd all agree. Why shell out the big bucks to caterers when the Community Fund could put the money to better use?"

And so on and so forth. That's our Jessica!

Part 6

Monday, 9:45 P.M.

Dear Diary,

My sister needs frantic activity and excitement in her life just as she needs air to breathe. She's already up and running with a new scheme, even though she's barely had a chance to catch her breath after the centennial picnic. The cheerleaders are looking for a way to raise money for new uniforms, and Jessica came up with one: hold a rocking-chair relay, with all the cheerleaders signing up pledges and taking thirty-minute shifts. They'll rock in the gym with a huge party going on at the same time—a "Rock Around the Clock" party, naturally. The gang talked it over at lunch today, and everybody had to admit it was a pretty original idea—just wacky enough to work!

Jessica's already asked The Droids to play at the party, which reminds me that I should mention their song-writing contest in my next newspaper column. They're looking for a new hit—anyone at school who's written an original song can submit a tape of it. Should be interesting—I bet they discover a lot of hidden talent in the Sweet Valley High student body. I wish I could sing—maybe I'd set one of my poems to music. Like this one:

> *Rainy Sunday,*
> *Foggy Monday,*
> *Closely creeping fears,*
> *Can't take much more of this.*
> *Drive east, drive fast,*
> *Until at last*
> *Desert rainbows dry my tears*
> *Like a kiss.*

But, Diary, as my family never hesitates to tell me, I have a voice like a seagull— squawk, squawk, squawk. Oh, well!

During lunch at school today, I noticed Lynne Henry sitting all by herself. She looked so lonely; imagine, in that whole crowded cafeteria, not being able to find one single person to talk to! I never see her hanging out with anybody—she's just so quiet and awkward. I found myself worrying about her. I spend a lot of time worrying about people, don't I? Maybe instead of worrying I should just look for an opportunity to get to know her better.

193

Ken had some big news for me today. Guess where he's going?? Burlington, Vermont, to visit Todd! We have a long weekend from school, in a couple of weeks, and he's taking two extra days so he'll have five altogether. I'm so envious I could die. Mom and Dad agree that I should wait until summer vacation before I fly out, and then they'll pay half my plane ticket if I save up for the rest. I guess it's a fair, sensible arrangement. But . . . summer seems so far away! I called Todd tonight to tell him how much I wished I could pack myself into Ken's suitcase, and it was almost like the old days—I could just feel over the phone how much he wanted to hold me in his arms. I guess the love is still there, deep down inside both of us.

Friday, 11:15 P.M.

What a great day! After school the annual junior-class softball game was held at Secca Lake. Mr. Jaworski and Mr. Collins each "managed" a team, so it was the Patriots— because Mr. J teaches American history— versus the Bards—in honor of Mr. C's love of Shakespeare, naturally. I played first base for the Bards, and we won 11–8. We made this one great double play, but of course the game-winning play was Ken's in-the-park home run with the bases loaded. That sort of stuff doesn't happen in the majors, let me tell you! Afterward we all went swimming and pigged out on foot-long sub sandwiches. A blast, all in all. But I couldn't help remembering last year's sophomore game, when I played right field and Todd played center and we spent the entire time flirting and telling gross jokes.

Right before the game The Droids announced the Star-Search Song Contest, as it's being officially dubbed. Everybody was talking about it—I bet they get lots of great entries. Speaking of The Droids, I spotted Guy Chesney, their keyboard player, talking to Lynne Henry on the sidelines during the game, and I almost didn't recognize her. I really think it was the first time I'd ever seen her smiling—she actually looked pretty. That smile proved that her big clunky glasses aren't the problem with her looks. It's what's going on inside that matters, and most of the time she just looks so . . . forbidding. So closed off. So, smile more, Lynne Henry! Let it shine!

Monday, 8:45 P.M.

Dear Diary,

Enid came over this afternoon, and we hung out listening to Billie Holiday CDs—she's our new (old) favorite. Jess sat with us for a while. Well, actually she rocked. She seems to think she needs to practice this very difficult skill before the fund-raiser. What a nut! Needless to say, she couldn't do this without talking nonstop at the same time. We did our best to tune her out, but it was hard. We ended up just laughing out loud because she looked so funny rocking back and forth like crazy—like Whistler's mother gone haywire!

Later Jess was all in a huff because her cheerleading buddy Helen Bradley is moving to L.A. That means there'll be a vacancy on the squad, and Jess was moaning about this as if it were some kind of national disaster. When I suggested that the sun will probably rise tomorrow despite this tragedy, she just threw her dirty socks at me.

Wednesday, 4:30 P.M.

The entries for the songwriting contest keep pouring in—we're collecting them at the newspaper office, and we've had to empty the box twice. I can't wait to hear them on Friday—this is going to be great!

I ran into Lynne right outside the Oracle office at lunchtime, and she acted as if I'd seen her naked, she was so embarrassed. I tried to chat with her, just act friendly, but she hustled off while I was still in midsentence. What's up with that girl?

Todd called just a few minutes ago to tell

*me he missed me. It made my day. We talked
about how fun it will be when Ken visits—
Todd's really psyched to introduce his old
buddy to all his new ones. But he confessed
that he wished it was me flying out. I'll tell
you, just when I'm ready to write off this relationship . . . it's worth it. Todd is still the
funniest, sweetest, most adorable guy.*

> *Friday, 5:20 P.M.*

Dear Diary,
    *We have a new mystery on our hands at
Sweet Valley High. A bunch of us were hanging around on the lawn during lunch listening
to the song-competition entries. The first few
songs were pretty standard, but then Guy
popped in this one remarkable cassette. . . .*

"Just between you and me, I'm not that impressed
so far," announced Dana Larson, the Droids' vocalist,
as Guy rewound a cassette on his portable tape
player.

"We've only listened to four songs," lead guitarist
Max Dellon pointed out. "Let's give this thing a
chance."

Dana sighed. "I guess I'm starting to think we're
expecting too much. I mean, it's tough writing a good
song. Maybe we should have given the contestants
another week or two. What do you think?" she asked,
looking straight at me, Enid, Jessica, Ken, and
Winston, the only non-Droids present.

197

"The first four were just so-so," Winston agreed cheerfully. "That just means the winning song's still out there somewhere."

Guy hit the play button. "OK, folks, shush up. This one's called 'On the Outside, Looking In.'"

I lay back on the soft grass, my arms folded under my head, listening attentively. For a second the tape whirled silently, then we heard a couple of evocative minor-key chords. Then . . . the voice.

I sat up. "Wow," Guy whispered.

"Listen to her go," exclaimed Max. "What a melody. What a voice!"

Dana's brown eyes were glittering. "This is it. This is it!"

The haunting song wrapped around us, holding us all spellbound. It was over too soon; Guy rewound the tape. "She's incredible," he marveled. "I can't believe there's someone with that kind of talent at Sweet Valley High and we didn't even know about it!"

"Well, who *is* she?" asked Jessica, bouncing excitedly on the grass.

Guy examined the tape and the box it came in. "That's funny," he said. "She wrote the title on it, but not her own name."

"Anonymous," said Winston. "A mystery woman!"

Guy started the tape again. Again we listened in awed silence. "The lyrics," Guy hissed. "This time focus on the lyrics."

Whoever she was, she'd poured her heart and soul into this song. The rich, throaty voice vibrated with emotion; it soared, only to fall into deep, whisper-soft sorrow.

"Day after day I'm feeling kind of lonely,
Day after day it's him and him only.
Something in his eyes
Made my hopes start to rise
But he's part of a world that doesn't include me
Nothing he says could ever delude me.
I'll never win.
This is how it's always been.
I'm on the outside . . . looking in."

My eyes filled with tears. "It's so sad, and so beautiful at the same time."

Guy had been deeply moved by the song, too. His eyes were bright with excitement and his face flushed. "She can sing *and* she can write," he exclaimed. "What incredible talent!"

"Why wouldn't she want you to know who she is?" Jessica puzzled. "If I'd written that song, I'd want everyone to know!"

"So are we agreed?" Guy asked his fellow band members. "Is this the one?"

Dana, Max, Emily, and Dan all nodded enthusiastically. "We should listen to the others just to be fair, but I'm pretty certain this is the one," Dana confirmed.

"Then we have a mission," declared Guy, waving the cassette at us. "We've got to find this girl!"

❖   ❖   ❖

On the way home from school Jess kept pumping me about who the mystery singer is—she thinks it would be great to unveil this incredible new talent at the cheerleaders' "Rock Around the Clock" party. I told the truth: sure, I'm an ace reporter, but I haven't cracked this story yet. I don't know who she is—nobody does. It's funny, isn't it? I write things just for myself in my journal—poems and stories and reflections. I wouldn't want anyone else ever to see them—there's too much of the secret me in them—that's why it was so hard sharing that short story with Ken. Somewhere out there is another girl who I think feels sort of the way I do about her writing. That song is so incredibly heartfelt and private, she couldn't even bear to put her name on it when she entered it in the contest. But she did enter it—she is ready, then, for people to hear her story. I'm just as curious as Jessica and Guy and everybody else. Who is she??

Friday, 11:45 P.M.

We all went dancing at the Beach Disco tonight. One good thing about being single— you can dance with as many different guys as you please. I didn't miss a song—took a spin with Ken, Winston, Max, John, and Aaron. I

200

*really don't mind not having a boyfriend. So
why do I feel so empty?*

*At one point Guy hunted me up and
asked if he could talk to me. We went for a
walk by the ocean and he really spilled his
guts. It's the strangest, most romantic
thing—he's developed this huge crush on the
mystery singer. He doesn't know her name,
he's never seen her face, but I swear, it
sounds as if he's falling in love with her. . . .*

"Everybody thinks I should have tracked her
down by now," I told Guy with a rueful laugh. "My
reputation as a reporter is about to go down the
tubes!"

"I just thought, writing 'Eyes and Ears,' you always seem to have a jump on the rest of us when it
comes to knowing what's going on at Sweet Valley
High," said Guy, skipping a stone out over the
water.

"I don't know who she is," I repeated. "I wish I
did, but I don't."

Guy's arms dropped to his sides, and for a moment
he stood with his head drooping. Then he turned to
me, and even in the dark I could see the fiery glow
in his eyes. "I've *got* to find her, Liz," he declared.

"I know you want to give her the credit she deserves for writing the prize-winning song, but
maybe she—"

"That's not the only reason." Guy raked a hand
through his wind-tangled brown hair. "This isn't just

about the Star-Search contest, Liz," he confessed. "This girl . . . I have to find her, for *myself*. This probably sounds totally idiotic, but I've been playing that song over and over, and it just . . . gets to me." He put his fist to his chest, next to his heart. "Not just because it's a great tune and the lyrics are sharp and she's so obviously this immense talent just waiting to be discovered. That's how it strikes Dana and Max and the others. For me it's more . . . personal."

He shot a glance at me and I nodded sympathetically.

"It's something about her voice," he continued. "It's like I *know* it, even though obviously I don't because if I'd ever heard it before, I'd remember. And it's like *she* knows me. Like she's singing to me." He laughed wryly. "I'm nuts, right?"

"The song really moved you. That was probably the effect she was going for."

"It didn't just move me. It *changed* me." He stared out to sea, his eyes wide open to the mystery of the dark night. "It made me see a hole in my life that I never realized was there. And there's only one person who can fill it."

We stood for a moment in silence, listening to the waves crashing on the sand just a few feet away. The emotion in Guy's voice was as powerful as the ocean, and for a moment I was almost envious. The exhilaration of feeling something so deeply, of loving so recklessly . . . would *I* ever feel that again?

"I wish I could help," I said, "but I don't have a clue." *And if she doesn't want people to know who she is, we may never find out,* I almost added, but didn't.

"Thanks anyway, Liz. I'll just have to keep searching." Guy's voice vibrated with determination. "I'll just have to find a way to reach out to her the way she reached out to me."

What a romantic story, huh, Diary? But I have to admit, I ended up feeling lonely after that conversation. Guy's heart is taking flight like a free, beautiful bird. I remember that. I remember what it feels like to love and be loved as Guy loves this girl he's never met, and it makes me so, so sad to have lost it.

Will I ever really get over Todd? Will it ever stop causing me pain when he forgets to call, when his voice sounds distant, when he stops needing to hear every little detail of my life in Sweet Valley—when he stops needing to know me inside and out? And if I do get over him, will my heart ever take wing like that again?

Saturday, 3:45 P.M.
Dear Diary,
I stopped by the Music Center today to pick up a Billie Holiday CD, and I made the most astounding discovery. . . .

I found the CD I was looking for, but there were a couple of people waiting in line at the cash register, so I decided to browse a little more. Beyond the section of the store where they sell tapes and CDs is a display of musical instruments, and beyond that a lesson/recording studio. I wandered down the row of bright, glittery electric guitars, fantasizing about being a funky Dana Larson type and playing in a band. *Liz Wakefield, rock and roll sensation.* I stifled a giggle. *Yeah, right!*

I paused by the drum sets, thinking about Emily Mayer and how happy she was now that her family life had settled down and she'd started dating Dan Scott. Just then I heard two people talking in the lesson studio.

The door was ajar, and I stepped closer. "Press the strings down hard," a teenaged girl instructed. "It hurts your fingers a little at first, but they'll toughen up."

"Like this?" a little boy asked. He strummed a broken chord.

"Exactly." The girl strummed the same chord, and then another. "Soon you'll be able to put them together in a song."

Still strumming, the girl started singing. My heart just about stopped. The voice sounded familiar. . . . *It's her!* I realized, goose bumps prickling my arms. *It's the mystery songwriter!*

I eased up to the door and peered in. In a million years I never would have guessed who I'd see sitting there, giving a guitar lesson to a little boy. Lynne Henry.

"Lynne!" I cried.

Lynne glanced up from her guitar. She wasn't wearing her glasses; her eyes looked especially wide, and almost frightened. "Keep working on that," she instructed the little boy, getting quickly to her feet.

"Lynne, it's *you*!" I said, clutching her arm excitedly. "You wrote 'On the Outside, Looking In'! You're the anonymous songwriter!"

She put a finger to her lips. "Ssh. Oh, Liz, you have to promise not to tell anyone!"

"But, Lynne, why?" As I stared at her, I noticed something else. Not only was she wearing contact lenses instead of glasses, but she'd styled her unruly light-brown hair differently, and a touch of makeup made her green eyes look luminous. "The Droids are dying to find out who you are—they want you to sing with them tonight at the 'Rock Around the Clock' party. Don't you want to get credit for writing such a fantastic song?"

A rosy blush tinted Lynne's pale cheeks. "Do you really think . . . do people really think the song's that special?"

"Are you kidding?" I shook my head in disbelief. "You're the toast of the town. The Droids are desperate to track you down, seriously. Especially Guy Chesney."

Lynne's blush deepened and she dropped her eyes, all her shyness returning full force. Suddenly the lyrics from her song popped into my head. "Day after day it's him and him only . . ." *No wonder Guy got the feeling the mystery girl was singing to him,* I realized. *Because she was!*

205

"Lynne," I said gently, "I know you're shy, and maybe you don't have a lot of self-confidence. We all feel that way sometimes. This should prove to you that you don't need to hide yourself away—you have a really special talent."

"You just don't understand," Lynne said quietly. "You're an incredibly sensitive person, Liz, but you just can't know what it feels like to be plain and gawky, that tall, skinny girl whose name nobody can ever remember, to walk around school like I'm invisible, to sit alone in the cafeteria day after day, to never get asked to dances and parties." Tears sparkled in her eyes. "I'm not asking you to feel sorry for me, I'm just asking you to keep my secret."

"But, Lynne, it doesn't have to be that way! Everyone loves your song, and they'll love you, too, if you give them a chance. Let me tell Guy and the rest of the band."

"No," she insisted, a note of panic entering her voice. "You can't tell Guy."

"He's dying to know who you are, though," I told her. "Lynne, it's like a dream come true. You wrote that song for him, didn't you? And it's bringing him right to you! All you have to do is tell him that you're the mystery songwriter and—"

"And it'll be the biggest disappointment of his life," finished Lynne. "He doesn't want to meet *me*, Liz. He's expecting somebody gorgeous and exciting. I know because we talked about the song walking home from school yesterday. He's picturing a girl

206

who's sexy and exotic, a young Linda Ronstadt. That's the girl he wants to play backup for. If he finds out it's just me, it would only ruin the song for him." Once again her eyes filled with tears. "And it would ruin the song for me, too."

"It wouldn't happen that way," I argued.

She shook her head stubbornly. "It would, Liz, and it would just kill me. Please, promise you won't tell anyone."

I gazed at her for a long minute, but she didn't waver. "All right," I agreed reluctantly at last. "I promise."

It's so sad that Lynne thinks she's better off staying a nobody. Sure, there are risks involved with revealing her identity, but there's so much to be gained! The admiration and friendship of her classmates, artistic recognition, maybe even love. But I can't force her to reach out and grab hold of her future—she has to do it herself. A promise is a promise, and my lips are sealed. But what if Guy finds out the truth? I honestly can't guess how he'd react. Maybe he would be disappointed because Lynne doesn't match his fantasy. Then again, Guy's fallen in love with a voice, a soul. He's fallen in love with who Lynne is on the inside. Would it really matter to him that she's not the most glamorous girl in school?

I hate secrets, Diary. I absolutely hate them! You'll understand why in a minute.

"The Rock Around the Clock" party tonight was a huge success. The cheerleaders decorated the gym so it looked like a fifties-style sock hop, and everybody dressed up: guys with slicked-back hair and T-shirts with the sleeves rolled up, and girls in poodle skirts and cardigans buttoned up the back. The big rocking chair was up on stage with the band, so the cheerleaders were literally in the spotlight when they were rocking, which I'm sure suited my sister just fine. The Droids were great as usual. They haven't officially announced the Star-Search Contest winner, but they played Lynne's song. Lynne wasn't even there to hear it, though, which just seemed so sad. Guy dedicated "On the Outside, Looking In" to "the girl who wrote it," and I could just see on his face how much he wants to find her. Dana sang it so beautifully, it brought tears to my eyes, and Guy looked as if he wanted to cry, too. All I could think about was lonely Lynne sitting home by herself instead of going to the dance, and Guy on stage feeling lonely because he's lost his heart to a song, a voice on a tape, a ghost. Everyone's just so darned lonely . . . me included.

When the band took a break, Guy and I walked outside for some fresh air. Of course, we started talking about the mystery girl, and without meaning to I let slip that I knew who she was. . . .

"Don't get me wrong, Dana's the best there is," said Guy as we sat down on the grass outside the gym, tipping back our heads to look at the stars. "Her version of 'On the Outside, Looking In' was gorgeous, tender, heartbreaking. But it just wasn't the same. *She* should have been up there onstage singing it to the world. It's *her* song."

I bit my lip, feeling as if I were about to explode. I was dying to tell Guy the secret, but I'd promised Lynne, and I couldn't forget her tormented expression in the music store. She really didn't want to be found out.

"This is driving me crazier and crazier," confessed Guy, tearing up a handful of grass. "I just can't . . . function, not knowing who she is. I'm so distracted— I can't eat, I can't sleep . . . . I think I'll run an ad in *The Oracle*, Liz. Just for starters. And if that doesn't work—"

"It probably won't. She wants to be anonymous— she won't respond to an ad in the newspaper."

"How can you be sure that—" Guy broke off his sentence, peering intently into my eyes. "Liz! You know who she is!"

And I'm always giving Jess a hard time because she can't keep a secret for thirty seconds! "I . . . I do know," I admitted reluctantly. "But she made me promise not to tell anyone."

"You know who she is. You've talked to her!" Guy's eyes were as starry as the sky overhead. "I can't believe she's a real person, living and breathing and walking around. Liz, is she as wonderful as I think she is? Do *I* know her? What class is she in?"

My head was spinning from Guy's eager questions. It seemed cruel to leave him totally hanging. How much could I tell him without revealing Lynne's identity? "She's a junior," I said guardedly, "and I think you know her."

"I know her." He looked dazed at this. "I've talked to her? I've heard that voice with my own ears? Then why can't I figure this out on my own?"

"That's all I can tell you," I declared. I wanted more than anything to tell Guy the truth, but this mattered too much to Lynne—I couldn't interfere. "Can we just drop it?"

Apparently not. Guy gripped my arm tightly. "Just tell me why," he begged. "Why doesn't she want anyone to know who she is?"

"She's shy." That wasn't saying too much, was it? A lot of people were shy. "She doesn't believe she's talented, and when you and everybody else started raving about the song, it just made her more insecure. She's afraid she can't live up to the image everyone's formed of who this singer is—for example, what she looks like. She thinks that because she's not as hot as Linda Ronstadt, people will be disappointed."

"Not as hot as Linda Ronstadt . . ." Guy's eyes

widened. "She said that? Those exact words?"

"Pretty much. Why?"

"Oh, thank you, Liz!" Guy catapulted to his feet and started dancing around in circles. "Thank you, thank you, thank you!"

"But, Guy! What are you . . . I didn't . . . how could you . . . ?"

"Gotta get back to the band—our break's about over." Waving good-bye, Guy dashed back toward the gym. "You're an angel, Liz! I won't forget this!"

I stared after him, my mouth hanging open. He was acting as if he'd solved the mystery, as if I'd given him the deciding clue. *What did I say?* I wondered, completely baffled.

Monday, 10:30 P.M.

Dear Diary,
    Two incredible things happened today. First of all, Guy figured out who his mystery woman is, and he recruited me to help him reveal her identity to the world. . . .

"Just because I mentioned Linda Ronstadt, you figured out it was Lynne," I said on Monday right before lunch, shaking my head.

"Because when Lynne and I talked about the mystery songwriter the other day, I said that playing backup for her would be like playing for Linda Ronstadt," explained Guy, handing me a stack of mimeographed flyers. He rocked up and down on his toes, jittery and excited. "Suddenly it just clicked.

211

This really shy girl with so much hidden depth . . . I've sensed that about Lynne." He flushed, his eyes sparkling with hope. "God, I hope she doesn't freak out about this. I hope . . . I bumped into her just a few minutes ago, and I told her we were going to announce the Star-Search winner at lunch, and that we knew who she was—that I'd been able to describe her face to this friend of mine who's an artist, just from listening to her voice. That I'd fallen in love with her. Am I doing the right thing, Liz?"

I nodded emphatically. "You're doing the right thing. C'mon, let's get in there!"

The cafeteria was packed full of bodies. While Guy ran to hook up the microphone so he could announce the contest winner, I grabbed Enid and we started handing out the flyers Guy had designed. "Mystery Songwriter Wins Contest!" the flyers declared, and right underneath . . . an exquisite sketch of Lynne, her hair tousled, her eyes bright, a shy, dreamy, amused smile curving her lips. Lynne . . . the real Lynne.

The new Lynne. "Look at her—she must have had a makeover or something!" Enid whispered.

My eyes found Lynne in the lunch line, and I gasped at the transformation. She'd blow-dried her hair so instead of being frizzy, it was attractively wild and wavy. A light touch of muted eye shadow brought out the gold in her green eyes; stirrup pants, a loose colorful sweater, and dangly beaded earrings finished the look. "I always suspected there was a pretty girl under those old jeans and baggy sweatshirts," I told Enid.

And now Sweet Valley High was seeing Lynne Henry for the first time. Unbeknown to Lynne, the flyers were circulating, and suddenly she was mobbed. I watched from a distance, an ear-to-ear grin on my face, as people congratulated her. "Great song, Lynne!" "Where'd you find the inspiration?" "How long have you been writing music?"

Suddenly Guy's voice came over the microphone. "As you can all see," he said, his eyes fixed on Lynne, "we've found our Star-Search Contest winner. 'On the Outside, Looking In,' composed by Lynne Henry!"

The applause was deafening. "And now," continued Guy, "I'm hoping she'll sing her song for us. Lynne?"

Lynne stood frozen as a statue, her eyes wide. Guy stepped toward her and took her hand. I saw him lean close, whisper something in her ear. And then for a moment they just gazed into one another's eyes.

I heard Enid sigh. "Is this the most romantic moment you've ever witnessed or what?"

With Guy still holding her hand, Lynne approached the microphone. He dropped her hand in order to sling his guitar strap over his head, and then he strummed the opening chords of Lynne's song.

I saw her take a deep breath. A moment later her unforgettable voice filled the room. "Day after day I'm feeling kind of lonely, day after day it's him and him only. . . ." Just as she had on the tape, Lynne was singing to Guy. Only this time he was right there beside her.

213

My heart swelled with pride and happiness for my new friend. It looked to me as if Lynne Henry's lonely days were over.

Right after Lynne's impromptu perfor-mance, I saw the sweetest thing. Guy pulled her outside and took her in his arms for the most romantic kiss. Sigh. What a happy ending!

I told you two incredible things happened today. Now for the second. Are you ready for this, Diary?? Drumroll, please. Amy Sutton is moving back to Sweet Valley!!! Yes, my old best friend whom I haven't seen since sixth grade. Can you believe it? There was a letter from her waiting for me when I got home from school. WXAB offered her mom a sportscasting job, so they're moving back from Connecticut—they bought the Bradleys' house! I'm just bursting from the news. It's the worst when people you love move far away . . . but sometimes they come back. I'm so excited to see her again!

Part 7

Friday, 10:30 P.M.

Dear Diary,

Amy called today! She's moving in a week from Sunday. I can't wait to see her. It's been five whole years since her family moved to Connecticut—incredible. I wonder if she's changed. Will I even recognize her? I shouldn't worry. There's nothing like a friend who goes way back—just hearing her voice reminded me of so many great times we had as kids.

I hung out by the pool all afternoon with Jessica and Enid, trying to get them as excited as I am about Amy's arrival. I wish Enid had known Amy back then, but Enid didn't move to Sweet Valley until eighth grade, and we've been friends only since last year. Although of course we're best friends,

215

and Enid knows everything about me—it doesn't matter that we didn't grow up together.

Jessica's big concern right now is filling the vacancy on the cheerleading squad. They have to hold tryouts soon, and she's dreading it, because last time she schemed to keep Annie Whitman off the squad just because Annie used to have a "bad" reputation, and Annie was so upset she tried to commit suicide. Annie ended up on the squad, and of course she's terrific. I told Jessica nothing like that will happen this time if she's fair about tryouts and picks the girl with the best jumps and pep and whatever else it is they look for. Needless to say, Jess doesn't think she needs my advice—especially now that she and Cara are writing their own advice column for The Oracle. Did I tell you about it? It's called "Dear Miss Lovelorn"—is that perfect or what?? She read me and Enid a couple of the letters they've gotten so far, and I've got to admit, her responses are really on target. The Sweet Valley High dating scene will never be the same.

So I'm counting the days until Amy gets here! Only one problem. That's the same weekend Enid and I were supposed to go up to Lake Tahoe to her aunt Nancy's ski cabin. I hinted that I didn't want to miss

Amy's arrival, and Enid was great about it—she said we could go the following weekend instead, and invite Amy. Isn't Enid the most understanding, generous friend?

Monday, 8:45 P.M.

I was talking at lunch today about how great it is that Amy's moving back to Sweet Valley, and Lila had a few typically obnoxious things to say on the subject. She remembers Amy as a tomboy and a klutz who needed braces in the worst way; in other words, back in sixth grade Amy wasn't a vain, boy-crazy flirt like Lila. A point in Amy's favor, in my opinion! Lila changed the subject so she could talk about her supposedly gorgeous cousin Christopher who's coming for a long visit soon. She's planning a huge costume party two weeks from Saturday—a lobster bake (since he's from Maine), a live band, the works. Big deal, right? Like Lila doesn't throw "the party of the decade" practically every month!

Luckily, the rest of the gang is excited about seeing Amy again. I just can't wait for Enid to meet her. My two best friends! We're going to have so much fun as a threesome—I think they'll really hit it off. They have a lot in common—me!

217

Right after school today I dropped by Ken's house with a care package for Todd. Ken had a midafternoon flight to the East Coast— by now he's in Vermont! The care package wasn't much—just some chocolate-chip cookies, a collage of headlines and pictures from recent issues of The Oracle, *and a picture of me so Todd can see I haven't changed much since the last time he was out here. Oh, and of course a letter telling him how much I wish I could put myself right into the package! We had a really good conversation on the phone last night. Todd talked about Gina and admitted that they'd gone on a couple of dates together. But now they're back to platonic status—Todd said his heart just wasn't in it. I was so glad on both counts—glad he felt free enough to ask someone out, but also (even more!) glad he decided he didn't want a new girlfriend. He says no one can compare to me, and I still feel the same way about him. I guess that's a good sign!*

Saturday, 10:00 P.M.

Dear Diary,
Guess what?? Amy's here!!!

I had just stuffed some suntan lotion and a paperback book in my beach bag when the phone rang on

Saturday morning. *Maybe it's Enid,* I thought, dashing into the kitchen to answer it. We were supposed to meet at the beach in fifteen minutes—she could be calling to tell me she was running a little late.

Amy Sutton's cheerful voice greeted me instead. "Liz, hi! Did I wake you up?"

I laughed. "I've been up for hours—Jessica's the one who sleeps until noon. What's up, Amy? Taking a break from last-minute packing?"

"We're already *unpacking,*" Amy told me, an excited note in her voice. "Liz, I'm *here.* I'm in Sweet Valley!"

"You're kidding!"

"The movers made really good time driving cross-country, so we decided to fly out a day early to be here when they got to the house with all our stuff. You wouldn't *believe* the scene—*total* chaos."

"Amy, I can't believe it!" I squealed. "You're just a few miles away. I can't wait to see you!"

"You don't have to wait to see me," Amy said with a giggle. "That is, if you can find me in the middle of this huge mess. Come on over right now!"

"I'll be there in five minutes," I declared. "'Bye!"

Grabbing the keys to the Fiat, I raced into the garage. Stopping at Amy's house would make me a few minutes late meeting Enid at the beach, but I knew she'd understand. I couldn't let my old best friend arrive in town without going over in person to roll out the red carpet!

An enormous moving van was parked in the driveway of the sprawling stucco ranch house recently va-

219

cated by the Bradley family. Pieces of furniture still draped in packing blankets were scattered all over the lawn, brawny moving men hustled back and forth, and in the middle of it all stood Dyan Sutton, Amy's glamorous mother, directing traffic like a parade marshal.

"Hi, Mrs. Sutton!" I cried, hopping out of the car and hurrying toward her. "Remember me?"

Mrs. Sutton wrapped me in a warm, perfumed hug. "Look at you, Liz! Where's that little blond pixie who used to snitch brownies from the kitchen before they were cool?" she teased.

"I couldn't help myself—you made the best brownies," I said with a smile. "But where's—"

"Liz!" someone shrieked.

I whirled. "Amy!" I shrieked back.

We raced toward each other like freight trains and flung our arms around each other. We both started talking at once—we had so much to say! Bursting out laughing, we hugged again. Then I stepped back and gave Amy a long look. "Amy, you're a knockout!" I exclaimed.

My old friend, the skinny, bucktoothed tomboy, had grown up to be as breathtakingly beautiful as a fashion model. She was tall and willowy, with shoulder-length dark-blond hair; a skillful touch of makeup made her slate-gray eyes large and dramatic; she looked both sporty and feminine in a flowered Lycra miniskirt and oversized T-shirt.

Amy flashed me a bright-white, flawless smile. "What can I say, I had orthodontia!" she joked. "You and Jessica were always the cutest girls in school, and obviously you still are. Oh, it's just so good to see you!" She gave me another big hug. "I want to hear everything about Sweet Valley—it looks pretty much the same, but you have to tell me all the gory details. Which boys grew up to be cute? Is Ken Matthews still a doll? What about Bruce Patman? Is he as handsome as he is rich?"

I laughed. "You'll see for yourself. What should we do right now? Do your parents need help?"

Amy glanced over her shoulder as a moving man bent to hoist a pale-yellow dresser onto his broad back. "Remember that dresser, Liz? I have the same old bedroom furniture. Ugh! Maybe we could find someplace to sit and talk," she said, sounding doubtful at the prospect.

"I know!" I declared. "Come over to my house. Spend the day—spend the night! My family would absolutely love to have you. It would be a blast, a slumber party, just like old times!"

Amy brightened. "Let me ask Mom and Dad. I'm sure they'll be psyched to get me out from underfoot!"

Half an hour later Amy had hunted up her suitcases and thrown a few overnight things in a shoulder bag, and we were both in the Fiat, heading toward Calico Drive. Amy had a million and one questions about all her old Sweet Valley pals, but every time I started to answer, she'd vault on to another topic. We just had so much to say to each other!

"Are you dating anyone new since Todd moved?" she asked, twirling the knob on the radio until she found a lively rock station. "I bet the boys have been beating down your door. I hope you're taking advantage of your freedom and playing the field!"

"Well, actually, I—"

"You wouldn't believe the gorgeous hunk of man I left behind in Connecticut. John Norton. Absolutely a living doll with this wonderful curly blond hair and bright-blue eyes and a body like Superman. We've been inseparable for a couple months—I mean like *this*." She lifted a hand to show me two crossed fingers. "He is just so broken up about my moving, you know? But I told him I just couldn't make any promises. Long-distance relationships are the biggest waste of time!"

"Yeah, they're tough," I agreed. "But I think if you really care about—"

"Your house!" Amy squealed suddenly. "Oh, Liz, I could just cry. This takes me right back to childhood. It is *so* wonderful to be back!"

After braking in the driveway, I reached over to give her a hug. "And it's so wonderful to have you back," I said sincerely.

My parents and Jessica were just as happy to see Amy as I was. We had such a fun day, hanging out by the pool, laughing hilariously over old grade-school scrapbooks, and then Dad put together the greatest cookout dinner. Amy's sleeping over—she's in the other bed in my room right now, reading Jessica's Ingenue *magazine. It's just like our old slumber parties. I can't get over what a glamour girl she is—that's really a big change from sixth grade!*

There was only one shadow on this otherwise fantastic day. I totally blew off Enid. It sounds terrible, but I just forgot all about her. I tried to call a couple times today to explain, but no one was home. I hope she'll let me make it up to her tomorrow. Maybe she and Amy and I can all do something fun together!

Sunday, 2:30 P.M.

I apologized to Enid first thing this morning—she admitted she was pretty steamed yesterday when I didn't show up at the beach, but of course she understood as soon as I told her about Amy arriving early. I got the impression she's a little worried already about having to compete with Amy for my time, so I decided I shouldn't waste another minute getting the two of them together so we can become a trio of best friends. Enid met me and Amy at the Pancake House for brunch—Belgian waffles with fresh strawberries—yum! I was so excited about the two of them meeting each other, I could hardly eat, though. They got along fine, but . . . I don't know. Somehow it wasn't quite what I was hoping for. . . .

223

"I'll have the blueberry pancakes, sausage on the side, and a large orange juice," Enid announced. Closing her menu, she handed it back to the waitress.

"I'll have . . ." Amy scanned her menu for a second longer. "Half a grapefruit and coffee, black."

I raised my eyebrows. "That's all? Amy, you should really try the waffles. They're out of this world."

Amy shook her head, patting her perfectly flat stomach. "Maybe you don't have to count calories, Liz, but I would just double in size if I ate waffles. And sausage!" She shook her head, laughing. "No way."

Enid smiled wanly. "I figure what the heck, it's just once a week—why not indulge?"

"Right," said Amy. "But there are fifty-two Sundays in a year. I have to be strict with myself, or I'll blimp out and no guy will ever look at me again!"

In my opinion Amy was nuts to worry about her weight, but it really wasn't polite to quiz her about her order. She could eat whatever she wanted to. "Well, when you were a kid, you were a bottomless pit," I reminded her. "Remember that time we had an ice-cream-eating contest?"

Amy rolled her eyes. "I ate about a gallon of Rocky Road. Boy, I was tasting that for a week."

"We were always conducting these culinary experiments," I told Enid. "Amy's mom likes to cook, so they had the latest appliances and stuff at her house. We'd concoct the grossest, most inedible things and then force her parents to taste them."

224

"They were pretty good sports about it," Amy recalled.

"Sounds like fun," Enid said somewhat wistfully.

"Most of our adventures didn't take place in the kitchen, though," Amy assured her. "Don't think we were goody-two-shoes girly types!"

I laughed. "We got into more scrapes. One of us always had a scabby knee or elbow. Remember when you fell out of the tree at Secca Lake park? I thought you were dead, and then you popped up from the pile of leaves like a jack-in-the-box."

"Then there was the time we got lost riding our bikes and ended up about twenty miles from home. I couldn't walk the next day, my leg muscles were so tired."

"We were tomboys, weren't we?" I said fondly.

Amy grinned, her eyes sparkling slyly. "Well, girls have to do *something* to keep busy until they get old enough to notice boys!"

I laughed heartily at this quip. Enid laughed, too, but I could tell she was forcing it. I gave her one of those secret looks we have—"What's wrong?"—but she just smiled blankly.

The waitress brought our food. I nudged my plate of waffles, buried in fruit and whipped cream, toward Amy. "Try just a bite."

"Don't tempt me, Liz," Amy begged, glancing at Enid as she spooned into her grapefruit. Enid paused in the act of buttering her pancakes, her expression suddenly guilty.

We ate for a moment in silence. Then Enid

225

cleared her throat. "So, Amy," she said. "How does it feel to be back in Sweet Valley?"

I was glad Enid was finally participating in the conversation—I didn't want her to feel shy around Amy. But then, Amy was so warm and outgoing—how could Enid not feel comfortable around her?

"It feels great," Amy declared. "Connecticut was nice, but California is really home. And the guys here are *much* better looking." She winked at me. "Blond hair, muscles, suntans . . . I don't think it'll take me too long to get over John!"

I shook my head, smiling. "The guys at school are going to flock to you like bees to honey. You'll have to beat them off with a stick."

Amy batted her eyelashes. "Do you really think so? I'm pretty nervous, thinking about my debut at SVH tomorrow. What if people don't remember me? I get kind of shy when I'm in a new situation. What if no one talks to me?"

I laughed again. "Amy, you are *too* much. Just be yourself, and you'll be an instant hit."

"I really hope so," said Amy, tearing open a pink packet of artificial sweetener and shaking it into her coffee. "But at least I have one good friend already." She smiled warmly at me and then shifted her gaze to Enid. "Make that two!"

"Of course," said Enid.

Amy sipped the coffee. "This is still too hot to drink. I'm going to run to the ladies' room to touch up my makeup. Be right back!"

As soon as Amy was out of earshot, I leaned

226

across the table, smiling widely at Enid. "Isn't she great?" I asked. "Don't you just love her already?"

Enid pushed a sausage link around on her plate. "Sure," she mumbled. "She's . . . lively."

"Isn't she? It cracks me up that she worries about people liking her. She'll be the most popular girl at SVH in no time! Don't you think she's easy to talk to? Doesn't she have a great sense of humor? She used to make me laugh so hard when we were kids. And can you believe how *gorgeous* she is? Who'd have guessed she'd turn out so pretty? But it's her personality that really shines."

"It really does," Enid agreed.

I reached out to give her hand a squeeze. "I'm so glad you like her," I said. "I want so much for you two to become friends. We'll have the best times together!"

Enid smiled. Was it my imagination, or did the smile not quite reach her eyes? "I hope so."

OK, Diary, I'll admit it. The conversation was a little stilted at times. I was scrambling to find topics that both Amy and Enid seemed interested in. But it's worth the effort. Enid's just a little shy and insecure, and Amy's preoccupied with making a good impression. When they get to know each other better, I bet they'll be inseparable.

Ken's in Burlington at this very moment. I wonder if he and Todd are having fun. I wish I could see Todd's new house, his room, his neighborhood, his school, where he hangs out—meet his new friends. But my life is full and happy, Diary. I don't have a boyfriend anymore, but I have the very best, dearest girlfriends!

Wednesday, 9:30 P.M.

Things really do change in five years! Jessica and Amy are really hitting it off. It's so surprising—they didn't like each other at all in middle school. But now Jess has decided Amy's just the greatest, and Amy really seems to prefer spending time with Jessica over spending time with me. There, I said it—I'm a tiny bit jealous. What a baby, huh? Don't get me wrong—I'm really happy for Amy. Everyone's wild about her, including Cara and Lila and all Jessica's gossipy, shallow friends. She's made such a big splash, she's constantly busy, and today she spaced our date to meet for lunch. Of course, when I caught up with her later, she felt terrible. This afternoon I really wanted to show her around the newspaper office, but instead she let Jessica drag her to cheerleading practice. I can't help getting the impression that, given a choice, she'd rather hang out with the Pi Beta crowd than with me and Enid. Am I being totally self-centered and immature? I just didn't expect to have to share her with so many people.

The good thing is, Enid and I finally made definite plans for the ski trip. We'll drive up a week from Friday, and Amy's coming, too. Just the three of us—it'll be so much fun! Jessica thinks we're crazy to go away the weekend of Lila's party, but I think if you've seen one Fowler bash, you've seen 'em all.

Speaking of Jessica, I have to fill you in on her latest romantic scheme. This time she's really sinking to new depths, in my opinion. She won't admit it, but I'm pretty sure she's using her "Dear Miss Lovelorn" column in The Oracle to try to break up Jay McGuire and Denise Hadley so she can go out with Jay herself. The other day she and Cara printed two anonymous letters, one from a junior guy complaining that his senior girlfriend was bossy and out of touch, and the other from a senior girl complaining about her junior boyfriend being immature. Naturally, everybody at school immediately jumped to the conclusion that the letters were from Denise and Jay; meanwhile, "Miss Lovelorn" advised them both to find somebody new. How convenient for Jessica, who's waiting to pounce! Do you smell a rat, Diary?

Ken got back from Vermont tonight. I couldn't wait until tomorrow to see him, so I drove over to his house after dinner. He had a special message from Todd. . . .

"Hey, Liz. Come on in!" Ken invited.

I reached up to touch his nose, which was sunburned and peeling. "Looks like the skiing was pretty good, huh?"

"It was fantastic," Ken said with a grin. "I picked up some good tips from Todd's Vermont friends—they're practically born on the ski slopes out there. Boy, was it cold, though!"

"So how was Todd?" I asked eagerly. "Did you . . . did he . . ."

"We talked about you the whole time," Ken replied, steering me down the hall to the family room. "I got some pictures developed at a one-hour photo store while I was out there—wait till you see me and Todd on the slopes!"

Ken's duffel bag was open on the floor, and he dug through it for the pictures. We sat side by side on the couch. The first photo was of him and Todd standing by the windswept lake in downtown Burlington, mountains rising dramatically in the distance. "What a beautiful place," I exclaimed.

"It's about as different from Sweet Valley as you can get," said Ken. "Nice for five days, but I'm glad to be back where it's warm, let me tell you. Here's one of the gang at Gina's cabin."

I wrinkled my nose. "Gina's cabin . . . again." It wasn't hard to pick Gina out of the crowd—she was standing between Todd and Ken with her arms around both their waists. "She's cute."

"She's OK," said Ken, tickling me playfully. "She's a lot of fun. But she's no threat, believe me. They're

230

just friends. She's going out with this guy now." He pointed to a tall tow-haired boy in a jazzy red ski suit.

I stared at the photo, and suddenly a wave of nostalgia overcame me. "I wish it was the old days," I said softly. "I wish Todd was still part of *our* gang."

"Me, too," said Ken, slipping an arm companionably around my shoulder. "We had a great time, didn't we? Picnics and volleyball at the beach . . ."

"The time you, me, Todd, and Jess went snorkeling in Turquoise Bay and saw the shark," I contributed.

"Hanging out at the Dairi Burger having french-fry-eating contests," reminisced Ken.

"All the wild parties at your house." I rested my head against his shoulder and sighed. "Maybe he'll move back to Sweet Valley like Amy Sutton did," I said hopefully. "I just hope it doesn't take five years!"

"In the meantime I have something for you." Ken bent forward and pulled something out of the duffel. "Todd sent this along for your folks."

"A gallon of real Vermont maple syrup." I laughed. "Dad will be thrilled—he's the waffle king on Sunday mornings."

"And this is for you." Ken handed me something wrapped in tissue paper. "For when you go skiing at Tahoe with Enid."

I unwrapped the tissue paper. Inside was a scarf, hat, and mitten set knit in a beautiful white and pale-blue snowflake pattern. I held the soft wool against my cheek.

"Looks good with your eyes," observed Ken.

"You'll be a real cute snow bunny. Cuter than *any* girl in Vermont, by a long shot."

I smiled. "Thanks for the moral support."

"Not that you need it," said Ken, slumping back against the sofa. "Todd's a pretty loyal guy. You're still number one as far as he's concerned."

I could feel my cheeks glow with happiness. "So did he have any message for me?"

"I think he'd rather say the mushy stuff to you in person over the phone. He asked me to do something for him, though—he told me to look after you. I mean, he was partly just joking around, like, 'Make sure she doesn't go on too many dates, keep an eye on her.' But he was serious, too. He just wants to make sure someone takes care of you since he's not here to do it anymore."

My eyes filled with tears. I'd been so sad lately, but suddenly I was brimming with hope. Todd might be three thousand miles away, having the time of his life on the Vermont ski slopes with his new friends, every week putting more and more emotional distance between us, but even so, I was still on his mind—very much on his mind.

"Oh, Ken, that's the sweetest thing I've ever heard," I cried, throwing my arms around Ken's neck. "Thanks. Thanks for bringing Todd close again."

Monday, 10:20 P.M.

Dear Diary,
     Talk about a frustrating day!! I feel as if I'm stretching myself thin to reach out in

both Enid's and Amy's directions, but I don't seem to be making anyone happy, myself included. I just want to be a good friend. Why does that seem so tough?

The day started out with me and Jess driving to school. I got an update on her progress with Jay—she's watching him and Denise like a hawk, waiting for signs that their relationship is crumbling so she can swoop in and sweet-talk Jay into being her date for Lila's costume party. I hate to say this about my own sister, but she's blood-thirsty. Merciless!

Jess had some surprising news on another subject. Amy has decided to try out for the vacancy on the cheerleading squad! Jess reminded me that Amy twirled baton back in sixth grade. But a cheerleader . . . somehow that just doesn't fit the picture of the Amy I used to know. She loved sports—she liked to be out on the field playing, not watching from the sidelines. So as you might guess, my knee-jerk reaction was pretty negative, but then I realized I was being unfair. It's natural for people to change—a friend's role is to be supportive, not judgmental. I decided to go to the tryouts and cheer Amy on. That meant postponing a date with Enid to shop for ski gloves at the mall after school, but she was really understanding.

Amy was terrific—way better than the

twelve other girls trying out. She's athletic, and graceful, too, and her voice is loud and peppy. She didn't seem nervous at all—she brimmed with confidence and enthusiasm and really looked as if she was having fun. It didn't take Jess, Robin, and the rest of the squad long to make their choice—they all voted for Amy. I was so happy that she achieved her goal! I rushed over to congratulate her, but we could only talk for about five seconds because the cheerleaders immediately pulled her right into the group. Needless to say, when I invited her to join me and Enid at the mall, she said she couldn't make it—she wanted to start learning the cheers right away. I felt kind of depressed—she's already turned into a social butterfly, and now it looks as if she'll have even less time to hang out with me. But then she suggested meeting at the Dairi Burger after.

Shopping with Enid was a riot. We laughed hysterically at this middle-aged couple who were buying every ski accessory you could think of in the worst gaudy colors. We could tell just by looking at them that they'd never skied before, so maybe the bright colors will save a few lives—when they barrel down the slopes totally out of control, everybody else will see them coming a mile away!

We both picked out navy ski gloves, and I also bought a pair of red ones for Amy. Enid

said she couldn't go to the Dairi Burger be-
cause she had to get home and start dinner,
so I went to meet Amy by myself. I got the
distinct feeling that if the plan hadn't in-
volved Amy, Enid might have wanted to
come along. Hmmm . . .

When I went to meet Amy, I almost
wished I'd gone straight home to start
dinner. . . .

"Liz, there you are!" Amy shrieked, glancing impatiently at her watch. "I've been waiting for *ages*."

I stepped out of the Fiat, checking my own watch.
"It's five o'clock on the dot," I said. "I'm right on
time!"

"I'm in a hurry, that's all," Amy explained, rushing
over to grasp the passenger-door handle. "C'mon,
let's go!"

"Go where?" I raised my eyebrows. "I thought we
were going to sit down and have a soda, catch up with
each other. I want to hear how you like your teachers
and stuff."

Amy waved me back into the car imperiously. "I'd
rather get a ride home than a Coke," she declared.
"When I said I'd meet you here, I'd completely forgot-
ten that John's calling from Connecticut at five thirty!"

Reluctantly, I climbed back into the Fiat. *Thank
God Enid didn't come along,* I thought. *Talk about a
waste of her time.* "John's calling?" I started the engine back up. "I thought you didn't believe in long-
distance relationships."

"Oh, I don't," said Amy, angling the rearview mirror so she could check her makeup. "But why waste all that adoration? I just love hearing him tell me how much he misses me."

I glanced at Amy out of the corner of my eye. Could she really be as heartless as she sounded? "Don't you miss him just a little bit, too?"

She laughed. "I don't have *time* to miss him. There are so many cute guys here! I'm busy, busy, busy."

"But you're making time for this phone call." *Whereas, you're not making time for me,* I could have added.

Amy must have heard something in my tone. She placed a hand on my arm. "I was hoping you'd hang out with me at home for a while before dinner. We can gab just as well there as we could at the Dairi Burger, right?"

I nodded, mollified. *Don't be so selfish,* I chastised myself silently. *It's great that Amy's in such demand socially, that she's too busy to be homesick for Connecticut.*

The Suttons' house had undergone a remarkable transformation. All the boxes had been unpacked, and each room was beautifully decorated, right down to the smallest details. "Your mom has fabulous taste," I observed.

"Doesn't she?" said Amy. "Come on upstairs."

I tagged after her to her bedroom. The next thing I knew, I was seated at her vanity table, bobby pins holding my hair back so Amy could put makeup on me.

236

"You have the most spectacular eyes," Amy declared, her lips pursed in concentration as she outlined my eyes with midnight-blue pencil. Next came black mascara and a vibrant pink brush-on blusher. "Do you ever wear lipstick?" she asked, examining a few of her lipsticks before zooming in on me with one. "You really should, you know. Guys *love* red, luscious lips."

I blotted my lips with the tissue she handed me. "Well, sometimes I do," I said, "but nothing this dark."

Amy clapped her hands. "You're stunning," she declared. "A real femme fatale."

I looked at the new me in the mirror. My first thought was *yuck*. "It's a little much for daytime, don't you think?" I said, unable to disguise my skepticism.

"Oh, I don't know. I guess it's a good idea to save some of your secret weapons for really special occasions like parties and dances, but why not let the world see what you've got?"

Just then the phone rang down the hall in her parents' bedroom. "Johnny!" Amy squealed, leaping for the door. "Be right back, Liz."

As soon as she was gone, I reached for some more tissues so I could wipe the eye shadow from my lids. I glanced at myself in the mirror. I looked absolutely ridiculous. Did Amy actually think I'd leave the house with all that gunk on my face?

As I dabbed the makeup off my face, I wandered around my friend's bedroom. It hadn't taken her long to get the whole room wallpapered with posters of movie stars and framed pictures of herself and her old friends from Connecticut. Were her friends all boys, though? I didn't see one photo of Amy and a group of girls; it was always Amy with some guy's arm draped around her.

Prominently displayed over the dresser, which was cluttered with jewelry and makeup, was an eight-by-ten of her and a tall blond hunk. "John," I speculated, shaking my head. I couldn't help feeling sorry for the guy. I didn't think it would be much longer before Amy had found a new Mr. Eight-by-Ten in Sweet Valley. John would be out of the picture frame and into the trash.

Sitting on Amy's bed, I reached for the stack of magazines on her night table. They were all fashion-and-glamour magazines stuffed with brainless articles about how to have sexy hair, how to juggle two boys at once, how to accessorize your wardrobe. I glanced once more around Amy's room, remembering when her old room was decorated with sports trophies, scouting badges, stuffed animals, and books. *I guess Amy outgrew all that stuff*, I thought sadly. All that stuff we'd had in common. . . . Did that mean she'd outgrown me, too?

"Johnny's losing his mind, he misses me so much," Amy sang out happily as she burst back into the room a second later. "That big bad bear was practically in *tears* on the phone just now!"

"Poor guy," I said. "Maybe you should let him off the hook—give him the ol' heave-ho so he can start getting over you."

"No way," said Amy. "It's too much fun torment-ing him. And besides, he'll come in handy down the road." She smiled coyly. "I'll need someone to chauf-feur me around when I go back to visit my old friends in Connecticut!"

I laughed, shaking my head. I couldn't help think-ing how Jessica and Lila would applaud such a speech. "Well, Amy, I really have to run," I told her, taking a few steps toward the door. "I just wanted to give you this little present."

I handed her the bag from the sports shop. Amy removed the red ski gloves and gave them a quick look-over. "I love them!" she exclaimed, tossing them onto the bed. "Thanks a million, Liz!"

"Enid helped pick them out. She said to tell you how glad she is you can come with us to Tahoe this weekend."

Amy stared at me, and for a split second I thought she'd seen through my lie. Enid hadn't displayed nearly that much enthusiasm.

But Amy had something else on her mind. "*This* weekend?" she repeated. "Oh, Liz, I can't go skiing *this* weekend. It's Lila's big costume party!"

"Don't worry, there will be others," I promised. "Lila throws a big bash every couple weeks."

"But this one is special," Amy countered. "Her cousin Christopher will be there—aren't you just *dying* to meet him?"

"No, actually, I'm not."

"Well, I am," Amy declared passionately. "And it's the first big party since I moved back to Sweet Valley.

I really think I should make an appearance, especially since I'm on the cheerleading squad now. I'd be letting Lila down if I blew it off."

"I just wish you'd told me you were set on going to the party when we first made the plans," I said, unable to mask my irritation. "We can't keep changing the date on Enid's aunt—it's really rude."

"Please, Liz?" Amy batted her thick eyelashes. "I really do want to ski with you and Enid, but I want to go to the party, too. Can't you persuade Enid to push it back one more week?"

"Well . . ."

"It would mean the world to me," said Amy, squeezing my arm. "Please?"

I couldn't say no. Amy was my friend—I wanted to make her happy. *Of course she wants to go to Lila's party,* I thought. *She's new in town. She wants to see people—it will be fun for her.* As for Enid . . . "I'll see what I can do," I replied with a disgruntled sigh.

Amy beamed. "Thanks, Liz. You're the greatest!"

Well, leaving Amy's, I didn't feel like the greatest. I felt like a horrible person. What am I going to say to Enid? She'll totally blow her top—we've changed these plans half a dozen times already. And it will give her one more reason not to like Amy. . . . But do I really have an alternative? If Enid and I go to Tahoe this weekend without her, it will hurt Amy's feelings. Either way I lose, right?

I talked the whole situation over with

Jessica when I got home and she made me
feel a little better. . . .

I slammed into the house, hurling my book bag onto the kitchen floor. It was my night to set the table, so I started clattering around in the silverware drawer.

Jessica was sitting at the table, scribbling on a notepad. "Do you have to make so much noise?" she asked as I banged a stack of dinner plates down on the counter.

"Yes, I do," I snapped. "If I'm bugging you, you can go work someplace else."

Jessica dropped her pen and raised her eyebrows. "Geez, what's with you?"

"Do you really want to know?"

"Sure. Get it off your chest before you blow up!"

I gave her a quick summary of my afternoon with Enid and Amy, and the latest conflict between the ski weekend and Lila's party. "I feel like I'm in the middle of a tug-of-war," I complained. "Amy's really putting me on the spot."

"Give her a break," said Jessica. "She's brand new in town. You and Enid invited her on the ski weekend—what? Her first day here? She didn't even know about the party at that point—she didn't know about the cheerleading vacancy. She didn't know anything or anybody! It's totally natural she wouldn't want to miss a major social event like Lila's party. Can't you see it from her point of view?"

"I suppose you're right," I grumbled.

"Besides, she could have blown you and Enid off altogether," Jessica pointed out. "Obviously she *does* want to go to Tahoe. God knows why," she added under her breath. "A whole weekend in a cabin with Enid Rollins—what a snore!"

So Jess helped me put all of this into perspective, in her own inimitable fashion. I've got to keep trying with Amy—I don't want to lose what's left of the special friendship we once shared. Enid will just have to understand.

Just to ruin a bad day, I called Todd tonight and some girl answered. I could hear her whisper something as she passed the phone to him. Ick. Donna, Todd said her name was. He didn't offer any further explanation, of course, since Donna was sitting right there—on his lap, probably! Ken's keeping an eye on me . . . but who's keeping an eye on Todd?

Tuesday, 8:45 P.M.

Dear Diary,

I brought up the subject of the ski trip with Enid at lunch today. I was dreading the conversation, but I knew I couldn't put it off any longer. She was pretty upset and I don't blame her. It was wrong even to ask her to reschedule the trip again, but I just can't bear to leave Amy out. What kind of friend would do that? The worst part was that Enid tried to talk me into going up this weekend anyway, without

Amy. It was so clear she doesn't like Amy, and that really hurts my feelings. Finally, though, she agreed to put it off one more week as long as it's OK with Aunt Nancy, who's been pretty accommodating. Would you believe she actually said, "I hope Amy's worth it"??

To make myself feel better, I popped over to Ken's after dinner. I told him about Donna the Bimbo answering the phone at Todd's last night, and he burst out laughing. According to Ken, Donna's in a bunch of Todd's classes— they're friends, they get together to study, but they're definitely not a couple. "He doesn't have a new girlfriend, Liz. I repeat: HE DOESN'T HAVE A NEW GIRLFRIEND." We totally cracked up—what a relief. After that we sat around and gabbed for a while. Ken told me some more stories about his trip to Vermont—about how weird it was to sit in the bleachers at a basketball game and watch Todd play for a strange team in a strange uniform. We also talked about skiing—Ken passed on some of the hot tips he picked up on the slopes in Vermont. He is really the greatest guy—I enjoy his company so much. I'm so glad he dumped that horrible Suzanne Hanlon!!

Wednesday, 5:30 P.M.

Amy bailed on lunch again. I was really annoyed—I mean, I have better things to do

243

than sit around waiting for people who don't show up! When I hunted her down and confronted her about it, though, she practically burst into tears. I couldn't stay mad at her. She says she's just so distracted—being the new girl in town gives her too many things to do and think about. The latest is the sorority pledge season, which starts Monday. Amy's decided she wants more than anything to join Pi Beta Alpha, and Jessica and Lila are all fired up to nominate her for membership. I'm sure she'll be a shoo-in.

Amy might actually be as insane about guys as Jessica is. She's madly in love with Lila's cousin Christopher in spite of the fact that she's never met him. Go figure!

I just had an idea for a short story. A girl about my age lives in Seattle. Her name is . . . Colleen. Colleen O'Hara. When she was small, Colleen had a very special playmate, Camilla. But Camilla moved away when they were eight, so Colleen hasn't seen her for half a lifetime. Years later something really terrible has gone wrong in Colleen's life—her parents are getting divorced, or she's sick with some terrible illness, or one of her sisters or brothers is sick. And on top of that, her boyfriend just broke up with her and she's been doing poorly in school. So she's in despair, on the verge of doing something drastic when a girl appears out of the blue and saves her life . . . and it turns out to be Camilla! Only, Colleen doesn't recognize her at first, because they've both changed so much over the years. They become best friends again, and Camilla's true friendship gives Colleen the strength to cope with her problems. What do you think, Diary? A story about a pair of childhood friends, happily reunited . . . Hmm. Are you wondering why I didn't name them Elizabeth and Amy? I'm kind of wondering myself. Except . . . it just wouldn't be true. As much as I hate to admit it, it hasn't been all sunshine and roses having Amy back in my life.

Friday, 11:30 P.M.

I consider myself a pretty patient and understanding person, but I'm not a saint. Amy stood me up again—I'm really getting tired of this! We were supposed to see an old movie at the Plaza—it was her idea—but she showed up at my house two hours late. Full of excuses and sincere apologies, of course— her mom was having a dinner party, and she had to help, blah blah blah.

We'd had a really good talk on the phone last night; she'd apologized for blowing off all our lunch dates and told me how much she valued our friendship. "Let's do something tomorrow night, just the two of us." I decided *to give her one more chance. I treasure our friendship, too. But she let me down again. She's changed in the past five years, Diary. She's a different person—I just can't depend on her. But what am I supposed to do when she shows up at the door looking as if she might cry because she's so worried I'll be mad at her, and swearing it would break her heart if anything came between us? I don't know what to think anymore.*

Saturday night, late

This was a miserable night, Diary. One of the absolute worst ever. It started out badly and unbelievably, but it went downhill from there. First of all, my costume wasn't terribly creative. I dressed as a skier headed for Lake Tahoe: Lycra ski pants, a striped turtleneck, the wool scarf from Todd, and mirror sunglasses. I carried ski poles and my new gloves, and I roasted. The whole point was to send a message to Enid about how much I'm looking forward to Tahoe, and that I'm sorry for treating her as thoughtlessly lately as Amy's treated me.

It was supposed to be just Enid and me driving to Lila's. We always go to things like this together if neither of us has a date. But at the last minute Amy called to beg a ride. When I confirmed plans with Enid and men-

tioned that we'd have to swing by the Suttons', she said in that case not to bother picking her up—she'd get a ride from someone else. That really bummed me out. Why wouldn't she cut me some slack—why couldn't the three of us go to the party together? Why do they keep putting me in this position, making me choose between them? I was in a pretty rotten mood when I left home, let me tell you. I felt it in my bones . . . we were all heading for a big showdown.

My spirits picked up a little when Amy and I got to Lila's and I saw that Enid was dressed as a skier, too. We both got the message; we hugged, and I felt so relieved to be on good terms with her.

As usual Lila outdid herself. The patio and gardens looked magical, with candles floating in glass bubbles in the swimming pool, fresh flowers everywhere, and the Number One, a hot new L.A. band, already cranking out a tune. There were some fabulous costumes, too. Jessica was definitely the hottest as Cleopatra in a white sheet with a gold bandeau top and lots of black eye makeup—very sexy, and all for Jay's benefit. Amy was a beautiful ballerina, and Lila was Princess Diana in a short blond wig. Cara and Steven were Raggedy Ann and Andy—totally adorable. There were some rock stars, an astronaut, and quite a few SVH teachers—

including Chrome Dome Cooper himself!

As you know, every girl in Sweet Valley except me and Enid has been dying to meet Lila's cousin Christopher. Believe it or not, when Lila introduced him (and I have to admit it, he is gorgeous), it turned out he knew Enid from summer camp in Maine a couple years ago—he was the sailing instructor. Small world, huh? Christopher rushed right over to Enid, and they started talking a mile a minute. I think they had a crush on each other back then, and they hit it right off. I could tell Enid was really psyched, and I was happy for her. She didn't expect to meet Prince Charming at Lila Fowler's costume party! But my initial feeling about the night was right. We weren't fated to have a happy ending. . . .

"You two seem to be having a pretty good time!" I observed to Enid as I got ready to leave the party. "I don't suppose you want a ride home."

We hadn't said more than a word or two all evening because she'd spent so much time dancing and talking with Christopher. Amy had coerced him into a dance or two herself, but clearly Christopher preferred Enid's company.

Enid smiled. "Actually, Christopher said he'd take me home," she confessed, her cheeks pink. "We may go for a drive first."

"This is so romantic! He really seems terrific."

"He is," Enid agreed. "I can't believe he's related to Lila!"

We were both giggling over this when someone grabbed my arm from behind. It was Amy, a scowl darkening her pretty face. "I've got to talk to you, Liz," she declared, glaring at Enid. "Alone."

Before I could protest, Amy had yanked me halfway across the patio. I tossed an apologetic look over my shoulder at Enid, but she'd already turned her back. "Amy, I was in the middle of a conversation with Enid!" I cried, tugging my arm out of her grip. "That was pretty rude."

"Sorry." She flashed me a sugary-sweet smile. "I just wanted to let you know that I won't need a ride home with you. Christopher's going to drive me."

"Christopher?" My jaw dropped. "But Enid just told me . . ." In a flash of insight I saw how it had probably happened. Hadn't Amy manipulated me a dozen times that past week just by fluttering her eyelashes and sweet-talking me? "Did Christopher offer to drive you or did you ask him to?"

"What difference does it make?" Amy reached up to fluff her blond curls and adjust her tiara. "He's driving me home, and I plan to make it worth his while. He'll figure out pretty fast that he was barking up the wrong tree tonight. Lila wanted to fix him up with me in the first place, after all."

I put my hands on my hips, unable to hide my disapproval. "So what story did you give him? It must have been a good one, because I happen to know he'd already offered to take Enid home."

Amy smiled slyly. "I told him you didn't have room in the Fiat for me, and if he didn't take me, I'd have to walk home. In these silly little shoes." She extended her foot, toe pointed, and displayed a delicate satin ballet shoe. "Guys can never resist the damsel-in-distress routine," Amy concluded with satisfaction, "and Christopher's a real gentleman. Lucky for me!"

"Lucky for *you*?" I stared at her, absolutely flabbergasted by her selfishness. Was I supposed to laugh at this tale, think it was cute, egg her on? "I can't believe you lied like that, Amy. You know Christopher really likes Enid, and you're ruining this for her on purpose!"

"You're right, I am!" Amy cried. Her smile dissolved and her face twisted with fury. "And you know why? Because I'm sick to death of Enid Rollins! That's all I've heard from you since the first second I moved back here—Enid, Enid, Enid! When are you going to figure out that I don't give a damn about her?"

I was almost too shocked to speak. "Amy, how can you talk like—"

"Oh, that came out all wrong!" Amy burst into noisy tears. "I don't mind Enid all that much, Liz. It's just that I hate having to share you with her. You were *my* best friend, and I just want it to be the way it used to be, but she keeps coming between us!"

Before I could respond, Amy raced off, her tutu flouncing. I watched as, still crying, she said something to Christopher. Putting an arm around her shoulders, Christopher escorted Amy along the walk that led around the house to the driveway.

I wanted to run after them and give Amy a good hard slap across the face. *How dare she steal Christopher from Enid like that?* I fumed silently.

Enid's own voice jolted me back to reality. "Thanks a lot, Liz," she snapped. "I hope you and Amy are proud of yourselves!"

I whirled around. Enid's look of tearful fury told me that she'd seen Christopher and Amy leaving, too. "What are you talking about?" I asked.

"You went along with her story about not having room in your car," Enid accused. "You helped her steal Christopher away from me!"

"But, Enid, I had no—"

"Don't try to defend her, or yourself. Your actions speak for themselves." Enid choked back a sob. "Amy won. You two deserve each other!"

"Enid, wait!" It was too late. She was already racing off across the lawn. She didn't look back.

I stood rooted to the spot staring after her, frozen with dismay and confusion. I felt as if I'd been hit by a truck. What had just happened?

"Liz, are you heading home? Can I squeeze into the backseat?"

I turned to see my twin standing behind me, her bare shoulders slumped and a look of profound disappointment in her dark-lined eyes. Cleopatra had lost all her haughty glamour. "You don't have to squeeze," I informed her dryly. "Suddenly there's lots of room."

"What happened to Amy and Enid?" Jessica asked.

"You don't want to know," I assured her. "What happened to Jay?"

Jessica heaved a forlorn sigh. "He ditched me. He saw Denise with another guy and totally flipped out."

I hooked my arm through hers. "Come on, Cleo. I'll give you a ride down the Nile on my barge."

Ken caught up to us on the way out the door. He tried to cheer me up, but there was nothing he could say to make me feel better. I really blew it, Diary. I wanted nothing more than to have two best friends, and now I have none.

Sunday, 9:00 P.M.

I woke up this morning feeling incredibly crummy—I slept really late because I didn't fall asleep until the sun was coming up. I would've been so happy if what happened at Lila's turned out to be a bad dream! But it was real and I had to deal with it. My first priority was to clear things up with Enid, so I called her right away. . . .

"Enid, it's Liz," I said when she answered the phone.

"Hi," she answered, her tone clipped.

"I—I just wanted you to know I feel really bad about how things worked out last night." The words spilled out in a rush. "I don't know how I ended up in the middle of what was going on with you and Christopher and Amy—the last thing I'd ever do would be to hurt your feelings on purpose. Can I come over? Can we talk about it?"

"Actually, I'm on my way out the door." Her voice was still frosty. "And frankly, Liz, I don't see the point in talking. You've made it pretty clear where your loyalties lie these days. You're off the hook with me, if that makes you feel any better."

"Off the hook?" I repeated, baffled. "What are you talking about? I don't want to be let off the hook—I want to patch things up. You're my best friend, Enid!"

"Really?" She sounded skeptical. "You could have fooled me, Liz. You've got Amy now. Do you really need me?"

"Of course—how can you—I'd never . . ." I stuttered to a stop, tongue-tied by distress.

"Look," Enid cut in, "let's give ourselves a break, OK? Sleep on it. We can talk tomorrow at school. Now I've really got to run."

"But, Enid—"

My words dropped into a void. She'd already hung up the phone.

Next I tried to call Amy, but Mrs. Sutton told me she was at the beach with Jess and Lila. Can you believe it? They didn't even wake me up to see if I wanted to go along!

I was ready to crawl back into bed and stay there forever. Enid had never been mad at me. I'd never heard her sound so cold, and it broke my heart. Instead I did something smart—I dragged myself down to the kitchen and dumped the whole story on my mother. Moms are wonderful, aren't they? Mine, anyway. She is just so smart! By asking me a couple questions, she helped me see things clearly for the first time. Because of my old affection for Amy, I haven't been able to see that she's changed, and Amy's been clinging to our friendship just as stubbornly for her own reasons. But Enid sized up Amy pretty fast; most likely she was steering clear of us so she wouldn't have to pretend she liked Amy when she didn't. Not to mention the fact that Amy may very well have been sending out signals that she didn't want Enid around. After what Amy said last night at Lila's . . . So I guess Enid was just going to wait patiently until I figured it out on my own. I started to last night when Amy pulled that stunt with Christopher, but then things unraveled so fast, I couldn't absorb any of it. How could I have been so blind? I wish you could talk, Diary, so you could tell me what an idiot I'm being sometimes!

I knew I needed to talk to Enid right away, no matter what she'd said to me on the phone. I had to tell her I'd finally realized what had been going on with Amy, and how truly sorry I was. . . .

I rang the Rollinses' bell, wondering if Enid was even home. I was just about to turn away, swallowing my disappointment, when she opened the door. "Liz," she said, surprised.

"Enid, I know I'm probably the last person you want to see," I blurted out, "but I can't bear for you to be angry at me for one more minute. Everything that happened with Amy and Christopher—it's all my fault. I was trying so hard to preserve my old friendship with Amy that I didn't even see what kind of person she'd turned into. I thought you weren't giving her a chance, that if you only tried harder . . . I was so stupid! Oh, please just say you forgive me, Enid!"

We were both crying and laughing at the same time. Enid pulled me into her arms for a quick, fierce hug. "Of course I forgive you," she said. "I'd never hold a grudge against my best friend."

We retreated to the patio with a couple sodas and a bowl of pretzels. "What *really* happened last night at Lila's?" I asked Enid.

Enid heaved a deep sigh. "Well, you probably saw Amy cutting in on me and Chris every chance she got. It was almost embarrassing, because obviously Chris wasn't the least bit interested in her, but she just wouldn't give up. And then . . ." Enid bit her lip. "Then she just came right out and told me to get lost. She accused me of trying to steal Christopher from her . . . just like I'd been trying to steal *you*."

I blinked. "She said that?"

"It wasn't the first time, to tell you the truth,"

255

Enid admitted, her expression pained. "She said a couple nasty things to me at school the other day. She must have decided right off that I wasn't anybody she wanted for a friend, but she wanted you and she thought I was just competition."

"Enid, I had no idea." I shook my head. "You should have told me!"

"How?" Enid asked simply. "Maybe I don't like Amy, but you do. It didn't seem fair to make you choose between the two of us. Your friendship means too much to me to risk it that way. I thought if I just gave both of you some space, sooner or later . . ."

"I'd come to my senses. I just wish it had been sooner rather than later," I mourned. "Your feelings really got trampled in the process. And Christopher—"

A mischievous smile lit up Enid's face. "Actually, it's kind of a funny thing. Christopher doesn't like Amy, either! He couldn't wait to get rid of her last night."

"How do you know?"

"Because *he* called to apologize this morning, too." The smile became a grin. "And he's taking me out to dinner tonight!"

"That's great, Enid," I said sincerely.

"Isn't it?" She reached out to squeeze my hand. "This is turning into a fantastic weekend after all. The best part is, I've got my friend back."

I beamed at her, my eyes sparkling with tears. "It feels great, doesn't it?"

I feel so much better, Diary. Amy and I had a lot of fun when we were kids, and she'll al-

ways have a place in my heart—I cherish those old memories. But Enid's friendship is the real treasure, and I don't intend to let anything—or anyone—come between us ever again!

Monday, 10:15 P.M.

On the "all's well that ends well" theme, I should give you the wrap-up on Jessica's advice column and her heartless scheme to break up Jay and Denise. I congratulate myself on playing a devious role. . . .

"Where are they?" Jessica demanded, bursting into the *Oracle* office during study hall.

"Where are who?" I inquired, looking up from the computer screen.

"Not where are *who*—where are *what*! The letters. Miss Lovelorn's letters! The ones from 'Heartbroken' and 'Missing Her.'"

"Oh, those. Well, I guess you and Cara didn't know we were printing a special early edition of *The Oracle* this week. You hadn't turned in any copy by Friday, so Penny asked me to write the column— there was a stack of letters, and I just grabbed the two that were on top."

"Not 'Heartbroken' and 'Missing Her'!" Jessica cried.

"'Fraid so." I couldn't keep from grinning. "Why? Did I do something wrong? I thought you'd be grateful. I saved your skin—if I hadn't thrown something

257

together, Penny would have cut the column."

Jessica collapsed into a chair, her face a mask of melodramatic despair. "The letters were from Denise and Jay, saying they made a mistake breaking up and they want each other back," she wailed. "If they read them, they'll get back together!"

"What a coup for Miss Lovelorn!" I exclaimed. "She really *does* give good advice, doesn't she?"

"Oh, I could shoot you, Liz," Jessica declared, jumping to her feet and stomping from the room. "And for your information, there *is* no more Miss Lovelorn. She's through with the newspaper business!"

We distributed the newspaper in the cafeteria, and about five minutes into lunch Jay and Denise were back in each other's arms. I'd printed Denise's letter, from "Heartbroken," first and then printed Jay's "Missing Her" as a response. And it worked! It was really sweet to see how happy they were . . . and how mad Jessica was! Maybe she'll learn a lesson. Listen to me. Who am I kidding??

I made up with Amy today, too, and I actually invited her one more time to come with me and Enid to Tahoe this weekend. You'd like to tell me I'm an idiot, Diary. I know, I know. But it gave me a chance to get things really clear between us, once and for all. Amy said she couldn't come, or rather that she didn't want to—she admitted that Enid isn't her cup of tea.

When she asked if I was mad at her, I told her I wasn't. And I'm really not. A little disappointed and hurt, sure. But not mad. We all change over time, and sometimes when we grow up, we grow apart from people we used to feel close to. Amy is who she is, and I can't hold that against her. I'm glad she's having so much fun with Jess and Cara and Lila. And I'm grateful to her for something. She doesn't know it, but she helped me see what real friends are . . . and what they're not.

Part 8

Dear Diary,

At brunch this morning Mom reminded us that Steven's coming home from college for a week's vacation starting Friday. I'm really psyched to hang out with him, although now that he and Cara are so hot and heavy, he might have better things to do! Jess and I promised we'd plan something special for him.

There was a Pi Beta Alpha meeting at Lila's this afternoon, and Jess dragged me along—it was so important that I put in an appearance because it's the start of a new pledge season, blah blah blah. I don't know how she can take PBA so seriously, but she does. So I went to the meeting and Sandra Bacon nominated Jean West and Jess nomi-

nated Amy and naturally they were both sec-
onded, and I'm sure they'll coast through the
pledge period. Whoop-dee-do.

I got out of there as fast as I could and
met Enid at the beach. It's so good to be back
to normal! We had a blast at Tahoe last week-
end—I can't believe I almost let Amy ruin
everything. Anyway, lying on the sand, I had
a great idea for Steven—a surprise party! He
has a lot of old Sweet Valley buddies that he
doesn't see much now that he's in college—
we'll invite absolutely everybody.

Ken stopped by after dinner—a great sur-
prise. I was just thinking about Todd and
wishing it wasn't three hours later on the
East Coast so I could call him, and the door-
bell rang. We went to Casey's Ice Cream
Parlor and ate hot-fudge sundaes—yum! I'm
so glad Ken and I came through that thing
with my short story with our friendship in-
tact. If anything, we're closer than before. . . .

Ken spooned into his hot-fudge sundae. "I hope
it's OK that I stopped by without calling first," he
said. "I mean, it's not like I'm taking it for granted
you're sitting around with nothing better to do than
go out for ice cream with me."

"Please." I rolled my eyes. "I don't have a boyfriend right now and you know it! I'm a total old
maid. I'm thrilled to have a guy like you ringing my
doorbell!"

261

We laughed heartily. "We're both between romances right now, huh?" observed Ken.

I nodded as I picked the maraschino cherry off my sundae. "It's not so bad, is it?"

"Nah. I kind of like it." He grinned. "I don't have to worry all the time about whether my face is scruffy or my socks match and do I need a breath mint since I had a chili dog for lunch. I'm not trying to impress anyone."

"You know, Ken," I began. "No, never mind."

"What?" he pressed.

"I probably shouldn't . . . well, we're good friends. I can risk a little honesty. I'm glad you blew off Suzanne," I declared. "She didn't deserve you."

Ken slumped comfortably in his chair. "I was so worried that *I* didn't deserve her—that I wasn't good enough. Smart enough. It's not supposed to be that way, you know? You should be able to relax with the person you're dating."

"I totally agree. If you have to pretend you're someone you're not, then something's wrong."

"Take us, for example," said Ken. "Right here, right now. You're so easy to talk to. It's not like being with Suzanne. I had to watch every word out of my mouth so I didn't sound *uncouth*."

I laughed. "That's because we're friends."

Ken nodded thoughtfully. "Yeah. I guess Suzanne and I were never friends."

"Love isn't really love unless there's friendship, too," I said. "At least that's my opinion."

We finished our sundaes in companionable si-

262

lence. As we left Casey's, Ken asked, "So, Liz. Do you think about dating other guys or are you happy being single?"

"Well, there was that thing with Nicholas Morrow," I reminded him. "Sometimes you just need someone, you know? But most of the time I feel OK being on my own."

"It's the same with me," said Ken.

I get the feeling Ken's a little lonely since he broke up with Suzanne, even though she was a jerk and he's better off without her. Why else would he take me out for ice cream?? We had fun, though. I'm glad we're such good friends. I'm sure he'll fall in love with someone new one of these days. He needs a girl who'll appreciate him . . . she's out there somewhere!

Monday, 9:15 P.M.

Today Jess and I started inviting people to Steven's surprise party. It'll be a week from Saturday, the day after the Friday-the-thirteenth party at school. Everybody's psyched, especially Cara. She'd better not spill the beans!

I called Todd and we had a nice chat. I wasn't even that upset when he told me he's going with some girl named Diane to a dance at his new school this Friday. She asked him,

263

they're just friends and he doesn't want any-
thing more than that with her, it's better than
sitting home alone, etc. I reassured him that I
understood completely. And I guess I do. Not
that I want to think about it all that much—
I'm glad I'm busy planning Steven's party! I
suppose if I get too worried about this Diane
chick, I can ask Ken if he met her when he
was out there, and maybe he'll tell me she's a
total drip.

Friday, 10:30 P.M.

Steven's home, but it's not exactly the joy-
ous occasion we all expected. We were sitting
out on the patio having this great cookout
supper when he dropped a humongous
bombshell. . . .

My father reached for the platter of barbecued
chicken. "So how are your classes going?" he asked
Steven.

Steven tipped back in his chair, directing an intent
gaze at Dad. "Actually, this is probably as good a time
as any to tell you. I've decided . . ." He cleared his
throat. "I've decided to leave school."

"What?" I squeaked. My mother dropped her
fork.

We all stared dumbfounded at Steven. "What
happened?" my dad demanded. "What's the matter?"

"Nothing's the matter." Steven forced a careless

264

laugh. "It's just something I've decided I want to do. College isn't for me."

"But, Steven, you're only a freshman," said my mother. "I know prelaw courses are tough, but don't you think you should give it another semester or two before you—"

Steven waved his hand. "I don't need another semester to know I'm sick of studying," he declared. "All I've done all my life is go to school! I want to travel. I want to have a job, find out what it feels like to earn a living. I can always finish my degree later."

"I take it you have some kind of plan," my father said, folding his arms sternly.

"As a matter of fact, I do." Steven leaned forward with his elbows on the table and smiled excitedly. "You know my roommate Bob? Well, his father owns a cruise ship that operates out of L.A., the *Bellefleur*. Bob's taking time off from school to work for his dad for a while, and he talked me into signing on with him. I'm going to sail around the world!"

"Wow," I breathed. Jessica looked downright envious.

Not surprisingly, though, Mom and Dad were skeptical. "What kind of work would you do on the ship?" Dad pressed.

"I don't know." Steven shrugged. "Bartender or waiter. What difference does it make? This is the chance of a lifetime. I can't pass it up!"

My father glanced at my mother. She pressed her lips tightly together. "I'm not sure this is a wise move, Steven," Dad said.

"We're just thinking about your future," Mom interjected, placing a hand on Steven's arm.

"I think you, your mother, and I should discuss this," said Dad. "Alone."

"There's nothing to discuss," Steven insisted. "It's *my* life, Dad. It's my decision."

"We're not about to let you drop out of school on a whim," my father countered. "As for working on a cruise ship, I hardly think—"

"It doesn't matter what *you* think!" Steven shoved back his chair, his eyes flashing. "I'm sorry if you don't approve, Dad, but my mind's made up. Like I said, it's my life!"

I got the feeling, watching him stride toward the house, his broad shoulders square with determination, that he meant what he said. He'd made up his mind; how were we going to change it?

> *As you can imagine, we were all pretty upset. Everyone but Jessica, that is. Forget Steven's plans to be a lawyer like Dad—in her opinion working on a cruise ship would be a lot more glamorous, like the* Love Boat *or something. Then I came up with a brilliant idea, if I may say so myself. . . .*

"Maybe it's just a phase," my mother said hopefully.

Dad nodded. "Maybe he's burned out from studying for exams. He just needs a week off."

"I don't know," I said. "He sounded pretty serious to me!"

Dad turned to Mom and spread his hands in a helpless gesture. "What do we do, Alice?"

She lifted her shoulders. "I don't know. I get the feeling if we forbid him to do this, he'll only want to do it more."

"That's it!" I cried.

Everybody stared at me. "What's it?" asked Dad.

"That's what we have to do, then," I explained. "Practice a little reverse psychology!"

"Reverse psychology?" repeated Mom.

I nodded eagerly. "What if instead of throwing a fit over this, we all pretend to be totally supportive, act like it's no big deal—like we can't wait to say good-bye and see him set sail!"

"We'll turn his surprise party into a bon voyage party!" Jessica added. "Mom, you take him shopping for luggage—Dad, you get out the atlas and show him all the places he should make sure to visit on his round-the-world tour. It'll totally burst his bubble."

"It could work," my dad admitted, his expression brightening. "Maybe he's just trying to prove that he's old enough to take charge of his own life. If we don't throw up any roadblocks, this dropping-out business could lose its appeal."

"It's awfully risky," Mom said, her forehead still furrowed with worry. "What if we push him out the door . . . and he actually goes?"

Jessica and I glanced at each other. "He won't," she declared with confidence. "Take our word for it. We know teen psychology!"

Dear Diary,

We've already put the plan into action. Last night I asked Steven if I could use his computer while he's gone, and Jessica promised to buy him some airmail stationery. Mom and Dad announced that on second thought, they're behind him 100 percent. College isn't for everyone, and he was wise to recognize early on that he's not cut out for it. Why waste the tuition money? Steven's pretty flustered by all this—obviously it's not at all the way he expected us to react on "second thought" or even third or fourth thought! We've even enlisted Cara to the cause. Tonight she's going to tell him that she doesn't believe in long-distance relationships, so this is it for them. Poor Steven!

Saturday, midnight

Ken called me this afternoon and we went to a movie tonight. It almost seemed like a Saturday-night date, but of course he's just looking after me as Todd asked him to. Still, when he dropped me off at my house afterward, I was startled by the way I felt as I looked into his eyes to say good-bye. . . .

"This was a lot of fun," I told Ken as we stood on the front step of my house. "Really. I don't know when I've had such a good time."

It was true. We'd had a riot at the movie, a horror film that kept us both on the edge of our seats the whole time. Then we'd gone to Guido's for a pizza, where we'd chattered for hours about every topic under the sun.

"My pleasure," Ken said with a grin. "I love going to scary movies with a girl who doesn't shriek and dig holes in my arm with her fingernails."

I laughed. "I *did* shriek at one part."

"Yeah, but I was screaming, too, so I didn't notice."

"Well . . ." I looked up at Ken. His blond hair glimmered in the moonlight; there was a warm glow in his eyes. My breath caught in my throat, and I felt my heart thump with extra force. For an instant, gazing into Ken's eyes, I knew how Suzanne felt when she was with him. I knew why she'd clung to Ken so stubbornly even though they weren't right for each other. *She probably looked up at him in the moonlight, just like this,* I thought, *and he was so handsome and strong, she just wanted him to wrap her in his arms and never let go. . . .*

"Well, good night," I squeaked, clutching the doorknob.

"'Night, Liz."

Ken put a hand on my arm. What were we supposed to do now? Shake hands? Peck each other on the cheek? I turned back to face him and he gave me a quick hug. I hugged him back, laughing to hide my awkwardness. "See you in school, Ken."

With a good-bye wave, he sauntered down the walk to his car, which was parked by the curb. I followed him with my eyes, drinking in the graceful lines of his broad, muscular back, his long, lean legs. A shiver chased up my spine. *That's Ken Matthews you're thinking about,* I chastised myself as I slipped into the front hall. *Your buddy. Todd's best friend. So cut it out!*

I must be tired, I decided as I tiptoed up the stairs. I must be feeling especially weak and vulnerable. Because my heart was still doing backflips; there were goose bumps on my arms from where Ken had touched me.

> *Pretty weird, huh, Diary? If I didn't know better, I'd think I was falling for Ken. But it's just because we've been spending so much time together—talking about Todd, mostly! I feel especially close to him these days.*

Sunday, 6:45 P.M.

Dear Diary,

I think Steven is already weakening. Jessica brought him a whole pile of brochures on the Far East and started babbling about the exotic gifts she expects him to pick up for her from all over the globe. He really looked as if he wanted to punch her. Cara's holding up her end of things valiantly. Steven's really hurt that she's being so cool and matter-of-fact about breaking up as soon as he heads off to sea, but Jess and I pointed out that that's a natural response, and after all, it's

270

not as if he talked any of this cruise-ship stuff over with her—he just dropped the bomb. Why shouldn't she protect herself from further pain?

Right before dinner I picked up the phone to call Ken to see if he'd heard from Todd, then hung up without dialing. Was that really the reason I was calling him?

Tuesday, 8:00 P.M.

I had lunch today with Jess and Lila and a bunch of other Pi Betas, including Amy and Jeanie, the new pledges. They were all buzzing about Jean's scheme to publicly humiliate Tom McKay to get into the sorority. I guess one of her pledge tasks was to ask him out— he used to like her once but she blew him off, so they figured it would be a tough assignment for her. As it turned out, Tom said yes but then he stood her up—he said he was at the hospital with food poisoning. When she called the hospital, though, there was no Tom McKay registered there. The PBAs decided Jean should go for major revenge. So Jean's not letting on to Tom that she knows he lied to her about the hospital. Instead she's pretending she really likes him. The plan is to ask him to the Friday-the-thirteenth dance and then totally burn him—she and Dana Larson get to start off the dancing because Friday is their

271

birthday, and Jeanie will just announce some other boy's name over the microphone. Classic Pi Beta, wouldn't you say? I'm actually surprised Jean's going along with it. I don't know her that well, but she always seemed like a really sweet girl to me. I guess some people will do anything to get into a sorority, even compromise their own values.

All systems go for Steven's party Saturday! We're pretending it's a bon voyage party. It should be the straw that breaks the camel's back—he's completely depressed about how cheerful we all are at the prospect of his sailing off into the sunset.

I'm sort of avoiding Ken at school. I just don't want people snooping around and asking why we're hanging out so much together lately. The Sweet Valley High rumor mill gets so out of control sometimes.

Friday, 12:30 A.M.

The Friday-the-thirteenth dance was fun. Ken and I danced just about every song together. Usually I miss Todd at events like this, but tonight I have to confess I didn't think of him once. . . .

"Let's take a break and sit one out," I suggested to Ken as the DJ put on a slow song. "I'm pretty breathless, aren't you?"

The mood in the gym had changed along with the music. All around us couples drew closer, wrapping their arms around each other. Romance seemed to fill the air like a perfume.

Ken grasped my arm, preventing me from stepping away. "One more," he said. "Slow dances aren't too strenuous!"

Laughing, I stepped close again. Ken put his arms around my shoulders and I circled mine around his waist. Gingerly, I rested my head against his chest. *Have we ever slow danced before?* I found myself wondering. I didn't think so. I didn't think I'd ever been this physically close to Ken Matthews. . . .

He was right—slow dancing wasn't that strenuous. But for some reason I still felt breathless. Why was my pulse racing? Why was my face so hot?

"You know, Ken," I murmured, not meeting his eye, "you should ask some other girls to dance. I know you're just looking out for me, but I'll be OK."

Ken's arms tightened around me. "What if I don't *want* to ask other girls to dance? What if I only want to dance with you?"

We were silent, our bodies swaying together to the slow, sensuous music. I couldn't answer Ken's question; I wouldn't. What if . . . ?

I know what's happening to me, Diary. I wasn't born yesterday—I've had feelings like this before. But I can't give in to them. Ken is Todd's best friend! I have to nip this in the bud. But it's hard. When Ken's arms were around me, my body pressed against his . . . I could feel his heart pounding—we were both generating an awful lot of heat. Thank God no one noticed.

He offered to drive me home, but I turned him down and I hope he knows why. I hope he's making a resolution, too—we simply can't follow up on this attraction. It'll pass if we ignore it. By the way, you'll be glad to know the Jeanie West thing had a happy ending. Jess filled me in on all the details when we got home. When the moment came for Jeanie to pick some other boy to dance with, she said Tom's name instead. All the Pi Betas were livid and ready to dump Jean, but then Sandra Bacon spoke up and confessed that she'd tried to sabotage Jean's chances to get into the sorority even though Jean's her best friend. I guess Sandy's always been a little jealous of Jeanie because Jeanie gets better grades, is so cute, has a fabulous wardrobe, and everything else. Sandy feels that Jean's always one-upping her, and PBA was the only thing Sandy had that Jeanie didn't and she wanted to keep it that way. So Sandy told Tom that Jean was just using him, and that's why he gave Jean the food-poisoning excuse. But then Jean and Tom fell in love anyway, and Jean really did do the right thing, putting her feelings for Tom before PBA. As a result, she got into the sorority, she straightened things out with Sandy, and she won Tom's heart.

Aaron Dallas brought this new guy with him tonight. His name is Jeffrey French—he just moved here from Oregon and he's starting at SVH on Monday. He and Aaron knew each other from soccer camp, or that's the story going around, anyway. I think Enid may have fallen in love with Jeffrey at first sight—one glance at him and she was incoherent for the rest of the night! He is pretty cute—tall, blond, athletic—but frankly, I had a hard time focusing on him. My gaze kept straying to another tall, blond, athletic guy, initials K.M. . . . DON'T DO THIS, LIZ!!!

Saturday night, late

Dear Diary,

Steven's party was a huge success. He and Cara had been off someplace together, and on their way to dinner she came up with some excuse to stop at our house. There were about fifty people hiding in the living room. . . .

"Ssh. I think I hear them!" Jessica hissed.

People were whispering and giggling in the dark, but now everyone quieted down. Sure enough, I heard a key in the front door and then Steven's and Cara's voices. "It doesn't look like anyone's home," Steven remarked.

"Jess said she left the sweater upstairs for me,"

said Cara. "Why don't you wait in the living room? I'll be right down."

Holding my breath, I listened to Steven's footsteps. One, two, three . . . He hit the light switch. "Surprise!" we all yelled in unison, leaping up from our hiding places.

Steven staggered backward. "What the . . ." He started to smile, and then I saw his eyes travel to the big banner draped over the fireplace. BON VOYAGE, STEVEN! was printed in huge red letters. Steven's smile faded.

Jessica and I bounded forward to throw our arms around him. "Bon voyage, Steve!" I cried, squeezing him tight. "We'll really miss you."

"What's the matter?" Jessica asked him. "Don't you like the party? We thought you'd want to see everybody one last time before you set sail!"

Steven stuck his hands into his trouser pockets, his shoulders slumping. "That's just the thing," he mumbled. "I've decided . . . I've decided not to go. I'm going to tell Mr. Rose I've changed my mind."

"You're kidding!" Jessica looked over her shoulder at our parents. "Did you hear that, Mom and Dad?"

I don't know when I've seen my mom look happier. "Well, gee, Steve," I said, pretending to be crestfallen. "I guess we planned the wrong kind of party. What can we do about that, Jess?"

My sister tipped her head to one side, as if pondering. "Let me think. . . . Hold on. I've got an idea. C'mon, Liz!"

Steven stared after us as we pushed through

the crowd toward the fireplace. Unpinning the banner, we lowered it so we could flip it over. Then we pinned it back up with the reverse side showing.

Everyone at the party shouted out the banner's new message. "Welcome home, Steve!"

Now Steven really looked confused. "But how did you . . . !"

"We thought we should be ready for any possibility," I explained. "And we were hoping and praying for this one!"

"Actually, we did more than hope," Jessica confessed.

Cara stepped forward and slipped her arm around Steven's waist. "It was a pretty grueling campaign," she admitted.

Steven stared down at her. "You mean you were all in on this? You didn't really want me to go?"

"Are you kidding?" exclaimed Cara. "It would've killed me!"

Mom and Dad moved in for a hug. "I really thought no one cared what I did," said Steven, his eyes damp.

"We *did* care, but we wanted it to be your decision," Dad explained. "You were right about that much, Steven. You're an adult now."

"But we're so glad you've decided to stick with your education, and with us," added Mom. "I don't know what we would have done if you went so far away from home!"

"I have a funny feeling you guys were behind

this," said Steven, smiling at me and Jessica through his tears. "And I just want to say . . . thanks."

Jeffrey French stopped by the party with Aaron. He really seems like a nice guy. Enid is now officially infatuated with him. I wonder if anything will start up between those two?

Speaking of sparks, I almost don't want to write this down. I hope no one ever finds out about it. I can't believe I let myself get so carried away . . .

"It's turning out to be a great party," Ken said. "I'm glad your brother's bagging the *Love Boat* idea."

We were in the kitchen; Ken was helping me load up another platter with foot-long submarine sandwiches. "Me, too," I said, laughing. "I really couldn't see Steven as a bartender on a cruise ship. He would've been bored to death after about five minutes."

I unwrapped the last sandwich; the platter was ready to go. "There," I announced somewhat unnecessarily.

Ken and I both looked at the platter. Then we looked at each other. Something in Ken's eyes told me I should take a step backward, away from him. *Pick up the platter,* I commanded myself. *Carry it into the living room.*

"Liz," he said, his voice deep.

He clasped my hand and my resolve melted. Instead of backing away I let him pull me outside to the patio.

The backyard was dark, and we slipped eagerly into the shadows. Without another word Ken folded his arms around me, lifting me slightly so his mouth could find mine. I kissed him hungrily, my fingers tangling in his hair. Meanwhile, his hands were on my neck, my shoulders, my back. We couldn't seem to stop touching each other—maybe because for weeks we'd been dying to do this, but holding back.

After a long, recklessly delicious moment, I pulled away, breathless. "Ken, we really shouldn't—"

"Ssh." He placed a finger gently against my lips. "Don't say it. Let's not think about . . ."

It was too late. It was already out there. Guilt crept into my heart, momentarily chilling my passion. Todd trusted Ken and me—how could we do this to him?

Ken reached for me again. If his hand so much as brushed my skin, I knew I'd throw myself back into his arms. Whirling, I ran away, back into the house.

Where will this end, Diary? Because it's finally started. Ken and I have let our feelings for each other show. There's no going back now. . . .

Part 9

Dear Diary,

Todd called this morning. I couldn't be-lieve the timing—it's almost as if he knew. But of course he doesn't; he was perfectly cheerful and casual. "So is Ken looking after you like I asked him to?" he actually said. I just about died. When I answered, I was sure he'd hear the guilt in my voice, but he didn't seem to suspect anything. Why should he? I'm his girlfriend, and Ken's his best buddy. If he can't trust us, who can he trust?

"It won't happen again"—that was what I was telling myself when I hung up the phone with Todd. I decided there was one surefire way to get rid of the guilt: stay away from Ken. It was just one kiss, after all— Todd probably kissed that Diane girl after

280

*the dance, so that makes us even. It wasn't
too late to draw a line with Ken—I knew
he'd agree with me that it was the best thing
to do. We'd just pretend it never happened.*

*Who was I kidding?? I might as well
have told the ocean to stop crashing on the
shore. I had to see Ken, and he felt the same
way. We met at the beach tonight—I told my
family I was going over to Olivia's to study
for the French test. Diary, I've never felt so
bad—and so good—at the same time. . . .*

"I think we should talk about this," I said to Ken
as we fell together onto the beach blanket he'd just
spread out in the shelter of a sand dune.

Ken kissed my face, my throat. "Go ahead," he
whispered, his lips near my ear. "I'm listening."

The night wind sighed through the dune grass;
just a few yards away the surf crashed rhythmically
on the sand. "Oh, Ken, I . . ." I held him close, burying my face against his neck. "This is all I think
about—holding you, kissing you—but it's *wrong*.
Don't you see?"

He cupped my face in his hands, his deep-blue
eyes shining in the dark. "All I see right now is you.
This incredibly sweet, beautiful girl I've always ad-
mired more than anyone I know. Only now I don't
just admire you—I adore you."

He kissed me gently. I shook my head, pressing
my lips tightly together. "What about Todd?" I asked
bluntly.

281

Guilt flickered in Ken's eyes. Sighing, he lay back on the blanket. "I always thought Wilkins was the luckiest guy on earth," Ken confessed, "because he was going out with you. I didn't expect this to happen. I didn't mean to take advantage of his trust."

I nestled against his side. "What are we going to do?"

Ken rolled over to face me. "We both know what we *should* do. And we both know what we *want* to do."

"And the problem is, they're not the same thing," I whispered. He pulled my body close to his. Our lips met in a deep, searching kiss, a kiss that exploded like fireworks inside me, flooding my whole body with a fierce heat. A kiss that, for now, said it all.

Friday, 4:45 P.M.

I ate lunch on the lawn with Jessica and Lila and Enid today. Always a fun foursome! I'm trying really hard to act normal around Ken so no one guesses what's going on between us—he was sitting inside with a bunch of guys, and I just tossed him a casual little wave. Do you think anyone can tell? I feel as if it's written all over my face like a billboard: I'M CRAZY ABOUT KEN AND HE'S CRAZY ABOUT ME! But I guess we're being discreet—even Jessica doesn't seem to suspect anything, and she's got a nose for these things. I'm not sure how much longer I can deal with the stress of secrecy, though.

Ken and I have seen each other a couple nights this week, and it means fibbing to our parents and sneaking off someplace where we think we won't run into anybody we know. If Todd ever found out . . .

Anyway, while we were eating lunch, we spotted the new guy, Jeffrey French. Enid's face turned pink as a rose—it was so sweet. She and I have been brainstorming all week about how to get her and Jeffrey together. But the worst thing happened. Lila took one look at Jeffrey, whom she hadn't even met yet, and decided then and there that he was the boy of her dreams. . . .

"Who is that?" Lila asked, adjusting her sunglasses for a better look.

I shaded my eyes. "Jeffrey French. The new kid from Oregon."

"Wow." Lila whistled. "What a bod! How come no one's introduced me?"

Uh-oh. When Lila Fowler goes on the prowl . . . I shot a glance at Enid, and I could see her thoughts were on the same track. "Oh, you wouldn't be interested in him," I told Lila, who was known to favor sophisticated older guys with trust funds. "He's a farm-boy type. Kind of on the dull side."

"Socially, he's a little backward," Enid contributed. "I think he spent most of his time while he was growing up talking to animals. Milking cows, slopping pigs, that kind of stuff."

Enid knew as well as I did that Jeffrey grew up on a tree farm, but I didn't correct her!

"Hmm." Unfortunately, Lila didn't seem discouraged in the least. She watched with appreciation as Jeffrey leaped to catch a Frisbee Aaron had just tossed his way. "Well, I'll say this for life on a farm—it gives a person *great* muscles!"

"Yeah, muscles." I shrugged this off. "Supposedly he *lives* to play soccer. Another sports-crazy guy. Who needs 'em?"

"Well, I'll tell you," said Lila, still ogling Jeffrey. "I'm tired of country-club guys. I'm in the market for a more down-to-earth type." She winked at Jessica. "And I'd be pretty psyched to get back to nature with Jeffrey French!"

"He'd be *perfect* for you!" Jessica squealed. I wanted to kick her. "Come on, Li. I'll introduce you right now."

And she did, the little brat. Something about the whole scene, I guess the way Lila thinks she can have anything and anyone she wants with a snap of her fingers, really made me mad. Enid saw Jeffrey first, and he's much more her type! I'm determined to do everything I can to make sure Lila doesn't steal him away from her.

So I really gave Enid a pep talk on the phone just a few minutes ago. . . .

"You've got to have more confidence in yourself,"

I encouraged my friend. "You've got a million things going for you, Enid, and as soon as Jeffrey gets to know you, he'll fall head over heels in love with you—take my word for it."

"But how can I compete with Lila? She's rich, she's sexy, she's glamorous. . . ."

"She's *Lila*," I pointed out. "Would *you* want to go on a date with her?"

Enid giggled. "No. About five minutes at a time is all I can stomach of that girl."

"So there."

"But guys are different. A lot of them flip for girls like Lila."

"Not Jeffrey," I argued. "I have a feeling about him. He's not the type to fall for superficial qualities. But that doesn't mean we can count Lila out of the running. She's making a massive play for Jeffrey. We can't just sit around twiddling our thumbs. We've got to counterattack!"

"Counterattack?" Enid sounded skeptical. "Are we talking love or war here?"

"You know the old saying," I reminded her. "All's fair . . . Do you want to sit by and watch Lila waltz off with Jeffrey when she doesn't deserve him and will only make him miserable?"

"No," said Enid. "But I might not deserve him either. Who's to say *I'm* his type? Maybe I should let things unfold naturally. If he notices me, fine. If not . . ."

"An attitude like that will get you nowhere," I declared. "Look, it's been long enough since George. You're ready to start fresh with someone new, Enid. You really are. Don't deny yourself a chance at happiness."

"It's just . . . scary to put your heart on the line, you know?"

I bit my lip, thinking about Todd. Thinking about Ken. "I know," I said softly.

So I talked Enid into going for it with Jeffrey. I should try out for the cheerleading squad!

The big news at home now that Steven's back to normal is that my cousin Jenny's arriving any minute from Dallas for a two-week visit. I confess to you, Diary: I'm not thrilled. She's a year younger than me and Jess, and she's a royal pain in the you-know-what. Jessica's even more bent out of shape about it—she chewed my ear off the whole way home from school. Last time Jenny visited, she followed Jessica everywhere like a puppy dog. So of course Jessica's worried that entertaining Jenny will interfere with her efforts to set a romantic snare for Eddie Winters, this really cute senior on the swim team. I told her not to worry—an obstacle or two only makes the chase that much more fun!

Thursday, 10:30 P.M.

This is turning into the most exhausting week of my life. Jenny's as much of a pill as

286

ever. Thank God she's sleeping in Jessica's room, not mine! It makes it a little easier to sneak off to meet Ken, but I'm running out of stories to tell people about where I'm going and who I'm with. I can't help feeling that it's only a matter of time before someone spots us together and the cat's out of the bag. Ken is incredibly special, but . . . is this really worth it? If we can't care about each other out in the open, if underneath the happiness there's always a cutting edge of guilt? I got a letter today from Todd, and a package, too—a big cuddly University of Vermont sweatshirt. "Something to keep you warm," he wrote, "since I can't be there to put my arms around you." I just started crying, and for the first time in weeks I didn't run straight to Ken for comfort.

Sunday, 3:30 P.M.

I am absolutely furious. I am livid! I just found out from Jenny that Lila had a big pool party yesterday and invited just about everyone in Sweet Valley but me and Enid. It just slipped out—Jessica had sworn Jenny to secrecy. Jessica was in on it—the slimeball! Of course, the whole point of the party was for Lila to flaunt herself in front of Jeffrey in the skimpiest bikini ever seen. I'm sure she was absolutely shameless. Oops, the phone's ringing—be right back.

That was Enid. She heard about the pool party from Olivia, who confirmed our darkest suspicions: Lila spent the whole time flirting outrageously with Jeffrey. I could just throttle Jessica! She's the most devious, conniving . . . ooh! Well, I'll tell you one thing, Diary. If that's the way Jess and Lila are going to play this game, then Enid and I will just have to fight fire with fire. Jess isn't the only matchmaker in this family! And I have a great idea for getting Enid and Jeffrey together during the volleyball game against Parker High tomorrow night.

Sunday, 11:15 P.M.

I saw Ken tonight—we drove down the coast to the Moon Beach Cafe for a burger. I felt even guiltier than usual when I got home because Jenny had scribbled a message for me—Todd called while I was out. I wish I had someone to talk to about this, Diary, but I don't dare tell anyone—not even Enid. Ken is as torn up about it as I am, and over dinner tonight we both agreed that we had to end it. We had this really calm and reasonable discussion—we even shook hands to seal the deal. From now on no more secret rendezvous, no more late-night phone calls. But the next thing we knew, we were strolling along this deserted strip of beach near the restau-

288

rant, and Ken took my hand, and suddenly all our resolutions flew out the window. We just crumpled to the sand in a passionate embrace—he kissed me as no one's ever kissed me before. It was almost scary, being overpowered by my emotions that way.

But it doesn't change anything. It's still wrong. I just have to be stronger. I'll tell Ken I can't see him anymore. I'll tell him tomorrow . . . or the next day.

Monday, 10:20 P.M.

"The best-laid plans of mice and men . . ." This evening didn't exactly turn out the way I'd hoped. First of all, I wimped out and didn't break things off with Ken. What can I say? Despite the guilt, despite the heartache, I like being with him. I need him. He makes me laugh. He keeps me from feeling lonely. But we're really walking a fine line. At lunch today a bunch of girls including Jess and Amy were speculating about who Ken has his eye on these days, seeing as how he's currently one of SVH's most eligible bachelors. I felt as if I were going to throw up. Couldn't they see that the girl Ken has his eye on was sitting right next to them?

Second of all, my brilliant Enid-Jeffrey matchmaking scheme was a total bust. It started out great, when Mr. Collins asked

289

me to show Jeffrey around the Oracle *office this afternoon. I'd already heard that Jeffrey was interested in joining the staff as a photographer, and it looked like the perfect opportunity.* . . .

"So, Jeffrey, you want to take pictures for the newspaper," I said cheerfully. "That's terrific—really a good way to get involved. And we can really use you. There's lots going on right now!"

Jeffrey smiled, his green eyes twinkling with friendliness. "Like what?"

I pointed to the papers scattered all over my desk. "Like, in addition to the usual weekly paper, we're putting together a special supplement about the fund-raising activities going on in town for Food Drive Week."

"Cool." Jeffrey nodded enthusiastically. "What can I do to help?"

I liked his attitude. "Tell you what," I said, after pretending to think for a moment. "You know what you might do. You might put in an appearance at the volleyball game tonight. Bring your camera. Allen Walters will be there taking pictures, but you could snap a few, too."

"Sounds like fun," agreed Jeffrey. "But you know, I'd be happy to cover more than just sports events and dances and stuff. I like to try new things, to challenge myself. This is a passion with me," he confessed with an engaging smile. "I'd like to be a professional photographer someday."

"I know what you mean," I exclaimed. "I feel the same way about writing."

"What do you write for *The Oracle*?" he asked, edging his chair a little closer.

"A gossip column called 'Eyes and Ears.'" I laughed. "Needless to say, at this school I always end up with about a hundred times more material than I can use! Who's going out with who, which couples are on the rocks, and on and on."

"What about you?" asked Jeffrey. "Do you have a boyfriend?"

His frankness took me by surprise. I thought about my stolen moments with Ken, and my face turned bright red. "No, I don't. So, anyway, Jeffrey, I'm glad you're going to the volleyball game, because I'd promised my best friend Enid Rollins that I'd join her there, but now it turns out I have to do something with my cousin Jenny, so I can't make it. Remember Enid from the party at my house the other night? Curly brown hair, gorgeous green eyes?"

Jeffrey nodded. "Sure. But—"

"Good. Keep an eye out for her, OK? I think you'd really enjoy getting to know her. She's a *terrific* girl."

"I bet," he said easily. "But how about you? Why don't you bring your cousin to the game? We could all sit together."

"I think Jenny's made other plans," I fibbed. I looked at my watch, suddenly feeling uncomfortable with the kinds of questions Jeffrey was asking me, and the way he looked at me with those intense green eyes. "Um, I've got to run."

Jeffrey rose to his feet. "Can I give you a ride home?" he offered. "We could stop at the Dairi Burger for a shake on the way."

Ordinarily, nothing can tempt me like one of the Dairi Burger's chocolate milk shakes. It would be fun to keep chatting with Jeffrey about the newspaper; he was an interesting guy and I enjoyed his company. *But Enid's the one he's supposed to be taking out for a milk shake,* I reminded myself. "Thanks, but I've got my own car," I told him. "Don't forget the volleyball game tonight, OK? It's not a real assignment or anything, but you could get your feet wet. And Enid's great company."

Jeffrey gave me a somewhat quizzical smile. "I'll try to make it," he replied. "Thanks for your time, Liz."

"No problem!"

Something about the conversation made me feel a little funny, but basically I felt it had gone pretty well. I drove right over to Enid's to give her the scoop. . . .

"Tell me exactly what he said when you told him I'd be at the volleyball game," Enid demanded, her eyes sparkling with interest.

"He said . . ." I sat down on Enid's bed and tossed a stuffed animal in the air to hide my discomfort. Fixing people up was an awkward business. I was sure Jeffrey would fall for Enid as soon as he spent

292

some time with her, but he hadn't exactly bubbled over with enthusiasm when I was hinting around in the *Oracle* office earlier. "He remembered you from the party at my house, Steven's surprise party."

"He did?" Enid pretended to swoon. "Wow. I can't believe he noticed me!" She turned to her closet and started to rifle through her clothes. "God, what am I going to wear to the volleyball game?"

She held up a pair of black stirrup pants and an oversized sweater for my inspection. I gave the outfit the nod. "Well, he didn't say *definitely* that he could make it to the game," I reminded Enid. "He said he'd *try.*" I didn't add that I'd gotten the impression that he might have been more definite if I'd been planning to go to the game, too. "I encouraged him to bring his camera and consider it kind of a practice photography assignment for *The Oracle*. So if he doesn't show up, don't take it personally, but there's probably a pretty good chance. . . ."

"Oh, Liz!" Enid gave me an impulsive hug. "I'm so excited! Just think—tonight I'm going to sit next to Jeffrey French at the volleyball game. I'm going to *talk* to him." She flopped back on her bed, her arms flung out and a goofy grin on her face. "What if he asks me out? God, he is *so* cute! Thank you, thank you, thank you, Liz. You're the best friend in the world!"

"Don't thank me yet," I cautioned her, an uneasy feeling sputtering in my stomach. Enid's enthusiasm was such a contrast to Jeffrey's total nonchalance. . . . *Why did I get mixed up in this?* I asked myself, watching Enid scramble around in search of the perfect accessories for her outfit. *If Jeffrey and Enid are meant to be together, won't it happen without my help?* I wanted to be optimistic for my friend's sake, but I couldn't shake the premonition that nothing good was going to come of this matchmaking experiment.

I'd told Jeffrey I was doing something with Jenny tonight, but actually, Jenny went out somewhere with Jess. I sat around at home waiting for Enid to call and tell me how it went at the volleyball game. I hung up the phone with her a few minutes ago, right before starting to write this. . . .

"Enid, what's the matter?" I asked.

"Liz, I feel like the biggest fool," she moaned.

"Why? What happened?"

A worst-case scenario flickered through my brain. Enid and Jeffrey had talked briefly at the game, but he'd blown her off because he wasn't interested in her. He'd told her he'd rather get to know her friend Elizabeth Wakefield.

"He never showed up," Enid explained.

A wave of relief washed over me. "Oh, is that all?"

"What do you mean, is that all?" Enid cried. "I really had my hopes up, Liz, but obviously he doesn't want to have anything to do with me."

"Remember, he didn't tell me for sure that he could go to the game," I said soothingly. "He might have had other plans. Or maybe he's just shy. Maybe he *did* want to see you, but he chickened out."

"Do you think that could be it?" Enid asked, sounding a bit less distraught.

"I'm sure that's it," I declared, liking this theory more and more all the time. "You're a really pretty girl, and he just didn't have the nerve to go up to you in the middle of a big crowd. We'll have to find another way to throw you two together. Don't give up, Enid, OK?"

"OK," she promised. "I won't."

Monday, 11:00 P.M.

So, Diary. The plot thickens!

Jenny just got home from the Beach Disco, and guess who was there tonight? Jessica, Eddie, Lila . . . and Jeffrey! Among others. Can you believe it? Boy, am I steamed. According to Jenny, Jeffrey and Lila danced just about every song together, including all the slow ones. They couldn't keep their hands off each other, and the rumor is they're falling madly in love. Just hearing about it made me want to puke. I almost started crying, I was so disappointed for Enid's sake. Lila just doesn't deserve a guy as smart and sweet and interesting as Jeffrey. He should be with Enid!

Tuesday, 4:00 P.M.

Dear Diary,
I did it. After school just now Ken and I went for a walk in the park, and I broke things

295

*off with him. We both got choked up about it,
but I know deep in our hearts we feel the exact
same way. He's lonely and I'm lonely and we
just kind of naturally turned to each other, but
entering into an actual out-in-the-open relationship would have been impossible and wrong.
We could never have felt good about it. . . .*

Our fingers interlaced, Ken and I strolled into the
shadowy green forest. The path was deserted. When
we came to a wooden bench under a spreading oak
tree, we sat down.

Ken slipped an arm around my shoulders. "It's
pretty here, isn't it?" he commented. "Peaceful."

"It is," I agreed. "But, Ken . . ."

He turned his face to me. There was a sad shadow in
his usually bright-blue eyes; he knew what I was going to
say. "We can't do this anymore," I said softly. "Coming to
the park because we know no one will see us here . . .
not being able to go to the movies, to go out to dinner, to
hold hands at school. Hasn't it been driving you nuts?"

He laughed wryly. "Yeah, I guess. But I keep telling myself I'd be even more nuts if I couldn't spend
time with you."

Lifting a hand, I touched his face. "We can still
spend time together," I pointed out. "In public, too.
If we do it as friends."

"You mean . . . go back."

There was a ragged edge to his voice. I could tell
he was close to tears. I nodded, blinking back tears of
my own. "Yes. Go back. To the way we were before."

Without speaking Ken pulled me to him. We held each other for a long moment. For once it didn't get us all heated up, being so close; the embrace was just incredibly tender and sweet. We were ready.

"You're a wonderful girl, Liz," Ken whispered into my hair.

I pressed my damp cheek against his neck. "You're a one-in-a-million guy, Ken."

"I'm not sorry, you know. I'll never forget what we've shared."

"Me, either," I said. And lifting my face, I kissed him softly, for the last time.

I think, Diary, we'll be able to stay good friends. There aren't any hard feelings. I know Ken cares for me deeply, and I'll always have a place for him in a secret part of my heart. And we promised each other: under no circumstances will we ever tell anyone about what happened between us. Never, ever.

So I'm on my own now, Diary—really on my own. And you know what? I think I'm ready to put my heart back together and move on. I think I'm going to be OK.

Wednesday, 5:00 P.M.

I feel good about how things ended with Ken, but meanwhile this Jeffrey French thing is getting stranger and stranger. . . .

297

"Liz, wait up!"

I stopped next to a shade tree in the courtyard outside the lunch area. Turning, I saw Jeffrey French jogging toward me.

I clutched my notebook to my chest, my cheeks flaming. *What does* he *want?* I wondered, irritated just at the sight of him. *Is he going to make excuses about the other night?*

"I'm glad I found you," he said, panting slightly.

"How come?" I responded, my tone far from encouraging.

Jeffrey gestured at the shady patch of green lawn. "I thought maybe we could eat lunch together."

I blinked at him, not sure whether to believe my ears. Lila and Enid were engaged in a duel to the death over this guy, and he wanted to have lunch with *me*? "Sorry, but I need to study for a biology quiz," I said coolly, turning away and dropping my books onto the ground.

Any other person would have gotten the message, but instead of beating a hasty retreat, Jeffrey squatted next to me and peered closely into my face. "Liz, did I do something wrong?" he asked, his tone concerned and friendly.

"As a matter of fact, you did." Before my better judgment could prevail, I blurted out, "I can't believe you went dancing at the Beach Disco with Lila two nights ago when Enid was expecting you to meet her at the volleyball game!"

"Enid—expecting me . . . ?" Jeffrey's blond eyebrows shot up. "But I never said—and I didn't go dancing with Lila," he declared. "There was a whole gang of people, and frankly, when she called and said she and Jessica were planning to take your cousin Jenny there, I just assumed . . ." Jeffrey flushed slightly, but he didn't lose his cool. "I thought you'd be there, too. After all, you told me the reason *you* couldn't go to the volleyball game was because you had to hang out with your cousin."

He waited patiently for my response. I dropped my eyes, too flustered to put words together in a grammatical sentence. "Oh. Well, I . . . hmm." I tried an accusing glare. "But you had a pretty good time at the Beach Disco, from all accounts."

"It was OK." He shrugged. "But it would have been a lot more fun if you'd been there." Standing up, he tossed me a casual good-bye wave. "Good luck on your quiz, Liz. See you around!"

I watched him saunter off, my head spinning. Jeffrey had made it pretty clear. He didn't go to the volleyball game to see Enid because he thought he'd see *me* at the Beach Disco!

How did I get us into such a state of confusion, Diary? I'd be happy to become friends with Jeffrey, but instead I feel really uncomfortable around him. This isn't working out at all the way I planned. How could he be interested in me? Enid would be so crushed if she knew. . . . What a rotten friend I am! I just hope I can find a way to get a happy ending out of this tangle. After what

299

*I've been through with Ken, I don't need any
more complications in my life right now.*

Wednesday, 9:45 P.M.

*Until about fifteen minutes ago I was hav-
ing a relatively peaceful evening. I really feel
so much better now that Ken and I have resolved things. But I'm feeling worse and worse
all the time about the situation with Jeffrey.
Enid called tonight to talk about strategy for
getting Jeffrey's attention. I tried to persuade
her that she and Jeffrey would be better off
without a matchmaker, but she begged me not
to abandon her. What could I say?*

"You don't need my help, Enid," I insisted, twisting the phone cord around my finger. "You're not getting anywhere with me in the middle. I think you
should just look for casual ways to talk to Jeffrey.
Bump into him in the hall, sit with him in the cafeteria, stuff like that."

"I can't fight Lila on my own!" said Enid desperately. "She's really going all out for him. You wouldn't
believe the latest!"

"What did she do now?" I asked, my blood pressure shooting up in anticipation of another outra-
geous stunt.

"She gave Jeffrey this incredibly fancy camera and
tripod," related Enid. "But Olivia said Jeffrey told
Lila he couldn't accept such an expensive gift."

I exhaled with relief. "That's a good sign. I'm sure he sees right through her—subtlety's never been her strong point. He's not going to let her buy him."

"Buy him . . . wait a minute!" Enid shrieked. I held the phone away from my ear. "That gives me a great idea!"

"What gives you a great idea?"

"I'm going to buy Jeffrey!"

"Enid, what are you *talking* about?"

"The charity auction on Friday," Enid elaborated breathlessly. "You know, the one where everyone bids cans of food instead of money, for the food drive. A lot of people are donating services like lawn mowing, baby-sitting, a back rub, a haircut, stuff like that, right? What if Jeffrey donates a date with himself . . . and I place the highest bid?"

I laughed out loud. "A date? At the auction?"

"It's been done before. I bet Jeffrey would go for it, too. And that's where you come in."

"Me?"

"You see him around the *Oracle* office, don't you?"

"Yeah, but—"

"So all you have to do is talk him into participating at the auction. Easy!"

"Don't make me do this, Enid," I begged, wondering if now was the time to remind her of what happened to Miles Standish in Puritan times when he asked John Alden to court Priscilla Mullens on his behalf. Priscilla fell in love with John instead.

"It's not such a big favor, is it?"

"It won't work," I argued. "How can you outbid

301

Lila, the richest girl in southern California?"

"I can't," Enid conceded, "so I'll just have to make sure she doesn't show up at the auction. I'll take care of that if you take care of Jeffrey. Please, Liz?" she wheedled.

"Well . . . OK," I relented at last. "But I'm going to feel really stupid doing this." Especially since Jeffrey was bound to get the wrong idea . . . and think I wanted him to auction off a date with himself so I could bid for it!

Thursday, 3:30 P.M.

Dear Diary,

Why am I letting myself get so worked up about this? I'm just involved because of Enid—otherwise, I wouldn't care who Jeffrey French dates. Guess I have to try harder to stay detached.

Jeffrey came by the newspaper office this afternoon, and I put the auction plan into motion. Once again I got a sinking feeling that no matter how hard I try, I'm sending Jeffrey all the wrong signals. . . .

Jeffrey and I were the last ones working in the *Oracle* office for the second time that week. *Now's my chance to bring up the auction,* I thought, crossing the room to look over his shoulder.

I had to lean close to see the tiny images on the contact sheet he was examining. "You got some terrific pictures at the track meet!" I exclaimed, impressed.

302

"Do you really think so?" he asked, looking straight into my eyes.

"Sure." With an effort I tore my gaze away from his, looking back at the contact sheet. "It'll be a tough choice, deciding which of those to use."

"I think I'll circle a few and let John pick one," said Jeffrey, "since he wrote the article."

Straightening up, I stepped away from him. "It'll be great having you on the staff," I said sincerely. "You're an excellent photographer."

"Thanks, Liz." Jeffrey's dark-green eyes glowed with pleasure. "It means a lot to hear you say that."

I'm just being friendly, I wanted to tell him. *Don't get the wrong idea!*

Instead I retreated to my desk. "I'm writing an article about the auction for the food drive tomorrow afternoon," I remarked. "Were you planning to go?" Jeffrey nodded. "How would you like to snap a few pictures while you're at it?"

He nodded again. "I'd love to be your partner on this."

Suddenly my face felt sunburned—I could tell I was blushing furiously. How annoying! This was just so contrived; I felt like a total idiot. "You know, there's another thing you could do to help," I told Jeffrey. "Winston's the auctioneer, and he was telling me just this morning that they still need some more things to auction off. Would you like to contribute something?"

"You mean like old furniture or sports equipment or toys or something?"

"Well . . . how about offering something personal?

Bruce Patman's offering a private tennis lesson, and Winston's auctioning off his services as a clown for a child's birthday party. You know, at past auctions the wildest bidding happens when somebody gets up there and sells a date with him- or herself."

"A date?" Jeffrey laughed. "You're kidding!"

"It really makes things lively." I smiled at him. "So what do you say?"

"You want me to auction off a date with myself?" he asked in disbelief.

"Sure! You'd be a big hit," I predicted. "Take my word for it, lots of girls at this school would be psyched to bid for a date with you."

Jeffrey wrinkled his nose. "You mean it wouldn't look totally cocky? Like I think I'm so hot or something? Or maybe so desperate!"

We both cracked up. "No, everybody knows this is just for fun. It's generous of you—you'll help collect a lot of canned food for the needy."

Jeffrey rubbed his chin thoughtfully, his eyes on my face. I felt myself blush again. "And *you* really want me to do this."

I silently cursed Enid for putting me in this ridiculous position. "Yes, I do. It's for a good cause."

"OK, then." Jeffrey gave me a knowing wink. "And may the best woman win!"

> *Talk about humiliating, Diary. Obviously he thinks I talked him into doing this so I can bid on a date with him. Once we got that subject out of the way, though, we had a fun con-*

304

versation about Jeffrey's first impressions of his classes and teachers. You wouldn't believe what happened after that, though. Just as we walked out to the parking lot together, Lila zoomed in in her lime-green Triumph waving two tickets to tonight's pro soccer game in L.A. It took about half a second for her to talk Jeffrey into going with her—he hopped into the passenger seat and off they went. That girl will do anything to get what she wants, and I must say, Jeffrey didn't exactly put up a fight. Maybe the reason he got so cheerful about the auction-date idea is because he assumes Lila will win the bidding. Why does this make me so angry? I'm mad on Enid's behalf . . . right?

Friday, 9:40 P.M.

News flash: Enid is on a date with Jeffrey even as I write! I can't sit still—she promised to call when she gets in, and I'm dying to hear how it went. I started a letter to Todd, and it feels good now that I don't have anything to hide regarding Ken, but I wrote only a couple of paragraphs. I'm just so restless.

Backing up a bit, as you can guess, Enid's plan went off without a hitch. She came up with a brilliant ploy to keep Lila and Jess away from the auction, and after that it was a piece of cake . . . or should I say a pyramid of cans??

305

I spotted Enid entering the auditorium a few minutes before the auction was scheduled to begin. "Do you need help?" I asked, hurrying to her side.

She staggered slightly, almost losing her hold on the cardboard box laden with cans of food. "There's another box in the car," she panted.

We carried that one in together. "Looks like you're not taking any chances!" I observed.

Enid smiled, pushing the hair back from her forehead. "There's no way anybody's going to outbid me, especially since I made sure Lila won't come anywhere near the auditorium this afternoon!"

"How'd you do that?" I asked as we searched for empty seats.

"I cornered her and Jessica in the hallway this morning and told them I was looking for two volunteers to help box up the cans to take over to City Hall after the auction," Enid explained with a mischievous glint in her eyes. "Suddenly Jessica had a special cheerleading practice she just couldn't miss, and Lila had a doctor's appointment. They couldn't come up with excuses fast enough!"

I laughed. "Nice going, Rollins."

Onstage, Winston, dressed in a tuxedo and top hat, stepped up to the microphone to announce the opening of the auction. Enid gripped my arm. "Wish me luck!"

The bidding was fast, furious, and funny. Three girls competed frantically for the private tennis lesson with Bruce—the winning bid was twenty-five cans. I bid fifteen cans for a home-cooked dinner to be served by Mr. Collins and his son Teddy, but Penny topped me. Roger Barrett Patman bought a pair of Number One concert tickets for twenty cans. With each minute that passed I found myself growing more and more nervous on Enid's behalf.

"I'd like to remind you all that we have yet to top last year's high bid of forty cans," boomed Winston. "So, ladies, don't be stingy when you're bidding for this next item . . ." Jeffrey emerged from behind the curtain, wearing crisp khaki trousers, a light-blue Oxford shirt with the sleeves rolled up, and a sheepish grin. ". . . a dream date this very evening with the new guy in town, Jeffrey French!"

There was enthusiastic applause and a few whistles. All around us I could hear girls murmuring with excitement. Enid was chewing her nails.

"Who would like to open the bidding?" asked Winston.

"I bid ten cans!" shouted Stacie Cabot, a cute sophomore.

"Fifteen cans!" shrieked Caroline Pearce, waving her hand.

"Twenty!" countered Stacie.

Caroline didn't hesitate. "Twenty-five!"

As this was going on, I watched Jeffrey. He looked down at his sneakers, a bemused smile on his face. Was he wondering why I wasn't bidding after I talked him into doing this crazy thing?

"Thirty cans!" Stacie shouted, and I saw Caroline shake her head.

Winston raised his gavel. "Going once, going twice—"

Enid was chickening out. I jabbed her in the side with my elbow. Her hand shot into the air.

"We've got another bidder!" Winston hollered.

People craned their necks in our direction. "I bid seventy-five cans," Enid declared, loud and clear.

"Yahoo!" Winston whooped, banging his gavel. "Sold, to Enid Rollins, for a record-setting seventy-five cans!"

The audience burst into applause. I clapped harder than anyone as Jeffrey stepped down from the stage to greet his date for the evening.

Friday, 11:30 P.M.

Enid finally called. It sounds as if her date with Jeffrey wasn't a huge success. First of all, he took her to the Dairi Burger—not the most romantic spot in town! They ended up at the Beach Disco, which was an improvement, but according to Enid, they just didn't click. They only talked about really casual, superficial stuff, and when Jeffrey dropped her off, he didn't even try to kiss her good night. "So that's it," she concluded. "I gave it my best shot, but it's just not meant to be." She didn't even sound that upset.

"You can't give up, Enid Rollins," I argued. "I won't let you!" And I won't. Jeffrey's a real prize—she can't let him slip through her fingers.

Diary, I am so full of emotions, I don't know if I can find a way to write them down. Maybe if I start at the beginning, you can help me make sense of this crazy day.

The Food Drive Week beach party got off to a crummy start. Both Enid and I ended up stranded at home without cars, so we had to take the bus, which meant we were practically the last people to show up. Lila was already dancing with Jeffrey when Enid and I arrived. I wasn't about to let her monopolize him; I dived into action. . . .

"I just can't stand to see them together!" I exclaimed, glaring as Lila and Jeffrey rocked out to a catchy Droids tune.

The beach party was in full swing. The PTA had set up a tent, barbecue grills, volleyball nets, and a temporary dance floor and bandstand—something for everyone.

"We've got to find a way to get Jeffrey out of Lila's clutches so you can spend some time with him," I continued, my hands on my hips.

Enid shook her head. "Look, Liz, I had my chance last night. It's just not there between us. Let's drop it, OK?"

"After all the trouble we've gone to? No way!" I declared.

"I told you, there was just no chemistry," Enid insisted, tugging on my arm to keep me from charging toward the dance floor. "Maybe Lila's not right for Jeffrey, but neither am I."

"Don't have such a negative attitude! So there were no fireworks on your first date—maybe there will be on your second date. But you won't *have* a second date if you don't assert yourself!"

"I've asserted myself plenty," said Enid. "It's just not—"

"I have an idea," I declared. "Jeffrey brought his camera, see? I'm going to have him put it to good use. Taking pictures of *you*, the head of the student committee for the food drive!"

"Please, Liz, don't—"

I didn't hear the rest of Enid's plea; I was already barreling my way through the crowd on the dance floor. "Jeffrey!" I shouted.

He and Lila both turned to look at me. "Ex*cuse* me, Liz, but in case you didn't notice, we're dancing," Lila snarled at me.

"Just let me steal Jeffrey away for a few minutes," I requested with an exaggeratedly sweet smile. "I need him to take some pictures for an *Oracle* article."

Jeffrey took a step away from Lila. She grabbed his arm. "You're not going to ditch me so you can go off and take stupid pictures, are you?" she demanded petulantly.

"I have a responsibility to the newspaper," Jeffrey told her. "It won't take long. I'll see you around, OK?"

As soon as Jeffrey shook his arm loose from Lila's claws, *I* grabbed him. "C'mon. Let's get a few shots of

310

the PTA members who organized this bash before things get too wild!" I suggested, bearing him off like a trophy of victory.

For the next twenty minutes Jeffery snapped pictures as I conducted quick interviews with the chairman of the food drive and others responsible for putting the beach party together. "How about a break?" he said as I hit the off button on my tape recorder. "I'll race you to the water."

He started to pull off his T-shirt. I blushed lobster-red at the sight of his bare chest. "Actually, there's one more interview," I said quickly, taking off in Enid's direction. "I'm going to leave you alone for this one."

"It's more fun doing it together, though," protested Jeffrey, striding after me. He touched my arm. "I think we make a pretty good team."

"Well, maybe, but I have to take care of something else," I mumbled, trying to ignore the way his hand made my skin tingle. "She's over there. Enid Rollins, the student food-drive committee chair. Just ask a few questions and take maybe ten pictures of her, OK?"

Jeffrey glanced at Enid, who was sitting on a beach towel and looking distinctly embarrassed. Then he looked back at me and narrowed his eyes, his smile fading. "Look, Liz, I'm not sure —"

"Thanks, Jeffrey," I cut in, spinning around to dash off across the sand. "I really appreciate this!"

I acted like a woman possessed. It was pretty clear that neither Enid nor Jeffrey wanted to be pushed on each other, but I

*went ahead and did it anyway. I don't know
what was the matter with me . . . no, actually, I do. I'm getting to that.*

*Right after I dumped Jeffrey on Enid, I
bumped into Jessica, who started yelling at
me for being so sneaky about the auction.
After I told her that Lila would never have
Jeffrey because I was going to make sure
Enid got him, I doubled back and found
Enid sitting by herself, practically in tears.
I demanded to know what Jeffrey had said
to her, but all she did was sniffle and beg
me to let the whole thing drop. Any normal
person would've given up at that point,
right? Not me. I chased Jeffrey down the
beach. . . .*

He was walking away from the party, bending
every now and then to pick up a stone and skip it
across the water. I had to jog to catch up to him.
"Jeffrey!" I shouted, raising my voice so he could
hear me above the pounding of the surf. "Wait up!"

He stopped but didn't make a move to backtrack
in my direction. I hurried forward, the wind whipping
my hair across my face. "Jeffrey, can I walk with you?"

He squinted at me, his eyes unsmiling. "I thought
you were so busy with something."

"Well, I was," I said lamely, "but I got everything
under control, and then I went back to see how you
were getting along with Enid and I—"

Jeffrey's right hand sliced the air in an impatient

gesture. "Whoa, let's stop right there, Liz. What's this all about, this Enid business?"

"What—what do you mean?" I stuttered.

"Practically from our first conversation, you've been bringing Enid into everything. 'Sit with Enid at the volleyball game, talk to Enid about photography, give Enid a call about a tour of Sweet Valley.' And just now . . ."

"Don't you think she's nice?" I asked.

"Sure, she's nice. But so what? What does that have to do with—"

"Spend a little more time with her and you'll see what a terrific person she is," I interrupted. "She's probably the nicest girl in Sweet Valley, and you'd be crazy not to—"

"Stop it, would you?" Jeffrey shouted, his eyes blazing.

His anger cut me like a lash, and I blinked, surprised. "But, Jeffrey, Enid really likes you. The least you can do is—"

"Listen to me, Liz." Jeffrey seized my bare shoulders and gave me a shake. "I don't need you or anyone else telling me who I should go out with. Enid's nice, but I don't want to date her. Can you get that through your thick head?"

With that he dropped his hands and strode off. I stared after him, my eyes blurring with tears. What had I done?

Jeffrey's anger had really shaken me up; my whole body was trembling. Letting my legs buckle, I sank to the sand. *Why didn't I quit when Enid asked me to?* I wondered, hugging my knees and staring out at the sparkling sea.

"Is this seat taken?" someone asked.

I looked up to see Jessica gesturing at the patch of sand next to me. I shook my head, smiling through my tears.

"What's the matter?" she asked. "It can't be anything as bad as what just happened to me."

"What happened to you?"

"Guess who's slow-dancing with Eddie Winters at this very moment when his arms are supposed to be wrapped around me?"

"Who?"

"Jenny." Jessica rolled her eyes tragically. "Our chubby, bratty baby cousin, Jenny!"

I burst out laughing. "I had to drag her along on all our dates," Jessica went on, "and instead of being annoyed by her, Eddie fell in love with her. Can you believe it?"

"What a bummer," I commiserated.

"God knows what I saw in him to begin with," Jessica declared philosophically. "If Jenny's his type, then he certainly isn't *my* type. But what's *your* sob story?"

I filled her in on my disastrous interventions with Enid and Jeffrey. "I made a total idiot of myself," I wailed, "and now Enid's upset and Jeffrey's furious and I've blown it for everyone."

"So big deal," said Jessica, digging a hole in the sand with her toe. "Enid knows you were just trying to help her, and who cares what Jeffrey thinks? If you

314

ask me, we've all been making too much of a fuss over him. He's really nothing special."

"He *is* special," I argued.

"Yeah, in what way?" Jessica challenged.

"He's smart and sensitive and he has a great sense of humor. And you have to admit he's been really cool about all these girls fighting over him—he's really tactful and polite and not at all egotistical. Which he could be, because in case you've gone blind, he happens to be the best-looking guy on this beach."

Jessica stared at me. Then her lips curved in a devilish smile. "Why, Elizabeth Wakefield," she teased. "I do believe you have a big, bad crush on Jeffrey French!"

"What? I do not!"

"You do, too. You should hear yourself!"

The simple truth of Jessica's words hit me like a thunderbolt. "Oh, no," I groaned, collapsing back onto the sand. "Oh, Jess, how could I be so stupid?"

"I really don't know," she said cheerfully, taking my hand to pull me upright again. "But there's no point wasting a gorgeous afternoon like this one. Why don't you go after Jeffrey? Start over from square one, and *this* time be your own matchmaker."

"How can I face him?" I shook my head. "It's too late."

"Take it from me. Where true love is concerned, it's never too late."

My twin sister spoke with utter confidence, and I knew she believed every word she said. But I wasn't

315

so sure. I'd really alienated Jeffrey. Was there any way I could make it up to him?

How could I have been so blind, Diary? This is another one of those times when I wish you could talk—you could have pointed out to me that I had a crush on Jeffrey French, and that the only reason I was so dead set on fixing him up with Enid was because I wasn't ready to acknowledge my feelings. I was still so mixed up about Ken . . . and Todd. . . . And then I felt guilty because I suspected Jeffrey was interested in me, but it would have been absolutely the meanest thing to steal him away from Enid. Ugh! At that moment, sitting on the beach, I think I was about as miserable as I've ever been in my life. It's as if I had this glimpse of something wonderful, but then a door slammed in my face, and it was all my own doing. At long last I understood my feelings . . . just in time to also see that I'd blown every possibility of something with Jeffrey.

I couldn't just sit on the sand all afternoon crying, so I did the first and most important thing. I apologized to Enid. . . .

I found Enid in the refreshment tent and tapped her lightly on the shoulder. "Hey, Enid. Can I talk to you for a minute?"

She whirled to face me, a startled, hunted look on

her face. "Liz, this had better not be about Jeffrey," she declared, poised to flee if I tried one more time to shove her in his direction. "Because I've had about as much humiliation as I can take for one lifetime!"

"Don't worry—I'm done interfering. I just wanted to say I'm sorry for the way I was acting before."

Enid's expression relaxed immediately. "It's OK, I know you were just trying to help."

"Well . . ." Taking her arm, I led her away from the mob of people. "Actually, my motives may not have been totally pure," I confessed. "What I mean is, I've been very . . . confused."

She wrinkled her forehead. "About what?"

"Promise you won't think I'm a terrible person," I begged.

Enid laughed. "I could never think you're a terrible person, because you're *not* a terrible person."

Side by side, we strolled away from the tent. "At first I was really happy at the thought of you and Jeffrey getting together," I began. "The matchmaking stuff was a little embarrassing, but I really wanted to make it work. Jeffrey seemed like a great guy, and you deserve a great guy."

"But he and I just don't have that much in common," said Enid.

"Right," I agreed. "But at about the same time that was becoming clear, I was getting to know Jeffrey pretty well myself—from *The Oracle* and everything—and I think I started to . . ."

Enid halted, staring at me with wide eyes. "Don't tell me *you* like Jeffrey, too?"

I nodded miserably. "But I didn't really recognize that that was what it was. I just felt mixed up. I was still really fixated on matching him up with you—it would have been too sleazy to make a move on him myself! So I think every time it started to dawn on me that I had feelings for Jeffrey, I shoved it right out of my brain."

"Poor Liz." Enid chuckled. "What a dilemma!"

"I wasn't even thinking straight enough for it to be a dilemma," I said with a wry smile. "If I'd acknowledged my feelings, I would have been overcome with guilt. So instead I tried even harder to make you and Jeffrey into a couple."

"It wasn't meant to be, and I'm more than happy to admit it." Enid tipped her head to one side thoughtfully. "But you and Jeffrey have a lot in common. You'd be great together! Why didn't we figure this out sooner?"

We both cracked up. "Poor Jeffrey," I said, my eyes straying to the dance floor. Jeffrey was dancing with Lila; the sight made my heart ache. "We've been batting him around like a tennis ball, and he's fed up with it, I can tell. That's why I'm backing off. I'm not going to push you on him, and I'm not going to push myself on him, either. Lila can have him."

"But what if he doesn't want Lila?" asked Enid. "Do you have any reason to think Jeffrey might be interested in you, too, Liz?"

A telltale flush crept up my neck to my face. "I don't know. Possibly . . ."

"Then you can't give up now," Enid declared, taking

my arm and propelling me toward the dance floor. "I'm giving your advice right back to you. Don't let this chance slide through your fingers!"

"Jeffrey doesn't want to have anything to do with me," I told Enid, digging my heels into the sand. "I've been such a pain! And what would I say? I can't just blurt out the truth."

"Just say what you need to say to straighten things out," Enid suggested. "Jeffrey will pick up your cue and take it from there."

She gave me a gentle shove. I started forward, my knees quaking. "Good luck!" Enid called after me.

Boy, am I going to need it! I thought.

Cutting in on Lila for the second time that afternoon was a daunting prospect. I stepped up, clearing my throat. "Um, can I . . . can I have the next song, Jeffrey?"

Lila's dark eyes pierced me like daggers. "Get a life, would you, Liz? Can't you see he's taken?"

Jeffrey intervened, his tone easy and genial. "Actually, Lila, I owe Liz a dance. It's traditional for the reporter and the photographer to take one spin together."

Lila held up a finger, her eyes still cutting me to shreds. "Just one," she snapped, flouncing off in a huff.

I bit my lip, trying not to laugh. Jeffrey caught my eye and we both grinned. "Sorry to spoil the mood," I said, suddenly feeling shy.

The Droids started a new song—a slow song. Jeffrey took my hand. "There was no mood," he replied. "Until now."

He pulled me into his arms, and instantly I relaxed. It felt so natural to rest my head against his chest, to feel his chin brush against my hair. Our bodies were a perfect fit. "Jeffrey, I need to say something."

"This better not be about Enid," Jeffrey warned, a note of amusement in his voice.

"I'm sorry about all that, Jeffrey." I lifted my face to his. "I didn't mean to be so pushy, but she's my best friend and I just wanted to—"

"Ssh." He placed a finger against my lips. "I think I understand. Let's just drop it, OK?"

"OK," I agreed, relieved. We continued to sway to the music. I could feel Jeffrey's heart beating.

"It was never going to work anyway, Elizabeth," Jeffrey remarked a moment later. "I mean, Enid's a cool girl—I hope she and I can be good friends. But my heart already belongs to someone else."

"It does?" My own heart sank to the floor at his words. *He already has a girlfriend,* I thought, *probably someone back home in Oregon.* I wanted to kick myself. Obviously Jeffrey just wanted to be friends with me, too; I'd read his signals wrong from start to finish. Disappointment filled my throat, choking me.

"Yep," Jeffrey confirmed. "But it's kind of frustrating, because I'm absolutely nuts about this girl, and I think she's nuts about me, but she doesn't seem to realize it."

We both stopped dancing. Jeffrey put his hand under my chin and tilted my face to his. Suddenly it clicked. We didn't need to speak; I found the answers

320

to all my questions in Jeffrey's warm, loving eyes. And in Jeffrey's tender, deeply satisfying kiss.

So, there I was, Diary, dancing in Jeffrey's arms, my heart doing backflips, and tears streaming down my cheeks. Why was I crying? It's hard to explain. I guess for the same reason I'm crying right now. For a long time, because of Enid, I refused to recognize my own feelings for Jeffrey. But I think there was another, even more powerful reason.

I think I was afraid to let myself really and truly fall for Jeffrey because it meant finally saying good-bye to Todd. The thing with Ken wasn't really a threat; it couldn't go anywhere. It was safe hanging out with him, hiding from the world. But with Jeffrey . . . I'm really putting myself out there, Diary, making myself vulnerable. Trying at last to open my heart to someone new, while knowing deep down inside that I may never love anyone the way I loved—still love—Todd. It scares me so much. But to find out if you can fly, you have to take that big leap, right?

Epilogue

The first light of dawn was breaking as I closed my diary. For another hour I sat with my eyes half-closed, reflecting on what I had read. *I'm only sixteen, and already my life has been so full!* I thought. Full of love and laughter, tears and disappointment, success and failure, fun and friendship. Every day, new experiences, new lessons to be learned.

Slipping on my bathrobe, I padded out into the hallway. Downstairs I had the kitchen to myself; the rest of my family was still asleep. Putting on a pot of coffee, I stood at the kitchen window, yawning. Then I rubbed my eyes. Was I seeing things, or was somebody lurking at the end of my driveway, watching the house?

I squinted to bring the figure into focus, and then my heart did a cartwheel. Todd!

He glimpsed me in the window at the same moment. We met at the door. "Liz, I . . ." He stepped into the house, and an instant later we were in each other's arms. "I'm so sorry we had a fight," he said hoarsely. "I couldn't sleep last night. I came over even though I knew no one would be up yet. . . ."

"I couldn't sleep, either," I said softly.

He squeezed me. "I shouldn't have blown my stack about the letter I should have explained right then and there. Michelle was the manager of the boys' basketball team. So we saw each other all the time and we got to be really close. We'd always flirt and joke around and stuff. But she was like a sister to me—nothing more. Don't you see?" He held me at arm's length so he could gaze earnestly into my eyes. "You and I dated other people while I lived in Vermont, but that couldn't change what we felt for each other. You're the only girl I've ever loved, Elizabeth Wakefield. And I'll love you forever."

I knew that every word Todd said was true . . . because I felt exactly the same way. I'd given a piece of my heart to other boys—to Ken, to Jeffrey. But Todd was the only one I'd ever cared for with *all* my heart.

And at that moment, looking up into his adorable brown eyes, my heart beat with a deeper, stronger love than I'd ever dreamed possible. "I'll love you forever, too, Todd Wilkins," I promised.

And, Diary, I know I will.

Bantam Books in the Sweet Valley High series
Ask your bookseller for the books you have missed

SIGN UP FOR THE SWEET VALLEY HIGH® FAN CLUB!

Hey, girls! Get all the gossip on Sweet Valley High's® most popular teenagers when you join our fantastic Fan Club! As a member, you'll get all of this really cool stuff:

- Membership Card with your own personal Fan Club ID number
- A Sweet Valley High® Secret Treasure Box
- Sweet Valley High® Stationery
- Official Fan Club Pencil (for secret note writing!)
- Three Bookmarks
- A "Members Only" Door Hanger
- Two Skeins of J. & P. Coats® Embroidery Floss with flower barrette instruction leaflet
- Two editions of *The Oracle* newsletter
- Plus exclusive Sweet Valley High® product offers, special savings, contests, and much more!

Be the first to find out what Jessica & Elizabeth Wakefield are up to by joining the Sweet Valley High® Fan Club for the one-year membership fee of only $6.25 each for U.S. residents, $8.25 for Canadian residents (U.S. currency). Includes shipping & handling.

Send a check or money order (do not send cash) made payable to "Sweet Valley High® Fan Club" along with this form to:

SWEET VALLEY HIGH® FAN CLUB, BOX 3919-B, SCHAUMBURG, IL 60168-3919

NAME_____
(Please print clearly)

ADDRESS_____

CITY_____ STATE _____ ZIP_____
(Required)

AGE_____ BIRTHDAY_____ /_____ /_____

Life after high school gets even sweeter!

Jessica and Elizabeth are now freshman at Sweet Valley University, where the motto is: Welcome to college – welcome to freedom!

Don't miss any of the books in this fabulous new series.

♡ College Girls #1 ....56308-4 $3.50/4.50 Can.
♡ Love, Lies and Jessica Wakefield #2........56306-8 $3.50/4.50 Can.

Life after high school gets even *Sweeter!*

Jessica and Elizabeth are now freshmen at Sweet Valley University, where the motto is: Welcome to college — welcome to freedom!

Don't miss any of the books in this fabulous new series.